Praise for Nancy Atherton and her
Aunt Dimity Series

Aunt Dimity and the Family Tree

"Perfect for curling up in front of a fire and reading and a great addition to the Aunt Dimity collection." —*Suspense Magazine*

Aunt Dimity Down Under

"This wonderful cozy is perfect to read while snuggled in bed. It's a cute, entertaining piece of escapism." —*Romantic Times*

Aunt Dimity Slays the Dragon

"One of the most charming entries in an enduringly popular series." —*Booklist*

Aunt Dimity: Vampire Hunter

"One of Aunt Dimity's most suspenseful mysteries. Loyal fans will be thrilled by every new revelation." —*Kirkus Reviews*

Aunt Dimity Goes West

"Just the ticket to ease out of a stressful day." —*Deadly Pleasures*

Aunt Dimity and the Deep Blue Sea

"The eleventh Aunt Dimity mystery is testament to the staying power of Atherton's cozier-than-cozy premise . . . Rainy Sunday afternoon reading." —*Booklist*

Aunt Dimity and the Next of Kin

"This is a book entirely without edge, cynicism, or even rudeness— this is the way life really ought to be if only we were all better behaved. Put on the teakettle and enjoy."

—*Rocky Mountain News*

"This is Atherton at her coziest. . . . Fans of the series will not be disappointed." —*Over My Dead Body!* (The Mystery Magazine)

"Cozy mystery lovers wouldn't dream of missing an entry in this series." —*Kingston Observer*

Aunt Dimity: Snowbound

"Witty, engaging, and filled with interesting detail that will make the cottage-in-the-English-countryside fanciers among us sigh . . . Just the thing to veg out on when life gets too much." —*The Lincoln Journal Star*

"The perfect tale for a cold winter's night." —*Publishers Weekly*

"Fans of this series will be delirious with joy . . . What a treat!" —*Kingston Observer*

Aunt Dimity Takes a Holiday

"A thoroughly modern cozy . . . The setting is delicious . . . A very enjoyable read." —*The Washington Post Book World*

Aunt Dimity: Detective

"Atherton's light-as-a-feather series is an excellent example of the (cozy) genre's traditions." —*The Seattle Times/Post-Intelligencer*

"Entertaining, comforting, and charming." —*Milwaukee Journal Sentinel*

Aunt Dimity Beats the Devil

"Nancy Atherton is a simply wonderful writer." —*The Cleveland Plain Dealer*

Aunt Dimity's Good Deed

"Atherton has a whimsical, fast-paced, well-plotted style that makes this book a romantic and graceful romp."

—*Houston Chronicle*

Aunt Dimity and the Duke

"Nancy Atherton is the most refreshingly optimistic new story-teller to grace the shelves in years. . . . Charming!" —*Murder Ink*

Aunt Dimity's Death

"A book I thoroughly enjoyed in the reading and which leaves me richer for having met charming people with the courage to care; and in places we all visit, at least in dreams."   —Anne Perry

A PENGUIN MYSTERY

AUNT DIMITY AND THE FAMILY TREE

Nancy Atherton is the author of fifteen other Aunt Dimity mysteries, many of them bestsellers. The first book in the series, *Aunt Dimity's Death*, was voted "One of the Century's 100 Favorite Mysteries" by the Independent Mystery Booksellers Association. She lives in Colorado Springs, Colorado.

Aunt Dimity
and the
Family Tree

NANCY ATHERTON

PENGUIN BOOKS

PENGUIN BOOKS

Published by the Penguin Group

Penguin Group (USA) Inc., 375 Hudson Street, New York, New York 10014, U.S.A.

Penguin Group (Canada), 90 Eglinton Avenue East, Suite 700, Toronto, Ontario, Canada M4P 2Y3
(a division of Pearson Penguin Canada Inc.) • Penguin Books Ltd, 80 Strand, London WC2R 0RL,
England • Penguin Ireland, 25 St. Stephen's Green, Dublin 2, Ireland (a division of Penguin Books
Ltd) • Penguin Books Australia Ltd, 250 Camberwell Road, Camberwell, Victoria 3124, Australia
(a division of Pearson Australia Group Pty Ltd) • Penguin Books India Pvt Ltd, 11 Community Centre,
Panchsheel Park, New Delhi—110 017, India • Penguin Group (NZ), 67 Apollo Drive, Rosedale,
Auckland 0632, New Zealand (a division of Pearson New Zealand Ltd) • Penguin Books (South Africa)
(Pty) Ltd, 24 Sturdee Avenue, Rosebank, Johannesburg 2196, South Africa

Penguin Books Ltd, Registered Offices: 80 Strand, London WC2R 0RL, England

First published in the United States of America by Viking Penguin,
a member of Penguin Group (USA) Inc. 2011
Published in Penguin Books 2012

3   5   7   9   10   8   6   4

Publisher's Note

This is a work of fiction. Names, characters, places, and incidents either are the product of the
author's imagination or are used fictitiously, and any resemblance to actual persons, living or
dead, business establishments, events, or locales is entirely coincidental.

THE LIBRARY OF CONGRESS HAS CATALOGED THE HARDCOVER EDITION AS FOLLOWS:

Atherton, Nancy.
Aunt Dimity and the family tree / Nancy Atherton.
p.   cm.
ISBN 978-0-670-02243-4 (hc.)
ISBN 978-0-14-312021-6 (pbk.)
1. Dimity, Aunt (Fictitious character)—Fiction.   2. Women detectives—England—Fiction.
3. City and town life—England—Fiction.   I. Title.
PS3551.T426A933   2011
813'.54—dc22
2010033598

Printed in the United States of America
Set in Perpetua   Designed by Alissa Amell

ALWAYS LEARNING   PEARSON

For Wyn,
who invited me to tea

Aunt Dimity and the
Family Tree

One

Fairworth House had good bones. Although it had been neglected for nearly fifty years by a succession of hapless owners, the basic fabric of the building had remained sound. I'd been mildly horrified when my father-in-law, William Willis, Sr., had informed me of his decision to purchase what appeared to be a two-hundred-and-fifty-year-old fixer-upper, but the engineer's report had proved that looks could be deceiving.

The slate roof required repair rather than replacement, the foundation retained its structural integrity, and the mellow limestone walls needed nothing more than patient pruning to rid them of the shaggy layers of ivy that had crept almost to the eaves. Though a handful of windows had been shattered by naughty children armed with slingshots, most were intact, and the splendid parquet floors had not fallen prey to dry rot, wood-worm, or water damage.

The superior skills of those who'd built the house and the quality of the materials they'd used had protected Fairworth from the elements, thus insuring that it would not descend with undue speed into an irretrievable state of decay. Fairworth House had aged, to be sure, but it had aged gracefully.

Fairworth wasn't palatial, but it would never be mistaken for a cottage. It was three stories tall, with no fewer than seven bedrooms, a conservatory, a billiards room, two reception rooms, a library, and a study. Any real estate agent worth his salt would have described it as "a pleasant country retreat for a gentleman of means." If he were honest, he would have added, "Needs work."

The chimneys were choked with soot, and the internal workings of the house were hopelessly out of date. After the purchase was completed, the plumbing, heating, and electrical systems received complete overhauls, as did the kitchen, the laundry facilities, and the bathrooms, and a small elevator was installed for the convenience of the staff as well as the new owner, whose knees weren't quite as springy as they'd once been.

By far the most significant alteration made to the building, however, was the creation, in the attics, of a self-contained, furnished apartment for the live-in servants who would, once they were hired, be responsible for the smooth running of the household.

The grounds, too, required serious attention. A professional landscape architect drew up plans for the lawns and the gardens that would be the focal point of the ten-acre estate, and a well-known landscaping firm turned his designs into reality. Barring unforeseen disaster, the kitchen garden would in a year's time be brimming with fruits and vegetables while the flower gardens flanking the house would produce enough blossoms to fill vases in every room.

With help from friends in the antiques trade, my father-in-law had, unbeknownst to me, started collecting eighteenth-century English furniture long before he had purchased Fairworth House. When the dust of renovation settled, he simply emptied his storage units into his new home. He worked closely with an interior designer to arrange each room's furnishings according to floor plans of his own devising, and he supervised the selection of appropriate paints, wallpapers, window treatments, upholstery, and bedding. At my suggestion, he placed a few historically inaccurate but cozier pieces of furniture here and there throughout the house, to make it feel less like a museum and more like a home.

By happy chance, some of Fairworth's original contents had been found stashed away in a dark corner of the old stables. A painting, a book, and a few pieces of bric-a-brac that had long kept company with spiders, mice, and bats were freed from their cobwebs and brought forth into the light of day.

The end result was spectacular, in an understated way. Fairworth House wasn't a flashy showpiece embellished with turrets, towers, and florid ornamentation. It was a solid, respectable Georgian house—classical, restrained, and relatively modest in size. The place I'd once thought an irreparable ruin had, in fact, been a tarnished gem that had needed diligent polishing—and a hefty infusion of cold, hard cash—to make it gleam.

The house suited its new owner to a *T*. William Arthur Willis, Sr., was the patriarch of a venerable Boston Brahmin clan whose family law firm catered to the whims of the wealthy. He'd been born into money, had made a great deal more of it over the course of his career, and would never want for it, now that he'd retired from his position as head of the firm. Although he was accustomed to the finer things in life, he disdained ostentation. Like the house he'd recently purchased, Willis, Sr., was solid, respectable, and thoroughly elegant—in an understated way.

He was also a devoted family man. Despite having the means to buy a much grander and far less derelict estate, Willis, Sr., had chosen Fairworth because of its proximity to his only child, a son christened William Arthur Willis, Jr., but known universally as Bill.

Bill Willis happened to be my husband. He and I lived with our seven-year-old twin sons, Will and Rob, and our black cat, Stanley, in a honey-colored cottage nestled snugly amid the rolling hills and patchwork fields of the Cotswolds, a rural region in England's West Midlands. Although Bill and I were Americans, we'd lived in England for nearly a decade. Our sons were more familiar with cricket than they were with baseball, and they celebrated Guy Fawkes Day with the same gusto as they did the Fourth of July.

Since Bill and I had no desire to uproot our happy family, Willis, Sr., had, upon his retirement, elected to entwine his roots with ours in England. Fairworth House was approximately two miles away from our cottage, a distance Will and Rob could traverse easily on their gray ponies, Thunder and Storm. To encourage their visits, Willis, Sr., had devoted the same care and attention to refurbishing his stable block as he had to restoring his house.

The nearest hub of civilization was Finch, a small village with no recognizable claim to fame. Local farmers patronized its shops and itinerant artists occasionally immortalized its buildings, but tourists seldom ventured down its narrow, twisting lanes, and historians ignored it altogether.

Thanks to its backwater status, Finch had defied modern trends and remained a tight-knit community in which everyone took a lively—some might say an obsessive—interest in everyone else's business. My husband, who ran the European branch of his family's law firm from a high-tech office on the village green, had learned early on to close his windows before making sensitive telephone calls because, in Finch, someone was *always* listening.

My father-in-law had provided enough grist to keep Finch's gossip mill churning merrily for months on end. Fairworth's graveled drive skirted the southern edge of the village, giving the locals an excellent vantage point from which to view the parade of heavy vehicles that had rumbled to and from the site during the renovation. Some of the villagers derided Willis, Sr., for throwing good money away on a decrepit dump. Others saluted him for restoring a historic home to its former glory.

Still others—a small but powerful minority composed principally of widows and spinsters of mature years—believed passionately that Willis, Sr., had made the best decision that had ever been made in the entire history of civilization. Hearts that had long lain dormant fluttered wildly at the prospect of welcoming a well-off, white-haired widower to the neighborhood.

My husband referred to these worthy ladies as "Father's Handmaidens," and it was they who were, in large part, responsible for the fantastic speed with which

Fairworth House was made habitable. Age and experience had given the Handmaidens an air of authority they did not hesitate to use. Every morning, rain or shine, they crossed the humpbacked bridge at the edge of town and marched determinedly up Willis, Sr.'s tree-lined drive to hover near the work site like a flock of demanding grannies.

Workers who arrived on time, took short breaks, and avoided visits to the pub were rewarded with fresh-baked cookies, home-cooked lunches, and the blissful silence that ensues when harpies cease to screech. Slackers were given lukewarm tea, icy stares, and, if necessary, a good talking-to.

The poor workmen were so eager to return to a world in which they could enjoy an evening's pint in peace that they accomplished in three months what should have taken them six. By mid-August, Fairworth House was fit for occupation. The library required fine-tuning, as did the billiards room and the conservatory, but the principal chambers were finished and furnished. Willis, Sr., would move in on Thursday, the twelfth of August, and I would throw a gala housewarming party for him on the evening of Saturday the fourteenth.

The only fly in the ointment was the absence of a live-in staff. Although Willis, Sr., had, with my assistance, interviewed a host of candidates sent to him by a reputable London employment agency, none had proven satisfactory. My father-in-law's preference for a mature, married couple had made the search ten times more difficult than it might otherwise have been.

Predictably, the Handmaidens had volunteered to do his cooking, his housekeeping, his gardening, and much more, but he'd politely refused their overtures, knowing full well that to choose one strong-minded woman over another would be to trigger a turf war whose reverberations would be felt throughout the village for years to come. To have all of them in the house at once, competing ardently—perhaps violently—for his attention, would be equally intolerable, so he set his sights on a competent couple who had no ties whatsoever to Finch. So far, no such couple had surfaced.

My father-in-law was discovering, as many had discovered before him, that good help was hard to find.

A good daughter-in-law, on the other hand, lived only a couple of miles away. It soon became apparent to me that, if reliable servants failed to materialize, I would be saddled with the difficult task of running two households simultaneously.

Cooking wouldn't be a problem—I could throw together healthy meals fairly quickly—and I could rely on my best friend, Emma Harris, to keep the gardens from dying an early death, but the mere thought of keeping up with two extremely active little boys while at the same time chasing dust bunnies from one end of Fairworth House to the other made me want to lie down in a dark room with a cold compress on my forehead.

I pleaded with the agency to find applicants who weren't too old, too young, too haughty, too flighty, too lazy, too rude, or simply too stupid to fill the well-paid posts, but as the fourteenth of August drew near with no likely candidates in sight, I began to lose hope.

On the day of the party, I rose with the sun, drove Will and Rob to nearby Anscombe Manor for their riding lessons, stopped at Fairworth House to make breakfast for Willis, Sr., and returned to the cottage to find Bill devouring a pile of toast he'd made for himself. I waved off the buttery slice he offered to me and headed straight for the old oak desk in the study to review my last-minute to-do list. The months I'd spent dealing with stationers, caterers, florists, and musicians were about to pay off.

At eight o'clock, two hundred guests would arrive at a flower-bedecked Fairworth House to savor an array of delectable nibbles and to drink champagne toasts to my darling father-in-law while a chamber orchestra played discreetly in the background. I might not be able to install plumbing fixtures or to pleach apple trees, but I know how to throw a good party. Thanks to my meticulous planning, Willis, Sr.'s housewarming was bound to be the most scintillating social event of the summer.

I was halfway through my checklist when Davina Trent, my contact at the employment agency, telephoned to inform me that a suitable married couple would arrive at Fairworth House before nightfall. The timing wasn't optimal, but beggars, I'd learned, couldn't be choosers.

"How suitable is the couple?" I asked suspiciously.

"Quite suitable," came the prim reply. "I will fax the particulars to you immediately, Ms. Shepherd."

Mrs. Trent earned bonus points for calling me "Ms. Shepherd." People who didn't know me well tended to forget that, while my sons and my husband were Willises, I'd retained my own last name when I'd married Bill.

"I give you my personal assurance," Mrs. Trent went on, "that your father-in-law will be delighted with the Donovans."

"We'll see." I sighed wistfully, thanked her, and hung up. I could squeeze an interview into the day's busy schedule somehow, but I wasn't expecting much. I'd been disappointed too often to believe that the delightful Donovans would live up to their billing.

As I stretched a hand toward the fax machine, the telephone rang again. This time, the caller delivered news that sent chills up my spine. I stared at the phone for a moment in dumbfounded disbelief, then threw back my head and howled, *"No!"*

The receiver dropped from my numb fingers and I slumped forward onto the desk as Bill came tearing into the study.

"Lori?" he said, rushing over to me. "What is it? Has something happened to the boys? Is it Father?"

"It's not William or the twins." I groaned. "It's the *caterers.*"

Bill heaved a sigh of relief, restored the telephone to its cradle, and put a comforting hand on my back.

"What's wrong with the caterers?" he asked.

"Food poisoning," I replied tragically. "The entire wait-staff is sick, the kitchens have to be professionally sanitized before they can be used again, and every bite of food has been *thrown out.*" I buried my face in my hands and moaned dolorously. "My canapés, my *beautiful* canapés, all of those finger sandwiches, the caviar, the lobster,

the smoked salmon, the petits fours, the itty-bitty eclairs, even the *crudités* . . . gone, all g-gone." My voice broke and I couldn't continue.

"Well," Bill said reasonably, "we wouldn't want to poison our guests, would we?"

"No," I whimpered.

"Can the caterers deliver the champagne?" he asked.

"Yes," I said limply. "They can bring the ice as well, but how . . . *how* are we going to *feed* everyone?"

"Easy," said Bill, with a nonchalant shrug. "Put out an S.O.S. to Father's Handmaidens."

I straightened slowly and felt the color return to my face.

"The Handmaidens?" I said, peering dazedly at the diamond-paned windows above the desk. "Of course. Why didn't *I* think of them?"

"You were in shock. I'm sure you would have thought of them eventually." Bill glanced at his watch. "I'll be in the office until noon, love. After that, I'm yours to command."

I jumped to my feet and kissed him soundly, then pushed him firmly out of the study.

"Go," I said. "I have to marshal my troops."

"Good luck, *mon capitaine*!" he threw over his shoulder.

I picked up the phone and began dialing, confident that the village's cadre of unmarried ladies would rally to my cause and produce a nontoxic feast for two hundred guests on time and under budget, if for no other reason than to impress the man of their dreams. I honestly believed that my greatest challenge would be to prevent food fights from breaking out among them as the evening wore on.

I hadn't the slightest inkling that, before the day was through, I would become embroiled in the greatest act of deception ever perpetrated on the good people of Finch.

Life in an English village is never dull.

Two

ews of the catering crisis spread through Finch faster than fleas in a kennel. Before long, offers of help were pouring in from all of my neighbors, regardless of age, sex, or marital status. The speed and urgency of their response didn't surprise me. The villagers were generous souls, always willing to lend a hand in an emergency, but a force more powerful than generosity drove them to salvage the housewarming party. As Lilian Bunting, the vicar's wife, put it: "They're quite simply *agog* to see what William's done with Fairworth House!"

I shared Lilian's belief that most of my neighbors regarded the party as a golden opportunity to sidle furtively from room to room, critiquing carpets, draperies, wall colors, and furniture arrangements while debating how much every painting, book, and bauble had cost. I was fully prepared, therefore, to handle the flurry of phone calls that came in from volunteers eager to roll up their sleeves and do whatever they could to ensure that the long-awaited show would go on.

I carefully doled out assignments, to avoid having too many pâtés and not enough profiteroles, then let the villagers take it from there. Those who could cook retreated to their kitchens. Those who didn't know one end of a piping bag from the other made themselves useful by fetching supplies from the village shops or from the big grocery store in the nearby market town of Upper Deeping.

Almost everyone gathered fresh herbs and vegetables from their own gardens, and a pair of local farmers drove from cottage to cottage, delivering eggs, poultry, bacon, milk, cream, butter, and cheese to those in need. By noon, Finch smelled so deliciously sweet and savory that I could have eaten the air.

Once the ball was rolling, I arranged for Will and Rob to spend the entire day at their riding school—the twins' idea of heaven—and moved my command post from the cottage to Fairworth House. After a brief search, I found my father-in-law settled comfortably in a leather armchair in his study, a light and airy room appended to the library.

Willis, Sr., was perusing an old and dusty volume embossed with the thrilling title: *Notes on Sheep*. I recognized it as the book we'd unearthed in the ruins of the old stables, along with a painting that was in dire need of cleaning. Willis, Sr., kept *Notes on Sheep* on his desk, but the painting leaned against the wall near the Sheraton sideboard, awaiting the ministrations of our local art restorer.

The painting wasn't merely soiled, it was hazardous—I'd nearly sliced my hand open on a shard of broken glass protruding from the frame's inner edge. God alone knew what it depicted, because no human eye could penetrate the layers of grime that obscured the image. Its filthiness struck a discordant note in an otherwise spotless room.

A refreshing breeze wafted in from the garden

through the open French doors, and the tall windows gleamed in the sunlight. Willis, Sr., inspired, perhaps, by the glorious summer day, was dressed as casually as I'd ever seen him, in a white flannel suit, a pale blue shirt, a yellow silk tie, white socks, and tasseled loafers. A silver tray on his walnut desk held a cut-glass pitcher filled with iced lemonade, and a glass of lemonade sat on the small satinwood table at his elbow. Although the weather was ideal for long walks across open meadows, my father-in-law clearly planned to spend the rest of the day indoors.

He closed his book and set it aside as I entered the room.

"I am considering the acquisition of a small flock of sheep," he announced.

"Sheep?" I said, caught off guard.

"Cotswold Sheep, to be precise," he said, "also known as Cotswold Lions, an ancient and threatened domestic breed endowed with a magnificent fleece. It would be a worthy endeavor to aid in the breed's preservation."

"Uh-huh," I agreed, and moved on to more pressing matters. When I began a breathless account of the sudden change in plans, however, Willis, Sr., raised a well-manicured hand to silence me.

"There is no need to explain," he said. "Bill came to see me on his way to the office. He informed me of the food-poisoning incident. It is a most distressing turn of events, to be sure, but I have no doubt that you will rise like a phoenix from the ashes and soar triumphantly over the hurdles that have been placed so inconsiderately in your path." He sighed contentedly as his gaze traveled around the sunlit room. "As you can see, I have chosen to follow my son's advice to, ahem, 'lie low until Hurricane Lori passes.'"

"Clever boy, that son of yours," I said with a rueful chuckle. "Why didn't you abandon ship and seek sanctuary in Bill's office?"

"I wished to be near at hand in the unlikely event that you should ask for my advice," said Willis, Sr. "Your manner suggests, however, that you have already solved the catering dilemma."

"As a matter of fact, I have," I said. "The villagers are pitching in to provide party fare. I don't know what they'll bring or when they'll bring it, and I have a thousand other arrangements to make before their contributions start trickling in, so there's bound to be a fair amount of chaos, but I'll see to it that no one bothers you in here. Your study will be off limits during the party, too. I don't want anyone rummaging through your desk."

Willis, Sr.'s eyebrows rose. "Who would have the audacity to rummage through my desk?"

"Anyone who wants to know how much you paid for your collection of miniatures," I replied bluntly. "The villagers have inquiring minds. It's best to lead them not into temptation."

He pursed his lips thoughtfully. "I will lock the study's doors when I leave. It may also be advisable to drape a decorative swag across the bottom of the main staircase, to discourage exploration of the upper stories."

"An excellent suggestion. I'll ask the florist to take care of it." I glanced at the cut-glass pitcher, wondering if a Handmaiden had dropped in to fuss over Willis, Sr., while I'd been fielding phone calls at the cottage. "Did Bill make the lemonade for you?"

"I cannot tell a lie," said Willis, Sr., his gray eyes twinkling. "I made it. I squeezed the lemons, added the sugar, poured the water, and stirred in the ice without assistance of any kind. You may find it difficult to believe, my dear Lori, but I am not entirely helpless."

"I don't think you're helpless," I protested. "But if you get hungry——"

"I shall make a valiant attempt to find my way back to the kitchen," Willis, Sr., interrupted, "where I have set aside a loaf of granary bread, a generous wedge of Stilton cheese, and a pair of ripe apples. I may be overly optimistic, Lori, but I believe that, with an effort, I will successfully avoid starvation."

"I get it," I said, smiling wryly. "Not helpless. Do you have your cell phone?"

"I do," he said, patting his breast pocket, "and I promise to use it to contact you if the need arises. In the meantime, I beg you to dismiss me from your thoughts. You have far more important business to attend to."

"You may have to attend to business, too," I said. "Davina Trent called to tell me that she found another couple for you to interview—the Donovans. She said they'll be here before nightfall."

"'Before nightfall' is a rather elastic time frame," Willis, Sr., observed, frowning. "Mrs. Trent is an exceptionally well-organized woman. I wonder why she was unable to be more precise?"

"I have no idea," I said, glancing at my watch. "Maybe the Donovans will tell us. Keep an eye out for them, will you?" I gestured toward the windows. "You have a clear view of the drive from here. If you see a strange couple pull up in an unfamiliar car—"

"—I shall use my cell phone to notify you." Willis, Sr., nodded patiently, then peered through the window closest to him. "Do the Donovans own a paneled van decorated with a floral motif?"

"A floral motif?" I followed his gaze and yelped, "It's the florists! They're early! And they're supposed to use the *back* door! I'd better get out there before they drip water on your beautiful floors. I'll touch base with you later, William." I glanced darkly at the grimy painting, then sprinted for the entrance hall to begin what would be a very long day of trying to be in too many places at once.

By six o'clock, the flowers were in place, the champagne was chilling, the musicians were seated in the library, and the kitchen was filled to overflowing with an astonishing array of finger food, all of it provided by my industrious and highly motivated neighbors.

Charles Bellingham and Grant Tavistock had closed their art appraisal and restoration business for the day in order to construct exquisite canapés featuring caviar, foie gras, truffles, and other splendidly high-end ingre-

dients. At the other end of the taste spectrum, Dick
Peacock, the publican, had turned out sausage rolls by
the score while his wife, Christine, had spent hours
sticking toothpicks into bite-sized pieces of cheese and
fruit.

Nineteen-year-old Bree Pym contributed miniature
pavlovas, which made sense, since she was from New
Zealand, and Emma Harris teamed up with Miranda
Morrow, the village witch, to make low-fat, vegetarian
hors d'oeuvres that, I feared, many would admire, but
few would eat.

Lilian Bunting had recruited a dozen volunteers to
work on a finger-sandwich assembly line in the old
schoolhouse, which, under normal circumstances,
served as the village hall. Her husband, Theodore Bunting, the mild-mannered vicar of St. George's Church in
Finch, presented the fruits of their labor to me along
with a fervent prayer for deliverance from food poisoning. Although I prayed with him, I also made sure that
perishable items were stored in the refrigerated truck
I'd rented from a restaurant supply company in Upper
Deeping. I was sure that God would understand. He
was rather keen on helping those who helped themselves.

The Handmaidens produced so many pastries that
Willis, Sr., could have opened his own bake shop.
Elspeth Binney, a retired schoolteacher, turned out hundreds of pastel-colored petits fours. Millicent Scroggins, a retired secretary, made madeleines, macaroons,
and meringues. Selena Buxton, a retired wedding planner, delivered a variety of dainty fruit tartlets. Opal

Taylor, who had the unfair advantage of being a retired professional cook, outdid them all by baking batch after batch of vol-au-vents filled with everything from smoked oysters to curried prawns.

The only villager missing in action was Sally Pyne, the energetic, grandmother-shaped widow who owned the village tearoom. When I heard Sally's hoarse voice and rasping cough on the telephone, I told her to go back to bed and to stay there. Her sixteen-year-old granddaughter, Rainey Dawson, was on hand to look after her, but even so, the timing of Sally's illness couldn't have been worse. She and Rainey would miss the party, which would be a great disappointment to them both. I was disappointed, too, because Sally would have been a model guest—she was the only widow in town who'd shown no interest in seducing my father-in-law.

The kitchen crew and the waitstaff I'd hired at great expense through a catering firm in Oxford arrived at half past six to set up food stations and to learn the layout of the ground floor. A young man named Chad appointed himself head butler and took up his post in the entrance hall, while his friend Rupert volunteered to act as car valet, a position that hadn't even occurred to me. Though Fairworth still smelled of fresh paint and damp plaster, we were as ready as we could be to welcome our guests. At seven fifteen, Willis, Sr., who'd exchanged his casual flannels for an immaculate black three-piece suit, gave me my marching orders.

I made a mad dash for the cottage, where, much to my delight, I found a pair of freshly bathed and neatly dressed little boys as well as a dapper husband. I took a quick shower, passed a blow dryer over my dark, curly hair, and slipped into the summery forget-me-not-blue silk dress I'd had made for the occasion.

Bill forced me to take a calming breath before he would allow me to join Rob and Will in our canary-yellow Range Rover. After I was seated, he took his place behind the wheel, paused to caress my cheek lightly with his hand, then hit the gas and gunned it all the way to Fairworth House while the boys egged him on from the backseat.

Rupert took Bill's car keys, Chad opened the front door, and Willis, Sr., greeted us in the high-ceilinged entrance hall. As we strolled into the morning room, I heard the faint strains of a Mozart concerto floating toward me from the library, breathed in the heady scent of tuberoses, and smiled as one fresh-faced young woman offered the adults champagne, another offered sparkling cider to the children, and still another presented us with a gleaming silver salver dotted with delicate canapés. I took a glass of champagne and turned to Willis, Sr., but before I could salute him, he raised his glass to me.

"To the heroine of the hour," he said.

"To Hurricane Lori," Bill added.

"To Mummy!" the twins chorused.

I blushed happily, accepted their accolades, and allowed myself to savor the first moment of peace I'd had all day.

It would also be the last.

*　　*　　*

By half past eight, I understood why houses had ball-rooms. Parties confined to one space were easier to monitor than parties spread through many separate chambers.

Since Fairworth House lacked a ballroom, I had to wander from one room to the next to reassure myself that everyone was having a good time. Fortunately, the rooms were connected to the main corridor and to one another by a series of arched doorways, which made it relatively easy for me to circulate. The buzz of lively conversation, the frequent outbursts of laughter, and the glow emanating from Willis, Sr.'s face as he welcomed family and friends eventually convinced me that all was well.

At nine o'clock I handed my hostess duties over to Emma Harris and Lilian Bunting—the most sensible women present—and threw myself into the challenging task of convincing my two thoroughly overexcited sons that it was time for them to go to bed. After much dis-cussion, Will and Rob agreed to return to the cottage with newlyweds Nell and Kit Smith, who'd volunteered to babysit. Since Kit and Nell got along well with the twins, and since they still preferred each other's com-pany to anyone else's, they were perfectly content to leave Fairworth House behind and enjoy a quiet evening at the cottage.

By the time I finished attending to my sons, the party was in full swing. A beaming Willis, Sr., was holding court in the drawing room, surrounded by new friends and old. Emma, who looked unusually alert, had positioned herself just behind him, but Lilian was nowhere to be found. When I ran into Bill in the billiards room, I asked if he knew where she was.

"Lilian's in the kitchen," he told me, "reading the riot act to the Handmaidens."

My stomach clenched. "Why? What did they do?"

"The minute you went upstairs they barged into the kitchen to fill trays with their own special goodies," he said. "Then they began to stalk Father. I shudder to think what would have happened if they'd caught up with him simultaneously."

"Dear Lord," I said, putting a hand to my forehead. "It would have been total war."

"Total war," Bill repeated gravely. "Vol-au-vents splattered on the ceiling, tartlets zipping through the air, innocent bystanders laid low by flying macaroons . . ." His words trailed off in a gurgle of laughter.

I dropped my hand and regarded him through narrowed eyes. "Have you ever tried to remove curried prawns from a freshly plastered ceiling medallion?"

"No," Bill replied, grinning, "and thanks to Lilian, I won't have to. She spotted danger approaching, headed it off, and herded the offenders into the kitchen for a refresher course on good manners."

"Leaving Emma to look after William," I said, as comprehension dawned.

"You chose his bodyguards well," said Bill. "I don't think the Handmaidens will cause any more trouble. Uh-oh." He looked past me and murmured, "Speaking of trouble . . ."

I swung around to see Peggy Taxman step through from the library into the billiards room. She scanned the room hastily, as though she were searching for someone, then made a beeline straight for me.

"Time to check on Father, I think." Bill spun on his heels and beat a hasty retreat to the drawing room.

"Coward," I said under my breath, but I smiled as I said it.

I couldn't blame Bill for steering clear of Peggy Taxman. Peggy was a formidable woman, a mover and shaker who ruled Finch with an iron hand and a stentorian voice. She ran the post office, the general store, and the greengrocer's shop, and she had a nasty habit of "volunteering" people to serve on the committees she invariably chaired. Village life would have come to a standstill without her, but no one could deny that she was officious, opinionated, overbearing, and, quite frankly, terrifying. When Peggy Taxman's majestic bosom and her rhinestone-studded glasses hove into view, most men—and many women—ran for cover.

"Hello, Peggy," I said brightly, bending sideways to smile at the nondescript man trailing in her wake. "I see you've brought your husband. Good to see you, Jasper. I'm glad both of you could come."

Jasper murmured something inaudible, but Peggy made up for his reticence by thundering, "Well, of course we came! Wouldn't have missed it for the world! Which is more than I can say for a certain friend of ours who is conspicuous by her absence."

"I noticed it, too," said Millicent Scroggins, appearing as if out of thin air at Peggy's elbow. "Haven't seen her all evening."

"Nor have I," said Charles Bellingham, coming up behind Millicent.

A circle of neighbors coalesced around our little group, drawn by Finch's special brand of social magnetism, and the conversation began to gather speed.

"We're trying to solve an intriguing mystery," Charles explained to the newcomers. "Where is *La Señora?*"

The villagers had referred to Sally Pyne as *"La Señora"* ever since she'd returned in late June from a trip to Mexico. Sally had won the ten-day, all-expenses-paid vacation by entering a contest in a travel magazine. Her friends might have been pleased for her if she hadn't spent the rest of the summer boring them stupid with her tales of adventure. To be sure, her stories were exciting. She had, apparently, kayaked across a laguna, swum in a subterranean river, zip-lined across a sinkhole, petted a stingray while snorkeling near a coral reef, and climbed the tallest Mayan pyramid in the world, among a great many other things. The trouble was, no one believed a word of it. Sally was a brilliant pastry chef and a champion gossipmonger, but an athlete she was not.

"I can't imagine *La Señora* missing a fiesta like this," Charles Bellingham commented, plucking a glass of champagne from a passing tray. "Perhaps you should have served tequila, Lori."

"And hired a mariachi band," Grant Tavistock put in. "Chamber music may be too tame for her now."

"Maybe she's in training for the Olympics," Christine Peacock suggested, rolling her eyes.

"Or getting ready to conquer Everest," said Dick Peacock.

"Or preparing to swim the Channel," chimed in Elspeth Binney.

"Flying a rocket ship to the moon, more like," said Selena Buxton, snickering.

"I reckon she's ill," said Mr. Barlow, Finch's kindhearted handyman. "Only thing that would keep her away."

"Do you think it could be something . . . tropical?" George Wetherhead asked worriedly. The shy model-train enthusiast did not have a robust constitution.

"Malaria, perhaps?" Opal Taylor offered hopefully. Opal resented Sally's success at the summer bake sale. "Or cholera?"

"Could be dengue fever," Grant Tavistock proposed. "Charles and I read an article about it last week. *Dreadful* disease. One bite from an infected mosquito and you're done for. *No cure*," he concluded somberly.

"N-no c-cure?" George Wetherhead stammered, his eyes like saucers.

"Most likely it's Montezuma's Revenge," said Mr. Barlow. "Sally ate some queer things over there—tacos and tamales and such. Bound to catch up with her sooner or later."

"Hold on!" I said, raising my voice to be heard above the clamor. "I can tell you why Sally's not here. She telephoned me this afternoon to tell me that she couldn't come to the party because she has a sore throat, a cough, and a stuffy nose. She has a summer cold, that's all, and

I'm grateful to her for not sharing it with William's guests."

"A cold?" my audience murmured disappointedly.

"Poor old Sally," said Christine, shaking her head.

"It's a good thing she's got her granddaughter staying with her," said Dick. "Girl's as bright as a button. Rainey'll have no trouble managing the teashop while Sally's under the weather."

"I'll stop by tomorrow morning to see if Rainey needs a hand with anything," said Mr. Barlow.

"I'll brew a slippery elm bark tisane for Sally," said Miranda. "Very soothing for the throat."

My mundane solution to what had been an intriguing mystery took the wind out of everyone's sails. They exchanged a few more ideas on how best to help Sally, then wandered off, leaving me once more alone with the Taxmans. Peggy, who had been uncharacteristically silent throughout the debate, waited for the others to disperse, then let out a derisive snort.

"Ha!" she said, tossing her head. "A summer cold, my aunt Fanny! You can believe what you want, Lori Shepherd, but I know why Sally's afraid to show her face in decent company."

"Do you?" I said, mystified.

"It's the *letter*," she said, leaning close to me.

"I see." I nodded wisely. "What letter?"

"The letter she picked up at the post office this morning," Peggy explained in what was, for her, an undertone. "The letter with the *Mexican stamp*! Blushed like a bride when I handed it to her. Opened it on the spot. I expected her to make a great show of reading it aloud, but instead she turned twenty shades of red, went white as a ghost, stuffed it back into the envelope, and trotted off without saying a word. And now she's not here." Peggy folded her massive arms and peered down at me through her glittering glasses. "Makes you wonder, doesn't it?"

"She sounded sick to me," I said hesitantly.

"She's faking," Peggy barked. "I told her that no good ever comes of foreign travel, but would she listen?" Peggy pursed her lips. "Mark my words, Lori, our Sally has done something she oughtn't."

"What sort of something?" I asked.

"I don't know yet," Peggy acknowledged. "But I will. I'll winkle the truth out of *La Señora*. I always do!"

A manic gleam lit Peggy's eyes as she sailed out of the billiards room. Jasper gave me a helpless look, then trailed meekly after her.

I had less than a minute to contemplate Peggy's tantalizing news before a trio of out-of-town guests—Sir Percy Pelham, Adrian Culver, and Nicholas Fox—swept me into the library, demanding that I show them the finest volumes in Willis, Sr.'s collection. I used the knowledge I'd acquired as a rare-book bibliographer to satisfy their curiosity, then allowed myself to drift aimlessly through the party's swirls and eddies. I ended up in the conservatory with Bill and his English cousins, Lucy and Gerald, both of whom worked for the family law firm. When they started talking shop, I excused myself and stepped out into the garden for a breath of fresh air.

A soft breeze cooled my brow as I strolled away from

the brightly lit house, and the cheerful cacophony of music, laughter, and talk dwindled to a distant hum. I was about to release a profoundly satisfied sigh when a hand clamped onto my wrist and dragged me into the darkness.

No one but my assailant heard me scream.

Three

"**S** top screeching, Lori!" said a voice. "It's me! *Me!*"

"R-Rainey?" I pressed a hand to my breast and stared wide-eyed at the long, narrow, and very anxious face of Sally Pyne's auburn-haired granddaughter. "For pity's sake, Rainey, you nearly gave me a heart attack!"

"I know and I'm sorry," she said earnestly, "but I couldn't think of any other way to speak with you privately."

Rainey Dawson was dressed like a cat burglar, in sneakers, dark jeans, and a black, hooded sweatshirt. She spoke in an urgent whisper as she pulled me deeper into the shadows cast by an ancient chestnut tree. Though she was a slender teenager, she had a grip like a lumberjack's.

"I can think of a dozen ways to talk to me," I said sternly, when we came to a halt, "beginning with the telephone."

"People eavesdrop on telephone calls," she retorted. "You know how *they* are."

Rainey didn't have to explain who "they" were.

"I realize that your grandmother's friends can be a bit intrusive at times," I conceded diplomatically, "but they don't eavesdrop at the cottage. We can talk there tomorrow, after I come home from church."

"No, we *can't*." She shook her head vehemently. "I have to speak with you *tonight*."

"What's wrong?" I said, suddenly alert. "Does your grandmother need a doctor or"—my heart constricted—"an ambulance?"

"Gran's not sick!" Rainey exclaimed. She clapped a hand over her mouth, as if to keep herself from shouting again, then spoke in a feverish whisper. "It was all *play-acting*, Lori! Gran doesn't need a *doctor*. She needs *William*."

I blinked at her incredulously for a moment, then said through gritted teeth, "Rainey, if you frightened me half to death for the sole purpose of telling me that your grandmother is secretly pining for my father-in-law——"

"It's not that," she interrupted. She glanced furtively toward the house before continuing, "Gran's gotten herself into the most frightful pickle, Lori, and she needs William's help to get out of it."

"What kind of pickle?" I asked.

"The kind only *Gran* could get herself into," Rainey replied, with a touch of asperity.

"Is she in some legal difficulty?" I asked. It seemed reasonable to assume that a villager at odds with the law might seek advice from an experienced attorney like Willis, Sr., whether he was retired or not. My guess, unfortunately, went wide of the mark.

"*If only.*" The girl groaned miserably. "I'm afraid it's much more complicated than that."

It was on the tip of my tongue to ask if Sally's complicated problem had something to do with her mysterious Mexican correspondent but Rainey jumped in before I could speak.

"It'll be much easier if Gran explains," she said. "Can she come here to see William after the party's over?"

"The party won't be over until dawn," I warned her.

"It doesn't matter," she said. "Gran won't get a wink of sleep tonight anyway. She's too upset. You can ring the tearoom after your guests have gone home." She shifted restlessly from foot to foot as she added, "Gran's in a dreadful state, Lori. She has to see William *tonight*."

"Okay," I said, recognizing desperation when I saw it. "I'll ask William to wait up for her and I'll call the tearoom as soon as the coast is clear."

"Thank you!" Rainey flung her slender arms around me in a grateful hug, then stepped back. "I'd better go. Honestly, Lori, when Gran goes off the rails, she *really* goes off the rails!"

As she faded silently into the darkness, I wondered if any of my guests could teach me the Spanish word for *pickle*.

The housewarming party ended much sooner than I'd predicted, out of consideration, no doubt, for Willis, Sr.'s advanced years. The locals, who tended to be early risers, were gone by half past ten and the last of the out-of-towners said their farewells just after eleven. A small group of close friends stuck around to help me and the Oxford crew with the cleanup effort, but by midnight, Bill, Willis, Sr., and I had the house to ourselves.

I called Kit Smith for an update on Will and Rob and

to let him know that Bill and I would return to the cottage as soon as Willis, Sr., had retired for the evening. Kit assured me that the boys were sleeping soundly and that he and Nell would wait up for us.

Willis, Sr., had consented to receive Sally Pyne in his study. Bill had earned the right to sit in on the meeting by informing us—a bit smugly—that the Spanish word for Sally's particular type of pickle was *"el aprieto."* I was there because wild horses couldn't have kept me away.

Our rendezvous with Sally had a cloak-and-dagger air to it, so I closed the drapes and dimmed the lights in the study while Willis, Sr., took his place behind his walnut desk and Bill seated himself in the leather armchair near the west-facing windows. I was about to make the prearranged telephone call to the tearoom when the doorbell rang.

"I'll answer it," I said. "It's probably Chad and Rupert, looking for a bigger tip."

"Give it to them," said Bill. "They did a great job."

Having bestowed a princely sum upon each member of the Oxford contingent, I was prepared to argue the point, but Willis, Sr., intervened.

"It is most likely Grant Tavistock," he said. He gestured to the grimy painting that had been found in the ruined stables. "I spoke with Mr. Tavistock earlier this evening and he agreed to take my neglected masterpiece to his studio for cleaning and evaluation. I imagine he has returned to fulfill his promise. He did not have his car with him at the time of the party, you see, and he could hardly carry the painting to Finch in his arms."

"He'll have to carry it to his car," I said grimly. "I don't want to get my new dress filthy."

"I am certain that he will oblige you," said Willis, Sr. "It is a lovely dress."

"Thank you, William." I curtseyed in a ladylike manner, then hiked up my lovely dress and set off for the entrance hall at a distinctly unladylike jog.

I didn't care for the painting in Willis, Sr.'s study. I had, in fact, developed a strong antipathy toward it, not only because it had tried to slice my hand open, but because it had left sooty streaks and smudges on carpets, walls, and anyone who handled it. Willis, Sr.'s "neglected masterpiece" was, quite literally, a dirty picture, and I resented it for soiling his pristine residence. I was so eager for Grant to take it away that I flung open the front door and began to thank him from the bottom of my heart before I realized that I wasn't speaking to Grant.

A pair of total strangers stood on the doorstep, smiling tentatively at me.

"Good evening," said the man.

"Hello," said the woman.

"We're the Donovans," said the man.

"The Donovans?" I stared at him blankly until the name finally clicked into place. "Oh! The Donovans! Davina Trent's Donovans! From the employment agency!"

"That's right," said the woman. "I'm Deirdre."

"And I'm Declan," said the man.

"I'm Lori Shepherd," I said. "Pleased to meet you."

Deirdre shook my proffered hand, saying, "Mrs. Trent has told us so much about you, Ms. Shepherd. It's a pleasure to finally meet you. I hope you'll accept our sincere and heartfelt apologies for arriving at such an inconvenient hour. We had car trouble."

"And our mobiles died," Declan added, holding up his cell phone.

"And we kept missing the turnoff," Deirdre went on.

"And by the time we sorted ourselves out, night had fallen," said Declan. "We would have waited until tomorrow to keep our appointment, but we couldn't find a guesthouse or a hotel."

"We're not familiar with the area," Deirdre interjected.

"So we came ahead on the off-chance that someone would still be awake," said Declan. "When we saw lights in the ground-floor windows, we thought . . ." He gazed at me imploringly.

"Better late than never," I said, moved as much by their fervor as by their plight. "Won't you come in?"

I studied the Donovans closely as they walked into the entrance hall. They appeared to be in their early thirties, a factor that might count against them, given Willis, Sr.'s preference for a mature couple. Declan was a stocky redhead with a barrel chest, light blue eyes, and a round, freckled face. His black suit, white shirt, and black tie needed pressing, but his untidiness was understandable, given the circumstances. He spoke with an unmistakable Irish accent.

Deirdre Donovan was another kettle of fish altogether. She was slender and almost a full head taller than Declan, and her accent was pure upper-class English. She was dressed ordinarily enough, in a short-sleeved summer dress and low-heeled pumps, but her looks were far from ordinary. She had a creamy complexion, high cheekbones, a strong, straight nose, and shapely lips. Her eyes were a rich, dark brown and their unusual almond shape was accentuated by a prominent mole near the corner of her right eye. She wore her luxuriant chestnut hair in a perfectly coifed French roll that seemed to add length to her swanlike neck, and she carried herself with the unconscious grace of a ballerina.

Deirdre must have sensed my scrutiny because a bashful smile suddenly lit her face.

"I haven't had a chance to freshen up for hours," she said, glancing guiltily at the scuff marks on her shoes.

"You look fine to me," I said, blushing. It was embarrassing to be caught staring at anyone, much less at a woman I'd just met. "But my opinion doesn't count because I don't live here. Fairworth House belongs to my father-in-law, William Willis, so you'll need his approval, not mine. Come with me and I'll introduce you to him. If you stay on, you'll have to get used to calling me Lori," I added, as the pair followed me out of the entrance hall and up the central corridor. "Everyone does."

"Happy to oblige, Lori," Declan said with a cheerful nod.

"I'm sorry you had such a hard time finding your way," I went on as we entered the library. "It's not unusual for people to get lost looking for Finch. It's such a small village that it doesn't even appear on some maps."

"Deirdre and I like small villages," Declan assured me.

"We were both raised in the country," said Deirdre. "We'd be lost in a big city."

I couldn't tell whether they were telling the truth or saying what they thought I wanted to hear, but they were winning me over. When Willis, Sr., totted up the pros and cons of hiring them, their fondness for the countryside might outweigh their relative youth.

I left them in the study with their potential future employer and retreated to the library with Bill.

"Declan looks strong enough to handle the gardening," Bill commented, lowering his voice. "Deirdre has a striking face and a reassuring air of competence about her. If you ask me, Davina Trent has sent Father a pair of winners this time."

"I hope he agrees," I said fretfully.

"You want to press your ear to the door, don't you?" said Bill, an amused smile tugging at his lips.

"Certainly not," I said indignantly. "I want to be inside the room, coaching the Donovans. Oh, Bill . . ." I sighed dismally. "What am I going to do if William doesn't like them?"

"We'll think of something," said Bill, pulling me into his arms.

I snuggled close to him and murmured, "If you so much as *mention* the Handmaidens, I'll—"

My threat hung unfinished in the air because at that moment Willis, Sr., emerged from the study, flanked by the Donovans, whose tired faces were wreathed in smiles. Bill and I broke apart and gazed at his father inquiringly.

"Lori? Bill?" he said. "Please allow me to introduce my new cook and housekeeper, Deirdre Donovan, and my new gardener cum handyman, Declan Donovan."

"Y-you hired them?" I stammered, unable to believe my ears.

"I believe I have stated that such is the case," Willis, Sr., replied. "I will telephone Mrs. Trent later today to inform her that her services will no longer be required. I would appreciate it if you would let it be known throughout Finch and the surrounding countryside that the Donovans—and the Donovans alone—will be responsible for engaging whatever daily or weekly help they might require."

My amazement gave way to admiration as I caught the meaning behind Willis, Sr.'s words. You sly old fox, I thought. From now on the Handmaidens will have to go through Deirdre to get to you.

"Bill," Willis, Sr., continued, "will you please show Mr. and Mrs. Donovan where to park their vehicle and assist them in conveying their possessions to their quarters?" He turned to the young couple. "Your pantry is not yet stocked, I fear, but we shall amend the oversight as soon as the shops open. In the meantime, please regard the downstairs kitchen as your own. Take from it whatever you need. You will find a wide selection of comestibles from which to choose."

His last comment was true, if understated. The kitchen was fairly bulging with party leftovers.

"Thank you, sir," said Declan. "With all of the confusion, we never did get around to having supper."

"Would you like me to prepare something for you, sir?" Deirdre inquired. "A midnight feast, perhaps, featuring a few of your favorite dishes?"

"I suggest that you tend to your own needs this evening," said Willis, Sr. "We can discuss mine after we've all had some rest." He caught my eye and said meaningfully, "Lori? Your presence is required in the study."

"Good night, sir," said Declan. "And thank you again."

"Thank you, sir," Deirdre echoed.

Willis, Sr., nodded cordially.

"Welcome aboard," Bill said as he led the Donovans out of the library. "I think you'll like your new digs. You'll be the first to live there."

I watched them go, then returned to the study with Willis, Sr. He resumed his seat behind his desk, but I remained standing, with my arms folded, eyeing him doubtfully. Part of me wanted to do a merry jig, but another part urged restraint until I'd heard the whole story.

"What happened?" I asked. "I've never known you to make up your mind so quickly. What did the Donovans do? Offer to work for free?"

"I can assure you that my decision was not made with undue haste." Willis, Sr., opened a desk drawer and removed several sheets of fax paper, which he placed upon the desk. "Mrs. Trent sent the Donovans' completed application form to me yesterday morning. Having spent most of the day contemplating their qualifications, I was well-prepared to conduct an interview. I saw no reason to prolong either their suspense or yours by subjecting them to unnecessary cross-examination."

"A job application isn't the same as a face-to-face meeting," I pointed out.

"Their demeanor and their appearance impressed me favorably," said Willis, Sr. "You need have no doubts about my decision, Lori. I am convinced that the Donovans and I will enjoy a long and pleasant working relationship."

"Right." I held out my hand. "May I see their application form?"

"Not now," he said firmly and returned the papers to the drawer. "My stamina, though remarkable for a man of my age, is not limitless. It has been a long day and it is not yet over. Please, I beg of you, *telephone Mrs. Pyne.*"

Four

I jumped to obey Willis, Sr.'s plaintive command, whipping out my cell phone and rapidly punching in the tearoom's number. Rainey Dawson answered on the first ring. The dialogue that followed could have come straight from a cheesy spy novel.

"The coast is clear," I murmured.

"Gran'll be right over," Rainey said tersely.

And that was it.

I relayed the information, such as it was, to Willis, Sr., and parted the drapes to watch for Sally's arrival, but turned away from the window when Bill came into the room.

"I can see why the Donovans had car trouble," he announced. "They drive a blue Renault camper van that should have been sent to a junkyard years ago. When I climbed inside to show Declan where to park, I was afraid my foot would go through the floor."

"Perhaps it will look better in the light of day," Willis, Sr., suggested.

"I doubt it," said Bill, easing himself into his armchair.

"Did you assist the young people with their luggage?" asked Willis, Sr.

"I carried a suitcase from the van to the elevator," Bill replied, "but Declan said he could take it from there. I think he felt awkward, having his boss's son lug gear for him, so I left him to it. Deirdre's already busy in the kitchen. They must be starving." He leaned back in the chair, stretched out his long legs, and loosened his tie. "Have you called Sally?"

"Yes," I said. "Rainey told me that Sally would come right over, so she should be here in five or ten min—" I broke off as the doorbell rang.

"Good grief," said Bill, frowning. "She must have run all the way."

I glanced at him and knew at once that we were thinking the same thought: *Sally Pyne? Run?*

I set off at a trot to answer the door. I should have been exhausted, but curiosity had banished my fatigue. I felt like a cub reporter on the verge of landing her first big scoop: *Legal Eagle in Covert Confab with La Señora.* I wasn't sure if Sally's pickle could live up to the hype surrounding it but I was champing at the bit to find out what it was all about. When it came to being a dyed-in-the-wool busybody, my neighbors had nothing on me.

I was halfway down the central corridor when Deirdre Donovan strode into the entrance hall from the morning room. She'd evidently discovered that Fairworth House offered a number of different routes to the front door, which meant that she'd already begun to explore her new domain. I gave her full marks for using her initiative and stood back to allow her to carry out what was now her duty rather than mine.

Deirdre had exchanged her scuffed pumps for a spotless pair and swapped her summer dress for a crisp white blouse and a high-waisted pencil skirt that flattered her curves. This picture of perfection opened the front door to a panting and perspiring Sally Pyne, who was clad in a mud-spattered brown sweat suit that made her look like a freshly harvested potato. If Deirdre was surprised to find a distraught and disheveled woman on the doorstep, she didn't show it.

"Good evening," she said pleasantly. "May I ask who's calling?"

Sally's mouth fell open, but no sound came out.

"Hi, Sally," I called, rushing forward. "Please allow me to introduce you to William's new housekeeper, Mrs. Donovan."

"H-housekeeper?" Sally managed. "Since when?"

I could almost see Sally's nose twitch as she caught the scent of fresh gossip. Although the poor woman was clearly beside herself with worry, she simply couldn't resist the urge to snoop.

"Since very recently," I replied shortly. "I'll take Mrs. Pyne through, Deirdre."

"Shall I serve tea in the study?" Deirdre inquired.

"Yes, please," I said gratefully. "As soon as possible."

Deirdre nodded and took off for the kitchen, her heels clacking loudly on the marble floor.

Sally Pyne looked as though she needed a pick-me-up. Her round face was beet-red, her short silvery hair stuck out in disorderly wisps all over her head, and a crumpled handkerchief dangled from the pocket of her sweatpants. I put my arm around her plump shoulders and guided her gently up the corridor.

"How recently?" she asked, clinging doggedly to the subject of Willis, Sr.'s new housekeeper.

"Less than an hour ago," I replied. "They got lost on the way to Finch."

"They?" Sally said sharply.

"Deirdre and Declan Donovan," I explained. "They're a married couple. Declan will look after the garden."

"Irish?" she asked.

"He seems to be," I said. "I'm not sure about her."

Sally nodded distractedly. "Is her beauty spot real?"

"I haven't tried to rub it off," I said, rolling my eyes, "but I'm fairly sure she was born with it."

"Exotic looking," Sally muttered.

"Striking," I commented, parroting Bill's words.

"Same thing," she retorted.

"Here we are," I said, and ushered her into the study. Bill and Willis, Sr., stood as Sally and I entered the room, but Sally didn't acknowledge them. Silently, and with downcast eyes, she lowered herself into the button-backed leather chair I'd placed before the walnut desk. I sat in the chair I'd arranged next to hers, the better to hear every syllable that passed between her and my father-in-law.

"Good evening, Mrs. Pyne," said Willis, Sr., and he and Bill resumed their seats. "Or shall I say, 'Good morning'?"

Sally pulled the handkerchief from her pocket and dabbed at her eyes. "What must you think of me, coming here in such a state, at such an hour?"

"I presume that you would not make such an assignation frivolously," said Willis, Sr. "Please, calm yourself, Mrs. Pyne. You are among friends. What is said in this room is said in the strictest confidence."

"B-but that's the t-trouble," Sally wailed. "There's no such thing as p-privacy in F-Finch!" She shook her head, buried her face in her handkerchief, and burst into tears.

There was a knock at the study door and Deirdre Donovan appeared, carrying a silver tray laden with a handsome Georgian silver teapot, a splendid Rockingham tea service, and a large box of plain white tissues. I looked from the box of tissues to Deirdre's pokerfaced expression and wondered if she was accustomed to dealing with hysterical visitors who arrived unannounced in the dead of night. If so, I thought, she must have worked in some very interesting households.

At a signal from Willis, Sr., she placed the tray on the Sheraton sideboard. Without being asked to do so, she moved his wastebasket from behind his desk to a spot near Sally's feet and set the box of tissues within Sally's reach, then stepped back and gazed expectantly at her employer.

"Will that be all, sir?" she asked.

"Yes, thank you, Mrs. Donovan," Willis, Sr., replied. "I will not require your services again until breakfast time."

"What time would that be, sir?" she asked.

Willis, Sr., considered Sally Pyne before replying, "Nine o'clock, I think."

"Very good, sir." Deirdre left, closing the door behind her.

I served the tea. Bill and Willis, Sr., sipped theirs, but Sally tossed hers back as if it were a shot of whisky. The hot, sweet drink seemed to bolster her courage. She mopped her face with a handful of tissues, dropped them in the wastebasket, straightened her shoulders, and lifted her chin, as if steeling herself to face an unpleasant task.

"Now, Mrs. Pyne . . ." Willis, Sr., spoke in the soothing tones of a highly successful attorney. "When you are quite ready, please feel free to describe the nature of the problem that appears to be troubling you."

Sally took an unsteady breath and asked in a quavering voice, "Have you ever been to Mexico?"

"Yes," Willis, Sr., answered. "I have been fortunate enough to visit Mexico on a number of occasions."

"I never expected to go there," she confessed. "I've been entering contests ever since I was a girl and I've never won anything, so I never thought I'd win something as grand as a trip to the Mexican Riviera! It seemed so wonderful when the *World Trek* lady—"

"World trek?" queried Willis, Sr.

"The travel magazine that sponsored the contest," Sally explained. "When the lady from *World Trek* rang to tell me I'd won, it was like a dream come true, except that I never dreamed of such a thing happening to me." She sniffed. "If I'd known what would come of it, I would have torn up the ruddy entry form and thrown it out with the rubbish!"

"Oh, dear," Willis, Sr., said sympathetically. "May I ask why?"

Sally seized another tissue and blew her nose.

"When I was in Mexico, everything was so . . . different," she said with a forlorn sigh. "The sun and the sea and the palm trees and all the bright colors . . . and *I* was different, too. I made a whole new set of clothes for the trip—resort wear, they call it in *World Trek*—because I wanted to fit in. I didn't want to look like a plain Jane who runs a teashop in a village no one's ever heard of. I wanted to look . . . glamorous . . . like someone who was used to cabanas and palapas and lounging by the pool all day. And I *did*." She turned to me. "You saw the things I made, Lori. They're lovely, aren't they?"

"They're splendid," I agreed, recalling the embroidered peasant blouses, the muslin skirts, and the flowing dresses Sally had shown me before her departure. "You're an amazing seamstress."

Sally reached out to give my hand a grateful squeeze, then turned back to Willis, Sr.

"Since I looked the part," she went on, "I thought I might as well act the part as well. I tarted up my accent and ordered fancy drinks and let the *camareros* wait on me hand and foot." She shrugged helplessly. "You know how foreigners are when they hear any sort of English accent. They think we're all lords and ladies living in castles and taking tea with the queen every other Wednesday. They made it easy for me to . . . to pretend to be grander than I am. It was just a bit of fun," she said, eyeing Willis, Sr., defensively. "There's nothing wrong with pretending to be someone else for a little while, is there?"

"It depends on what happens as a result of pretending," Willis, Sr., replied judiciously. "There can, of course, be serious consequences to assuming a false identity."

"You're so right." Sally nodded dejectedly. "Because on the second day of my trip, Henrique came along— Señor Henrique Cocinero." Her tear-streaked face softened as the exotic name rolled off her tongue.

I stared at Sally, enthralled. If she'd gone off the rails with a man, it would be the biggest scandal to hit Finch since Peggy Taxman had accused my former nanny of burgling the vicarage. Bill shifted his position in his chair, but I kept as still as a statue, for fear of distracting her. I was dying to know what, if anything, had happened between her and Señor Cocinero.

"Henrique is quite well-off," Sally went on. "He wears lovely white suits and Panama hats and he knows good tequila from bad and he's a real gentleman, too, with polished manners and perfect grooming and . . . and he took a fancy to me, so—just for fun—I went on pretending that I was the Honorable Lady Sarah Pyne, a wealthy widow who loves to travel." Sally managed a faint smile. "And it worked! Henrique actually believed that I came from the same sort of world he came from. We had the most wonderful time together. He took me with him to Coba, to climb the Mayan pyramid I told you about. We went kayaking across a laguna and snorkeling near a coral reef and . . ."

As Sally recounted her by-now familiar list of adventures, my doubts about her veracity slowly melted away. If love made all things possible—and I had reason to believe it did—then surely a holiday romance could propel a plump, silver-haired teashop owner to the top of a pyramid and beyond.

". . . and he bought this for me." Sally fished a delicate silver chain from the collar of her grubby sweatshirt and displayed a snowflake-shaped silver pendant embellished with a curious golden symbol. "It's the letter *S* in the Mayan alphabet," she explained. "*S* for Sarah."

"A striking adornment," said Willis, Sr.

"I told Henrique I'd treasure it always," she said wistfully, tucking the chain out of sight. "The nine days I spent with him were the happiest days of my life."

"And yet," Willis, Sr., observed, "you do not appear to be happy."

Sally reacted like a guilty schoolgirl, ducking her head and fixing her gaze on the floor.

"I haven't quite told you everything," she said, in a subdued voice.

"I thought not," said Willis, Sr. "Pray continue."

Sally cleared her throat. "You must understand, William, that once Kit and Nell were married, the only topic of conversation in Finch was Fairworth House. It was Fairworth House *this* and Fairworth House *that*, all day long, so naturally, Fairworth House was very much on my mind when I went away to Mexico." She kept her head down and clasped her hands together in her lap. "Which is why, when Henrique asked me where I lived, I told him . . . I told him . . ."

"You told Señor Cocinero that you live in Fairworth House?" Willis, Sr., hazarded.

"It just popped out!" Sally blurted, blushing furiously. "I didn't mean any harm by it, but one thing led to another and before I knew it, I'd told him that Fairworth was my family's ancestral estate and I . . . I invited him to drop in if he ever came to England." She looked pleadingly at Willis, Sr. "It seemed like the sort of thing rich people did. How was I to know that he'd *accept* my invitation?"

Sally burst into tears again. I patted her back, offered her tissues, and exchanged astonished glances with Bill, who was sitting in rapt attention on the edge of his chair.

"I had a letter from him this morning," Sally managed shakily, when her sobs had subsided.

"How?" Willis, Sr., inquired.

"Beg pardon?" asked Sally.

"How did he send a letter to you?" he clarified. "If Señor Cocinero addressed a letter to Lady Sarah Pyne of Fairworth Hall, surely it would have come to me rather than to you."

"Oh." Sally's face went scarlet and she stared at her hands. "I told Henrique that the villagers call me Sally— Sally of Finch—because I'm not a la-di-dah sort of snooty-nose who needs to show off her title all the time. He addressed the letter 'To Sally of Finch' even though he insisted on calling me Lady Sarah—to give me my proper due, he said. He's s-such a g-gentleman!"

Another teary downpour ensued, but it passed fairly quickly.

"As I was saying," Sally went on, dropping another wad of damp tissues into the wastebasket, "I had a letter from Henrique this morning. He arrived in England a week ago. He's touring the English countryside and he thinks it'll be such fun to spend three days at Fairworth on his way to Stratford." She gasped. "He'll be here on Monday!"

"Which leaves you one full day to prepare for his arrival," Willis, Sr., observed.

"How can I prepare for his arrival?" Sally wailed. "Henrique thinks I'm a grand lady who lives in a grand house. What will he think of me if he finds out who I really am?"

"He may be enchanted," said Willis, Sr.

"Don't be daft," Sally said, shaking her head mournfully. "He'll think I'm a big fat liar, because that's what I am. What's worse, he might think I'm some sort of *gold digger*, which I'm *not*. I may not be a grand lady, but I'm not a pauper."

"Of course not," murmured Willis, Sr.

"I could stand Henrique thinking ill of me," Sally said, twisting her hands in her lap. "It's what I deserve. But if word gets out about my little . . . charade . . . I'll never be able to hold my head high in Finch again. I'll be a *laughingstock*, William. I'll be the butt of jokes from now until the end of time. Peggy Taxman will *never* let me live it down. I'll always be Silly Sally, the ridiculous woman who put on airs and graces because she was too ashamed to be herself." She caught her breath and blinked back a fresh batch of tears. "I know how foolish I've been, William, but I won't be able to bear it if everyone else knows, too." She swallowed hard. "I'll have no choice. I'll have to leave Finch."

There was a pregnant pause. My eyes swiveled back and forth between Sally and Willis, Sr. I had absolutely no idea what would happen next. The suspense was delicious.

After what seemed an age, Willis, Sr., spoke.

"We must not allow that to happen," he said.

Sally pressed a hand to her mouth and peered at Willis, Sr., as if he were her last hope of salvation.

"Finch would be greatly diminished if it were to lose your excellent jam doughnuts, your skills as a needlewoman, and your effervescent personality, Mrs. Pyne." Willis, Sr., leaned back in his chair and tented his fingers over his immaculate waistcoat. "You must leave the problem with me. I will contact you as soon as I have devised a satisfactory solution to it. In the meantime, you are to remain incommunicado."

Sally blinked uncomprehendingly.

"You are not at all well, Mrs. Pyne," Willis, Sr., reminded her. "You are certainly too ill to receive visitors. You must remain sequestered in your sickroom, with the curtains drawn, until I telephone you. Do you understand?"

Sally nodded eagerly. "I'll keep out of sight. Rainey'll tell everyone I'm sick as a pig."

"A granddaughter can be a great support in times of strife." Willis, Sr., consulted his pocket watch. "I believe our business is finished for the moment, Mrs. Pyne. Please allow my son to escort you home."

"No, thank you," Sally said, getting swiftly to her feet. "I'll go back along the riverbank, the way I came. One person makes less noise than two."

"In that case, I will bid you good night," said Willis, Sr. "Get some sleep, Mrs. Pyne. I will be in touch. Lori? Will you see our guest out?"

"No need." Sally motioned toward the French doors. "I'll slip out through the garden. Good night, William. And *thank you*." She scurried across the room and was gone in a swish of draperies.

Bill crossed to sit in the chair Sally had vacated.

"I'm glad she mentioned the river," he said, grinning. "I was wondering where the mud came from. Well, well, well . . ." He gave a low whistle. "Who'd've thunk it? Sally Pyne, femme fatale."

"It's not funny," I scolded. "Sally has good reason to worry about the villagers. They'll make her life a misery if they find out what she's done."

"They will," he agreed. "Sally's dug a pretty deep hole for herself." He favored Willis, Sr., with a speculative gaze. "It sounds as though you intend to jump in with her, Father. What are you going to do?"

"I am going to go to bed," Willis, Sr., replied firmly. "I suggest that you do the same. We will reconvene here after church tomorrow—later today, that is—to devise a stratagem that will allow Mrs. Pyne to maintain both her friendship with Señor Cocinero and her standing in the community." He leaned forward, and though he addressed Bill and me, he looked only at me. "I wish to state once again, to both of you, that whatever is said in this room is said in the *strictest confidence*."

"My lips are zipped," I said, "and your son's a lawyer—he's trained to keep his trap shut."

"I'm ready to shut my eyes as well," said Bill, yawning. "Come on, Lori. Kit and Nell must think we've forgotten about them."

I glanced at my watch as we said good night to Willis, Sr. Although it was two o'clock in the morning, I still had enough energy to complete one more vitally important task. Bill could sail off to dreamland when we reached the cottage, but I planned to make a small detour.

I needed to speak with Aunt Dimity.

Five

Nell Smith was awake and absorbed in a book when Bill and I walked into our living room. She sat in the chintz armchair near the hearth, bathed in the pool of light cast by a single lamp.

Nell's beauty never failed to astound me, but it had somehow become even more ethereal since her marriage. The nimbus of soft golden curls framing her flawless oval face seemed to glow with a brightness that rivaled the sun's, and her midnight-blue eyes, darker and deeper than moonlit wells, were filled with a quiet contentment most souls yearn for but seldom find. The aura of happiness surrounding her was almost palpable.

Kit, who was every bit as beautiful as his young wife, was asleep with Stanley on the sofa, but he woke with a start when the sleek black cat used him as a trampoline to reach Bill. As Kit sat up and rubbed his eyes, Stanley wove in and out of Bill's legs, purring ecstatically. Stanley was very fond of me and the twins, but he adored Bill.

"Must've dozed off," Kit said, running a hand over his short crop of prematurely gray hair. "Did William enjoy his party?"

"Very much," I replied. "I'm sorry we're so late. A pair of potential employees arrived just after midnight and we wanted to stick around until William finished interviewing them."

"What's the verdict?" Kit asked.

"They're in," I announced. "Deirdre Donovan is William's cook/housekeeper. Her husband, Declan, will look after the garden and fix things that need fixing around the house."

"You must be relieved," said Nell, with a knowing look.

"I'm over the moon," I conceded. "Now that William has solved his servant problem, I can get back to my usual routine."

"I'm glad he's not alone anymore," Nell said thoughtfully. "Fairworth is too big for one person."

"I never liked the thought of him staying there by himself," I agreed. "I'll sleep better, knowing that Deirdre and Declan are on hand to look after him. Incidentally, William wants *everyone* to know that the Donovans are in charge of hiring extra help."

"In other words," Bill interjected, "he's posted guards at the gates."

Nell's eyes twinkled merrily and Kit laughed out loud. They were aware of the Handmaiden situation.

"Wise man," said Kit. "There's such a thing as having too much company."

"We'll spread the word," Nell promised.

She set her book aside, uncurled her long, slender legs, and rose gracefully from the chintz armchair, then put an exquisite hand out to her husband, who took it and got to his feet.

"We'll be off," said Kit, entwining his fingers with Nell's. "Will and Rob were as good as gold, by the way."

"They always are, when they're with you," Bill said

dryly. "It helps that you're their riding instructors. It gives you the kind of clout mere parents can only dream of."

We thanked Kit and Nell profusely and watched from the doorstep as they made their way down the flagstone path to their classic gray Land Rover. They were such an enchanting couple that it was hard to look away.

"Ah, young love," I said with a heartfelt sigh as they drove off.

Bill closed the door and put his arms around me.

"Old love's not so bad," he observed.

"Not bad at all," I agreed, kissing him.

"I'm for bed," he said, "but something tells me that you have other plans."

"You don't mind, do you?" I asked.

"Since you won't be able to concentrate on anything until you finish your business in the study," he said, "no, I don't mind. I'll look in on the boys before I hit the sack. Don't be too long." He nuzzled my neck in a way that made it quite difficult for me to let him go to bed alone, then went upstairs. Stanley gave my leg a friendly rub before padding faithfully after his favorite human.

I sped past the stairs and up the hallway, because Bill was correct: I wouldn't be able to sleep—or to concentrate on anything else—until I'd finished my business in the study.

Our study was smaller, darker, and much less formal than Willis, Sr.'s. Bookshelves lined the walls from floor to ceiling, and the only furnishings, apart from the old oak desk beneath the ivy-covered windows, were a pair of tall leather armchairs and an ottoman grouped before the fireplace.

The room was still and silent when I entered it. I paused to light a fire in the hearth, not for warmth, but for the cheerful companionship of the dancing flames, then smiled at the small, pink-flannel rabbit perched in a special niche on one of the shelves.

"Hi, Reg," I said, touching a finger to the faded grape juice stain on his snout. "Wait until you hear about Sally Pyne!"

A psychiatrist would have had a field day explaining why a woman in her late thirties spent time chatting with a pink bunny named Reginald, but it made perfect sense to me. Reginald had been my confidante and my companion in adventure for as long as I could remember. It would have been impolite to ignore him simply because I'd grown up.

"It's spectacular, Reg," I continued. "It's the juiciest story I've heard since we moved to Finch."

Reginald's black-button eyes glimmered with anticipation as I took a particular book from the shelf next to his and curled up with it in the leather armchair closest to him.

I'd inherited the book from my late mother's dearest friend, an Englishwoman named Dimity Westwood. My mother and Dimity had met in London while serving their respective countries during the Second World War. The bonds of affection they forged during that dark and dangerous time endured long after peace was declared and my mother sailed back to the States.

Though the two women never saw each other again,

they nurtured their deepening friendship by sending hundreds of letters back and forth across the Atlantic. My mother regarded those letters as her private sanctuary, a peaceful retreat from the daily grind of raising a daughter on her own after my father's sudden death. She valued her sanctuary so highly that she kept it a secret from everyone—including me. As a child, I knew Dimity Westwood only as Aunt Dimity, the redoubtable heroine of a series of bedtime stories that sprang from my mother's fertile imagination.

I didn't find out about the real Dimity Westwood until after both she and my mother had died. It was then that Dimity bequeathed to me a considerable fortune, the honey-colored cottage in which she'd spent her childhood, the letters she and my mother had written, and a curious book—a journal bound in dark blue leather.

It was through the blue journal that I finally came to know Dimity Westwood. Whenever I opened it, her handwriting would appear on its blank pages, an old-fashioned copperplate taught at the village school at a time when inkwells were considered useful rather than decorative. I was staggered the first time it happened, afraid that I'd unwittingly conjured up a creepy, demanding sort of spirit who would rattle chains and howl at inappropriate moments.

I couldn't have been more wrong. Aunt Dimity quickly showed herself to be a wise and kindly soul who wanted nothing but the best for her best friend's only child. I had no idea how she managed the trick, but by reaching out to me from beyond the grave, Aunt Dimity proved to me that love could indeed make all things possible. I simply couldn't imagine life without her.

I rested the journal on my lap and opened it, but before I could say a word, the familiar lines of royal-blue ink began to curl and loop excitedly across the page.

You're back very late, Lori. Am I right to assume that William's party was the success you hoped it would be?

"It was a smashing success," I assured her. "Against all odds, I might add. The caterers were smitten by food poisoning at the eleventh hour, but the villagers rushed to my aid."

I imagine some rushed more speedily than others. Were you able to keep the Handmaidens from thrusting their offerings on William?

I laughed. "You know Finch too well, Dimity. The dear ladies tried to ambush William behind my back, but Lilian and Emma kept them at bay."

Three cheers for Lilian and Emma! It's a pity they won't always be around to protect William from his overzealous admirers. I fear that he will be pestered incessantly, now that he's on his own.

"Ah, but he's not on his own," I said. "He has the Donovans to run interference for him."

Who, may I ask, are the Donovans? I don't recall a family by that name in Finch.

"Deirdre and Declan Donovan aren't from Finch," I informed her. "I'm not sure where they're from, but they showed up tonight to offer their services to William and he accepted. They're at Fairworth House right now."

Are they . . . suitable?

"William thinks so," I said. "I'm not sure what to think. He made up his mind awfully fast."

I've never known William to be impulsive.

"Nor have I," I said. "But I've never known him to talk about sheep before, either."

Sheep?

"Sheep," I said. "William told me this morning that he's thinking about adopting a flock of endangered sheep."

If he has enough land to support a flock of sheep, why shouldn't he adopt one?

"Because he's no more a shepherd than he is impulsive." I glanced pensively at the fax machine on the desk, then looked down at the journal again. "He's behaving oddly, Dimity. First he comes up with the sheep idea, then he hires the Donovans without a proper interview. I can't help wondering if he hired them just to please me and Bill. He knows how twitchy we've been about leaving him alone at Fairworth."

He may have hired the Donovans in order to allay your fears, Lori, but he won't keep them on if they fail to meet his expectations.

"They're doing all right so far," I said. "Deirdre Donovan didn't bat an eye when Sally Pyne showed up after the party, covered in mud."

Why on earth was Sally Pyne covered in mud? And why did she arrive after the party?

"You're going to love this, Dimity," I said, grinning. "I promised William that I wouldn't breathe a word of it to anyone, but you're not just anyone."

I appreciate the compliment, Lori, but I would appreciate a direct response even more.

"Your wish is my command." I hunkered down and gave Aunt Dimity a detailed account of the dramatic events that had taken place both during and after the party, from Rainey Dawson's startling entrance in the garden to Sally Pyne's stealthy exit along the riverbank. "I think it's fair to say," I concluded, "that Sally's pickle lived up to its hype."

I think it's fair to say that it surpassed my wildest expectations. Poor, dear, featherbrained Sally. Her first experience of foreign travel turned her head completely. She would have been better off if she'd won a seaside holiday at Skegness. No Englishman would have mistaken her for a grand lady.

"She wouldn't have pretended to be one if she'd stayed in England," I said. "But would she be better off, Dimity? It sounds to me as though she had the time of her life with Henrique. She may regret it now, but would she be happier if she'd missed it altogether?"

Are a few days of happiness worth years of regret? It is a vexed question, to be sure, but I believe Sally gave her own personal answer to it when she bared her soul so tearfully to William. If she could relive her Mexican holiday, knowing what she knows now, I'm certain that she would behave differently.

"Twenty-twenty hindsight's no fun at all," I said, nodding. "But why *did* she bare her soul to William? What did she think she'd gain from her confession, apart from sympathy?"

She hoped that William would solve her problem, of course.

"How can William possibly solve her problem?" I asked, smiling incredulously.

Let me see . . . The ormolu clock on the mantel ticked away the minutes while Aunt Dimity marshaled her thoughts. Finally, the handwriting continued. *If I were a gallant gentleman like William, I would continue the charade.*

"How?" I asked.

I would allow Sally to have the run of Fairworth House for a few days.

"You want William to move out?" I said, blinking in disbelief. "He's only just moved in!"

William doesn't have to go anywhere, Lori. He can introduce himself to Señor Cocinero as Lady Sarah's brother or, better still, her American cousin who is spending the summer with her in her beautiful home.

"It's a good start," I conceded, "but I can see a few stumbling blocks along the way. Sally has to keep the villagers from finding out about her Mexican swain. Even if William agreed to go along with the charade—a big *if*—how would Sally get from the tearoom to Fairworth House without anyone in the village seeing her? She can't keep crawling along the river after dark."

She needn't crawl at all. Sally requires careful nursing to recover from her recent illness. She has, for that reason, decided to stay with Judith Crosby.

"Who's Judith Crosby?" I asked.

Judith Crosby is Sally Pyne's youngest sister. She lives in Chipping Norton. Sally will stay with her until she is well again. Since Rainey must remain behind to manage the tea-

room, you, my dear, have volunteered to drive Sally to Chipping Norton.

"I have?" I said blankly.

You are a good and dependable friend, Lori. No one will question your desire to help Sally in her hour of need.

"Okay," I said doubtfully. "But you still haven't addressed the main issue: How will Sally get from Chipping Norton to Fairworth without anyone seeing her?"

You are being obtuse, my dear. You will not take Sally to Chipping Norton. You will bring her here, to the cottage, where you will remain for an hour or two.

"Won't work," I said instantly. "Will and Rob will ask too many questions if Sally hides out here."

You're quite right. Let me think. . . . The handwriting stopped briefly, then started again. *I have it! You will drive Sally to Chipping Norton, then turn around and come back to Fairworth House, thereby accruing the correct amount of travel time. As you approach Fairworth, Sally will lie flat on the backseat and conceal herself beneath a blanket.*

"I'll smuggle Sally into Fairworth?" I said, giggling.

You will. I suggest you do so as soon as possible. Sally will need time to acquaint herself with her ancestral estate. Please remember to tell her to pack her best clothes. If she is to be a grand lady, she must have something other than sweat suits in her wardrobe.

"Pack best clothes," I murmured, entering into the spirit of things.

In the meantime, you will inform the villagers that an important foreign client is due to arrive at Fairworth on Monday for an indefinite stay. Everyone knows that William practices international law.

"He doesn't practice any kind of law anymore," I pointed out. "William has retired."

Attorneys never really retire, Lori. There are always a few special clients who refuse to deal with anyone but the trusted family solicitor with whom their fathers and grandfathers dealt.

"I see," I said. "Go on."

You will describe the client as a boring old fusspot.

"Why?" I asked.

If you don't paint a picture for them, the villagers may surmise that William is entertaining a celebrity. A boring old fusspot will arouse much less interest than a celebrity.

"Very true," I said, impressed by Aunt Dimity's attention to detail.

You will let it be known that William is engaged in a highly confidential conference with his client, and that he must not be disturbed for any reason while the conference is under way.

"No visitors allowed," I said, nodding.

None whatsoever. You must make it clear that William and his client require complete privacy.

"The villagers will probably stay away if I tell them to," I said, "but what about the twins? If Rob and Will get the impression that Sally's moved in with Grandpa, they're bound to ask awkward questions."

Can you keep them away from Fairworth for a day or two?

"I can try," I said, "but it won't be easy. They love Grandpa's new house."

In that case, you must tell them that their grandfather wishes to spend some quiet time with an out-of-town guest. They do understand quiet time, don't they?

"Sort of," I mumbled, with a guilty parental grimace.

It will be up to Sally to keep Señor Cocinero from wandering into Finch.

"Again, it won't be easy," I said. "Remember all the kayaking and the snorkeling? Henrique sounds like an adventurous kind of guy."

The last time I looked, kayaking and snorkeling did not rank high on Finch's list of local activities. Sally can inform Señor Cocinero that, when at home, she prefers the gentler pursuits of taking tea and strolling sedately through her gardens.

"I've never seen Sally stroll sedately," I said, "but maybe Lady Sarah does."

William will have to explain the situation to the Donovans and impress upon them the need for absolute discretion.

"If you ask me, the Donovans are used to keeping secrets," I said.

What gives you that impression?

"Deirdre didn't bat an eye when Sally showed up," I reminded Aunt Dimity. "If she's used to finding hysterical women on her employer's doorstep in the wee hours of a Sunday morning, I'd say that she's had *plenty* of practice at keeping secrets."

A well-trained housekeeper keeps her opinions to herself, Lori. She certainly doesn't discuss her employer's affairs with all and sundry. Deirdre, it seems, is a well-trained housekeeper. William should have no trouble with her. I can only hope that her husband is equally discreet. The scheme cannot work without the Donovans' full cooperation.

"If they want to keep their jobs, they'll go along with it," I observed.

When Señor Cocinero departs, you will smuggle Sally out of Fairworth House and return her to the tearoom, restored to full health and ready to resume her vital role in village life. There was a pause before the handwriting continued. *Sally will have to be uncivil to Señor Cocinero, of course.*

"I beg your pardon?" I said.

Sally will have to conceal her affection for Señor Cocinero. Otherwise, he'll keep coming back. I doubt that William will agree to go through this more than once.

"I doubt that he'll go through it even once," I said.

He will. Gallant gentlemen can't resist the urge to help a damsel in distress.

"He may buy into your plan," I allowed, "but even if he does, it won't succeed."

Why not?

"Because, as you've told me on more than one occasion, nothing goes unnoticed in a village," I replied. "Secrets don't stay secret for very long in Finch."

There's a first time for everything, Lori. Consider the dreadful consequences of doing nothing. Can you imagine Finch without Sally Pyne's jam doughnuts?

"I didn't say I'd do nothing," I protested. I was quite fond of Sally's jam doughnuts, which bore little resemblance to the American pastries of the same name. Sally's were dense and submarine-shaped, rolled in coarse sugar, filled with thick cream, and finished with the merest dab of homemade raspberry jam. They were the stuff of which food fantasies were made.

"I didn't say I'd do nothing," I repeated, coming out of my sugary reverie. "I was about to ask if you have a role for me in your charade."

You'll play yourself, Lori. William stays with Lady Sarah because her home is so near his son's.

"Why doesn't he stay with us?" I inquired.

Your cottage is too small to accomodate him, whereas Fairworth House has rooms to spare. The closer we keep to reality, Lori, the easier it will be to pull the whole thing off.

"Lies are easier to coordinate if they're close to the truth," I agreed.

Lies told to spare a foolish woman persecution and ridicule may, I think, be forgiven. If the conspirators play their parts to the best of their ability, I believe that my scheme has a fair to middling chance of succeeding.

"I'll do *my* best," I promised.

I know you will. My dear, you've been racing like a greyhound for nearly twenty-four hours. It's time to curl up in your basket. Buenas noches, querida.

"*Buenas noches, Tía Dimity,*" I said, surprising myself with a few words of high-school Spanish that had until that moment lain dormant in a dusty corner of my brain.

I waited until the graceful lines of royal-blue ink had faded from the page, then closed the blue journal and returned it to the shelf. I threw a halfhearted glance at the fax machine, but shook my head.

"No," I said to Reginald. "I'll go cross-eyed if I try to read Davina Trent's faxes now. I'll check up on the Donovans after I've had some sleep."

A psychiatrist wouldn't have understood it, but I could tell by Reginald's expression that he approved of my decision. I twiddled his ears, banked the fire, and went upstairs.

Bill was, unsurprisingly, dead to the world by the time I climbed into bed. After persuading a reluctant Stanley to move from my pillows to a spot near my husband's feet, I lay back and stared at the ceiling while thoughts of Aunt Dimity's complex machinations rolled sluggishly through my brain. No one respected her craftiness more than I did, but I'd never heard of a plan in which so many things could go wrong.

"Not a snowball's chance," I murmured, and as dawn's rosy fingers touched the sky, I plunged into a deep and dreamless sleep.

Six

ill concurred with my dour assessment of Aunt Dimity's scheme, but he thought it was worth a try. He, too, was a big fan of Sally's jam doughnuts.

"We'll pick up Father on our way to St. George's," he said, as we dressed for church the following morning.

"It's a fine day," I said, peering through the bedroom window at the cloudless blue sky. "He'll probably want to walk."

"Fine day or no, he'll ride with us," Bill said flatly. "When we get to Fairworth, I'll keep the boys occupied while you run in and present the plan to Father. If he gives it the green light, we'll start the ball rolling in the churchyard scrum."

The "churchyard scrum" was Bill's affectionate term for the knot of chattering villagers that formed in the graveyard surrounding St. George's every Sunday after church. Wherever two or more were gathered in Finch there was bound to be gossip, so the scrum would be a perfect place to launch our disinformation campaign.

"And if William doesn't give us the green light?" I asked.

"We'll hope he comes up with a better plan." Bill straightened the knot in his tie, then opened the bedroom door, saying, "*Vámonos, muchacha!* If we stand around talking much longer, the boys will decide to drive themselves to church."

I followed him out of the bedroom, mentally rehearsing a condensed version of Aunt Dimity's complicated scenario. A full rendition would make us miss the morning service and a missed church service would raise eyebrows I didn't want raised.

Fairworth House glowed like old gold in the morning sun. Declan Donovan, clad in khaki shorts, a short-sleeved shirt, and scruffy work boots, was already tending to his duties, using a rake to repair the damage done to the graveled drive by the flotilla of cars that had come and gone the previous evening. He stopped raking and raised a hand to greet us as we piled out of the Rover. Bill took the boys over to meet him while I scampered up the steps and into the entrance hall, where I found Willis, Sr., who was about to leave for church.

"Such haste on a Sunday morning," he observed, clucking his tongue. "You are aware that the catering crisis is over, are you not?"

"Come with me," I said, ignoring his quip. "I have something to tell you and it can't wait."

I led him to the settee near the window in the morning room, closed the door, and relayed the essential points of Aunt Dimity's plan to him, shamelessly claiming them as my own. Although my father-in-law had known Dimity Westwood when she was alive, he was unaware of my ongoing relationship with her, and I had no idea how to explain it to him.

"Well?" I asked, when I'd finished. "What do you think?"

"An American cousin?" he said doubtfully. "I was rather hoping to play the role of the butler."

I frowned at him in confusion. "What are you talking about?"

"Great minds think alike, Lori," he said, smiling. "I devised a stratagem very similar to yours over breakfast this morning. Mrs. Donovan, by the way, is an excellent cook. My poached eggs were sublime. She is also knowledgeable about sheep."

"Never mind about sheep," I said impatiently. "What's all this about playing the role of a butler?"

"I have always wanted to buttle," Willis, Sr., replied wistfully. "My accent, alas, will not serve. The butler in an English country house would sound more . . . English. I admit it, Lori. Your scheme trumps mine. I am better suited to the role of Lady Sarah Pyne's American cousin."

"You mean . . . you'll do it?" I said incredulously.

"Of course I shall do it. Mrs. Pyne is depending on me. When Señor Cocinero arrives at Fairworth tomorrow, he shall find Lady Sarah Pyne entertaining her American cousin, William Willis, who is whiling away the summer months as a guest in her splendid home. It is a role I was born to play." He gave a satisfied nod before adding, "I have already taken the Donovans into my confidence and secured their full cooperation. As it happens, Mrs. Donovan is fluent in six languages, one of which is Spanish. She will be a most useful accomplice." He glanced at his watch. "You must telephone the tearoom immediately."

"No time," I said, shaking my head. "I'll explain everything to Sally after church."

"Mrs. Pyne may miss church this morning, but Rainey will almost certainly be there," said Willis, Sr. "The child will need a word of warning about the story we are about to unveil. For now, ask her merely to agree with everything we say. We will acquaint her with the details later, when we have more time." He stood. "While you are making the call, my dear, I will gather Bill and the twins. We shall await you in the Range Rover." He smoothed his impeccable waistcoat and left.

I stared speechlessly at his retreating back. My father-in-law was a methodical, meticulous thinker. His eagerness to grab a leading role in an absurd masquerade was as out of character as his interest in sheep and his hasty decision to hire the Donovans. I'd heard that retirement could be a liberating experience, but Willis, Sr., seemed to be taking it to a whole new level. It was a bit unnerving.

A series of blaring honks from the Rover's horn reminded me that I was supposed to be telephoning Rainey. I hit the speed dial on my cell phone and she answered on the first ring. Though mystified by my brief and cryptic message, she instantly agreed to follow our lead.

"I'll do anything to help Gran," she said earnestly. "She loves Finch. It would break her heart if she had to move to another village."

A granddaughter, I thought, smiling, can be a great support in times of strife.

*   *   *

Elspeth Binney was playing the first chords of the procession-al as Bill, Willis, Sr., Will, Rob, and I slid hurriedly into a pew. I nodded to Rainey, who was seated across the aisle from us, then tried to pay attention to the service.

Theodore Bunting's sermons were rarely stimulat-ing, and this morning's was no exception. It was all I could do to keep from nodding off as he elucidated yet another obscure biblical text, but I wasn't alone in my struggle. The previous night's revelries had taken a toll on almost everyone, and it was a subdued group of parishioners that shuffled into the churchyard at the ser-vice's end. The only people who appeared to be well rested were Will and Rob, who ran off to play hide-and-seek among the headstones, and Peggy Tax-man, who was sailing majestically toward me.

My cowardly husband took his father by the elbow and suggested that they pay their respects to the ceme-tery's newest residents, a pair of ancient and identical twin sisters named Ruth and Louise Pym, who'd been laid to rest beneath a single headstone less than a year ago. Similarly, most of the villagers shot off home, to peruse the Sunday newspapers over a leisurely breakfast beyond the reach of Peggy's voice. A select group, how-ever, streamed after Peggy, knowing that they could rely on her to ask questions they were too polite—or too sleepy-headed—to ask.

"George Wetherhead tells me that he saw a ratty old van drive through town last night, after the party was over," Peggy boomed as soon as she was within earshot. "He seems to think it was headed for Fairworth House. Did some of William's guests arrive late?"

"No," I replied. "His new housekeeper and his new gardener—a married couple—had car trouble on their way to Finch. They didn't reach Fairworth until the wee hours."

Eyes that had been drowsy brightened noticeably as the villagers digested my first news flash.

"Housekeeper? Gardener?" Peggy thundered. "What are they called? And why weren't they in church?"

"Deirdre and Declan Donovan," I told her. "And I don't know."

"Donovan, eh?" Peggy pursed her lips. "Sounds Irish to me. I'll wager they're at St. Margaret's in Upper Deeping."

"Possibly," I said, aware that it would be futile to point out to Peggy that not everyone named Donovan was a Roman Catholic.

"William must be pleased to have them," said Christine Peacock.

"He is," I assured her. "Now he can enjoy his leisure time and leave the management of the household to the Donovans."

"They'll be doing the hiring, will they?" inquired Mr. Barlow. The handyman was always on the lookout for odd jobs.

"That's right," I said, thanking him silently for leading the way to my second bit of news. "William has put them in charge of all matters concerning his staff. If the Donovans decide that they need extra help, *they'll* do the hiring."

"They'll need extra help," Opal Taylor opined. "One

solitary woman can't keep up with the dusting at Fair-worth House."

"Or polish the silver," said Selena Buxton.

"Or mop the floors," said Elspeth Binney.

"Or beat the rugs," said Millicent Scroggins.

"We'll see," I said.

"Bree Pym missed church again," Peggy Taxman bellowed. She jutted her chin toward the headstone over which Bill and Willis, Sr., were standing. "Ruth and Louise would turn in their graves if they knew how often their great-grandniece sleeps in on Sunday mornings."

"I'm quite sure that the Pym sisters know everything there is to know about their great-grandniece," said Lilian Bunting, who'd left her husband's side to join the throng. "I sense that Ruth and Louise are gazing down upon us from heaven even as we speak. I can almost hear them reciting one of their favorite verses: Judge not, lest ye be judged."

The villagers tittered, knowing full well that Lilian's minisermon had been aimed directly at Peggy.

"'Morning, all," Bree Pym said cheerfully, striding up to stand next to me. She was clad in a skimpy slip-dress, striped leggings, and black flip-flops—an unusual ensemble in Finch, where modest dresses were the norm on Sundays. She ran a hand through her short spiky hair and beamed at the world in general. "It's such a beautiful day that the vicar let me climb up into the belfry to listen to the service." She gave Peggy a sly, sidelong look. "I could hear *every word*."

The villagers eyed Bree with respect. They were used to the vicar's wife crossing swords with Peggy Taxman, but it took courage for a relative newcomer to take a swipe at her.

Bree glanced over her shoulder at Bill and Willis, Sr. "Auntie Ruth and Auntie Louise have company, I see. Think I'll pop over for a chat. My aunties like to know who's saying what in Finch."

Since Ruth and Louise Pym had threatened posthumously, via a letter read aloud at their funeral, to smite anyone who was unkind to their great-grandniece, Bree's words had a sinister tinge to them. While she sauntered off to sit cross-legged before her great-grandaunts' grave, the villagers glanced skyward and backed surreptitiously away from Peggy, as if they expected a bolt from the blue to strike her at any minute.

A lesser woman would have reeled from the verbal blows Lilian and Bree had landed on Peggy, but the uncrowned empress of Finch merely sniffed disdainfully and cast a scathing glance at Bree's tattoos and her nose ring. No one else in the village made a fashion statement quite like Bree's, and though many of us found it refreshing, Peggy did not approve.

"Sally wasn't in church, either," Peggy roared, moving on to an absent and therefore easier target. "Still under the weather, I suppose."

"She is," Rainey Dawson piped up. "Gran's sick as a pig. Couldn't stand on her own two feet this morning."

I caught Rainey's eye with a laserlike look and asked, "Is your grandmother still planning to go to her sister's?"

"To her sister's?" Peggy Taxman said sharply.

"To her sister's," I repeated firmly. "Sally rang me before church to ask me to take her to Judith's house this afternoon." I shrugged nonchalantly. "Well, it makes sense, doesn't it? Sally can't expect Rainey to run the tearoom *and* to look after her, so she's going to stay with her sister until she feels better. Isn't that right, Rainey?"

"Y-yes," Rainey faltered. She gulped, then said more decisively, "Yes, that's right, Lori. Gran will stay with Great-aunt Judith until she feels better. She's leaving this afternoon. With you."

"If your grandmother is so ill, why hasn't Dr. Finisterre been to see her?" Peggy challenged.

"Waste of money," Rainey replied, glaring defiantly at Peggy. "Gran doesn't need a doctor to tell her how sick she is."

A murmur of approval rippled through the group. Most of the villagers were habitual penny-pinchers.

"Why can't Judith drive over from Chipping Norton to fetch your grandmother?" Peggy demanded. "Seems silly to have Lori go all that way when Judith's perfectly capable of managing the trip herself."

"It may seem silly to you, Peggy," I said, with a sanctimonious smirk, "but I consider it a privilege to be able to help a friend in need."

"Good on you, Lori," said Mr. Barlow, patting me on the back.

"Do unto others . . . ," murmured Lilian Bunting, smiling at me.

Peggy's lips tightened dangerously, as if she sensed

that she was being outmaneuvered but could do nothing to stop it.

"My friends," said Willis, Sr., inserting himself into the space between George Wetherhead and Charles Bellingham, "I would like to thank each and every one of you for attending my housewarming party last night. You have always made me feel welcome as a visitor to Finch. Last night, you welcomed me as a member of your charming community. I will endeavor to live up to the honor you have bestowed upon me." He made a courtly bow before continuing, "Sadly, I must detach myself from you for a short time. A client, who prefers to remain anonymous—"

"Why?" Peggy interrupted.

"Please accept my apologies, Mrs. Taxman, but the dictates of my profession bar me from discussing the subject," Willis, Sr., said smoothly, "except to say that my client will arrive at Fairworth House tomorrow and stay with me until our business is concluded."

"Business? What business?" barked Peggy. "Haven't you retired?"

"One likes to keep one's hand in," Willis, Sr., responded modestly. "I will be conducting delicate negotiations on my client's behalf while he is at Fairworth. I must ask all of you to respect my privacy until I am once again at liberty to enjoy your delightful company. I can assure you that the prospect of being cloistered with my client gives me little pleasure." He sighed. "He is quite possibly the most tedious man in the world."

The villagers mumbled words of sympathy.

"William," said Grant Tavistock, "will it be all right with you if I pick up the painting today?"

My heart skipped a beat. I'd completely forgotten about the painting Grant was supposed to clean, but I knew for a fact that, if he came to Fairworth House while Sally was playing lady of the manor, the entire plan would crash and burn. Like everyone else in Finch, Grant would be incapable of keeping such a magnificent revelation to himself.

"Why spoil such a nice Sunday with work?" I said, throwing myself into the breach. "I'll bring the painting to you tomorrow. I'd like to hear your opinion of it."

Grant waved a hand toward Crabtree Cottage, saying, "Charles and I will be at home all day, Lori. Come whenever you like."

"Most kind." Willis, Sr., nodded genially to Grant, then addressed the group at large. "If you will excuse me, I will attempt to lure my energetic grandsons from their playful pursuits. We would not want to be late for the excellent luncheon Mrs. Donovan is preparing for us."

"We certainly wouldn't," I chimed in, though it was the first I'd heard of Deirdre Donovan's excellent luncheon.

Willis, Sr., strolled toward Will and Rob and the churchyard scrum began to break up. Rainey scurried back to the tearoom, Lilian headed for the vicarage, and Bree Pym sailed past me, calling a cheery "Bye, aunties!" to the late Ruth and Louise Pym. The others, as if satiated by the juicy tidbits Willis, Sr., and I had tossed their way, peeled off in twos and threes until only the Taxmans and the Handmaidens remained.

"Did you hear what William said?" Peggy growled, fixing her gimlet gaze on each of the Handmaidens in turn. "Stop pestering the poor man! He has important work to do!"

"I'm sure I don't know what you mean," said Millicent, blushing.

"I've never been one to intrude," said Opal, bristling.

"Nor have I!" Elspeth exclaimed.

"Judge not," Selena intoned, staring hard at Peggy, "lest ye be judged."

The four women tossed their heads contemptuously, passed in single file through the lych-gate, and marched across the lane to their cottages.

"Thanks, Peggy," I said, after they'd gone. "They might have ignored William, but they'll listen to you."

She regarded me shrewdly through her pointy glasses. "William's anonymous client wouldn't be from Mexico, would he?"

I doubted that Rainey could have withstood such a brazen frontal assault, but I was made of sterner stuff. Though I flinched inwardly, I laughed out loud.

"Mexico?" I said, chuckling merrily. "You've got Mexico on the brain, Peggy. If I hadn't promised to keep mum about William's client, I'd tell you where he comes from. As it is, I can't even tell you that he's *not* from Mexico."

"Humph," Peggy grunted. She flicked an imperious finger toward her husband. "Come along, Jasper. The Emporium won't open itself."

I smiled grimly as the Taxmans made their way out

of the churchyard, up the lane, and across the village green to their general store. It seemed to me that the first phase of Aunt Dimity's scheme had gone fairly well. Everyone but Peggy appeared to believe in Sally's fabricated illness and in Willis, Sr.'s nonexistent client, and Peggy didn't scare me. If Lilian and Bree could stand up to her, so could I.

With the disinformation campaign firmly under way, I told myself, it was time to move on to phase two. A phone call after lunch would bring Sally and Rainey into the loop. Then the smuggling operation would begin.

I called my menfolk to me and strode through the lych-gate with a militant swagger. Peggy's bullying tactics had gotten my dander up. I was bound and determined to make Aunt Dimity's plan succeed, if only for the pleasure of outfoxing the uncrowned empress of Finch.

Seven

After what was an indisputably excellent luncheon of exquisitely grilled dover sole, a goat cheese and heirloom tomato salad, glazed baby carrots, and a luscious raspberry compote, my family and I went our separate ways. Bill and his father took the boys off to explore a heavily wooded corner of the estate while I closeted myself in Willis, Sr.'s study and telephoned Sally Pyne.

Sally was so pathetically grateful to me for offering her a way out of her predicament that she could scarcely take in a word I said. To be on the safe side, I explained the plot all over again to Rainey, who promised to pack what she called "Gran's Lady Sarah clothes" and to have her grandmother ready to leave the tearoom at three o'clock.

I was still seated at the walnut desk, rubbing life back into my phone-numbed ear, when someone rapped on the study door.

"Come in," I called.

The Donovans entered the room, Declan in his work clothes and Deirdre in the full-skirted white shirtdress she'd worn while serving lunch. Her long chestnut hair was bundled tidily into a black snood at the back of her head.

"Sorry to disturb you, Lori," she said. "Mr. Willis asked Declan to put the painting in your car, and I wanted to make sure that he took the right one."

"It's pretty easy to identify," I said, waving a hand toward the Sheraton sideboard. "It's the nasty one sitting on the floor and the sooner it's out of here, the happier I'll be."

"Dear me," said Declan, grimacing as he caught sight of the filthy picture. "It has seen better days, hasn't it?"

"It must have hung near a fireplace that smoked rather badly," Deirdre observed. "Fetch a dust sheet from the storage room to wrap it in, Declan. Otherwise, you'll leave a trail of soot behind you."

"I hear and obey." Declan bowed to his wife with comic humility, then sauntered out of the room.

I crossed to stand beside Deirdre, who was peering thoughtfully at the painting.

"Was it in the house when Mr. Willis purchased it?" she asked.

"No," I replied. "The house was empty when William purchased it, but we found some stuff in one of the outbuildings—a book, a collection of paperweights—"

"The Murano paperweights in the morning room?" Deirdre interjected.

"That's right," I said. "The paperweights aren't worth a great deal, but William decided to display them as relics of Fairworth's history. The same goes for the brass compass in the billiards room, the enameled snuffboxes in the drawing room, and the flock of little silver sheep in the dining room. The silver sheep turned out to be Victorian salt and pepper shakers." I nudged the painting gingerly with my toe. "A workman found this monstrosity wedged beneath a pile of rubble in the old stables. If it were mine, I'd put it on the scrap heap."

"You may think more highly of it after it's been cleaned. I believe it's from the late Victorian period." Deirdre smiled briefly. "I could be wrong. I'm judging by the frame."

"You amaze me," I said, giving her a sidelong glance. "Where did you learn to date picture frames?"

"Oxford," she replied. "I took a first in art history. One of my tutors was fanatical about frames, so I learned quite a lot about the art of frame-making—the art that frames the art, as he was fond of saying."

I was beginning to feel a faint twinge of annoyance every time Deirdre revealed a new area of expertise. I couldn't imagine why a woman who cooked like Escoffier, spoke six languages, knew how to raise sheep, and possessed a degree in art history from an Oxford college would be content to work as a housekeeper.

"If you don't mind my asking," I said, "what brought you to Fairworth House?"

Deirdre tore her gaze away from the painting and faced me. "Haven't you read the papers Mrs. Trent sent to you?"

"Not yet," I told her. "I've been a little distracted lately, what with the housewarming party and all."

"I'll give you a thumbnail sketch," she said. "After Declan and I were married, we decided to go into business for ourselves. We opened a guesthouse in Connemara—in the west of Ireland, where Declan's people come from."

"Is that where you learned about sheep?" I asked.

"Yes," she said, looking faintly surprised. "You can't live in Ireland for any length of time without learning a thing or two about sheep. At any rate, our business ran smoothly for the first four years, but during the fifth year we were plagued with problems, major problems that closed us down and cost the earth to repair——a gale damaged the roof, a grease fire destroyed the kitchen. . . ." She shook her head ruefully. "After the boiler burst, we'd had enough. We sold up and started new careers."

"Why *these* careers?" I pressed.

"Why not?" she returned. "Declan and I enjoy working together and we're good at what we do. We're paid a substantial wage to live in a historic home in the heart of the English countryside, and we have a degree of independence without the burden of total responsibility." She surveyed the sunlit study and smiled. "I can't think of a much better life, can you?"

I thought my own life could run circles around hers, but I understood her point. Managing a country house beat punching a corporate time clock, and if the roof leaked, it would be up to Willis, Sr., to pay for the repairs.

"Makes sense," I said. "Thank you."

"Not at all," she said. "Feel free to ask as many questions as you like, Lori. I'd expect nothing less from a devoted daughter-in-law."

The study door opened and Declan returned. Deirdre and I stood well back as he proceeded to wrap the painting in a dust sheet.

"Mind the broken glass," I cautioned. "I would have yanked it out with a pair of pliers, but William insisted on preserving it in place."

"No harm done," Declan announced, wiping his hands on his jeans. "I'll put this rarity in your car, Lori, and you can take it away before the charade begins."

"Speaking of the charade . . ." Deirdre turned to me. "Mr. Willis informed me that he doesn't know when Señor Cocinero will arrive tomorrow, but I wondered if you could tell me when to expect Mrs."—she quickly corrected herself—"*Lady Sarah* to arrive today?"

"Lady Sarah will arrive at half past four or thereabouts," I said. It was a rough guess. I knew how long it would take to drive to Chipping Norton and back, but I had no idea how long it would take to get Sally and her luggage into the Rover. "Have you chosen a bedroom for her?"

"I have," Deirdre assured me. "Mr. Willis will retain the master suite, Lady Sarah will have the rose suite, and I'll put Señor Cocinero in the blue suite."

Willis, Sr., had, quite sensibly, named the bedrooms after their dominant colors. The rose and the blue suites were on opposite ends of the second story and across the corridor from the master suite. Deirdre's arrangement meant that Willis, Sr., would not have to share a wall with either of his guests. I was sure he would approve.

"Do you know what to do after Señor Cocinero arrives?" I asked.

"Mr. Willis has briefed us," said Declan, nodding. "We're to keep an eye on the Mexican gentleman and head him off if he makes a break for the village."

"We're to make him comfortable, but not *too* comfortable," Deirdre went on. "Mr. Willis wishes to discourage return visits."

"We're to bar the doors to visitors while he's here," said Declan, "and never breathe a word about him to anyone after he's gone." He grinned. "Should be a lark."

"A lark?" I said skeptically. "It'll be more difficult than you can possibly imagine. When it comes to spying, the villagers make the CIA look like a bunch of bumbling amateurs."

"Difficult's better than dull," Declan observed, laughing. He hoisted the painting into his arms. "Work to do, ladies. I'd best be off."

"You'll have to excuse me as well, Lori," Deirdre said. "Lady Sarah's suite needs dusting and the blue suite needs to be aired. After I've finished upstairs, I'll come back here and clean up the mess left behind by the painting. Lady Sarah would never approve of sooty smudges in her study."

A flutter of unease passed through me as the pair left the study. I should have been pleased by their good humor, their industriousness, and their willingness to follow what must have struck them as a very peculiar set of instructions, but I couldn't shake the feeling that the delightful Donovans were simply too good to be true.

Bill, Will, Rob, and I returned to the cottage around two o'clock. While I helped the boys to change from their Sunday best into shorts and T-shirts, Bill carried the painting into the study to make room in the Rover for Sally's luggage. He also removed the twins' booster seats from the backseat to make room for Sally, who would lie there, concealed beneath a quilt, while I smuggled her past the villagers on our way back from Chipping Norton. After a brief pause to catch my breath, I set out alone in the Rover, with a king-sized quilt folded discreetly on the backseat and a mind focused sharply on the job at hand.

I was so absorbed in my thoughts that I was scarcely conscious of my surroundings as I cruised past the curving drive that led to Anscombe Manor, negotiated the sharp bend near the redbrick house Bree Pym had inherited from her great-grandaunts, and passed the mouth of Willis, Sr.'s drive. I snapped out of my reverie, however, when I beheld the scene that greeted me as I drove over the humpbacked bridge and looked down on Finch.

The tearoom's curtains were drawn and a CLOSED sign hung ostentatiously on its front door. The village green, by contrast, was a buzzing beehive of activity. The Handmaidens were perched like a row of twittering budgerigars on the bench near the war memorial. Grant Tavistock and Charles Bellingham were weeding the flower beds that surrounded the memorial while their little dogs, Goya and Matisse, frolicked with Buster, Mr. Barlow's cairn terrier.

Mr. Barlow, George Wetherhead, and Miranda Morrow appeared to be discussing notices posted on the message board outside of the old schoolhouse, and the Buntings were passing the time of day with the Peacocks, who were seated on sturdy captain's chairs in front of their pub, with Grog, their basset hound, curled in a rumpled heap between them.

Last but never least, Peggy Taxman stood in the doorway of the Emporium, barking orders to her husband, who was manning the bins in front of the green-grocer's shop.

Conversations ceased and heads swiveled in my direction as I drove across the humpbacked bridge. I could tell simply by looking from one alert face to the next that my neighbors had gulped down their Sunday lunches in order to be on hand to watch Sally emerge from her sickbed.

I climbed out of the Rover, called hello to those who were near enough to hear me, waved to the others, and rang the bell near the side door Sally used to reach her second-floor flat. The door opened abruptly and Sally appeared, blinking owlishly in the sunlight and leaning heavily on her granddaughter's arm. Sally was swathed in a voluminous woolen cape and a thick felt hat, but she'd done nothing to conceal her face. It was a canny move on her part, because it allowed the curious to see just how dreadful she looked.

Two days of stress-induced weeping and a clever choice of outerwear had provided Sally with an impenetrable disguise. No one observing her splotchy cheeks, crimson nose, and swollen eyes could doubt that she was suffering from an exceptionally virulent head cold, and the sheen of perspiration on her forehead could plausibly be attributed to a high fever rather than to a decision to wear a wool cape on a hot summer's day. Sally strengthened the illusion of dire illness by emitting a series of rasping coughs and hobbling along as if she were one step away from a slab in Upper Deeping's mortuary.

Rainey handed her grandmother to me, then dragged an enormous suitcase from the doorway and loaded it into the Rover's cargo compartment. I boosted Sally into the passenger seat, climbed into the driver's seat, turned the key in the ignition, and lowered Sally's window, to give Rainey a chance to bid her grandmother a fond farewell.

"Sorry about the suitcase," Rainey murmured, rolling her eyes. "Gran *insisted* on cramming her entire wardrobe into it." In a louder voice, she said, "Say hello to Great-aunt Judith for me, Gran. And don't worry about the shop. I'll keep the kettle boiling and the pastries fresh."

Sally raised a pudgy hand to bestow a feeble pat on her granddaughter's cheek, then slumped in her seat and resumed coughing. I closed her window and drove the length of the village green, acknowledging with somber nods the cries of "Take care, Sally!" and "Come back soon!" that accompanied our departure.

"I can't wait to get out of this confounded cape," Sally grumbled as we passed St. George's. "I'm sweating like a horse."

"Keep it on until we're past Hodge Farm," I ordered. "I have a sneaking suspicion that Annie Hodge will be on the lookout for you."

"I did well, though, didn't I?" Sally asked, with a touch of pride. "The hat was Rainey's idea, but I came up with the cough."

"The cough was very convincing," I agreed. "But I'm not handing out any acting awards yet. Your most challenging role is still to come."

*   *   *

Peggy Taxman just happened to be standing on the highest point of the humpbacked bridge when I returned to Finch at half past four, with Sally lying flat on the Rover's backseat, hidden beneath my king-sized quilt.

I somehow doubted that Peggy was there to observe fish. While the rest of the villagers had abandoned the village green, the empress had placed herself in a position that would allow her to gaze down on the Rover as I approached the bridge and to scrutinize its interior as I drove past her.

"Stay under the quilt," I murmured, without moving my lips.

"Eh?" said Sally. She clearly hadn't understood a word I'd said.

"Stay put and don't move," I snapped, covering my mouth with my hand. "Peggy's trying to ambush us."

"Interfering old cat," Sally muttered. "Good thing we tucked my valise under here with me. Ugh," she grunted. "The blasted thing is digging a hole in my leg."

"Hush," I said urgently. I increased the pressure on the gas pedal and favored Peggy with a carefree smile as we bounced up and over the bridge. I could feel her hawklike gaze boring into the back of my head as I turned into Willis, Sr.'s drive and I wouldn't allow Sally to sit up until we'd rounded a curve lined with trees that effectively blocked Peggy's view.

"Look at me," Sally complained, as she pushed the quilt aside. "I'm swimming in sweat. Don't know why you had to use a quilt, Lori. A sheet would have been more comfortable in this weather."

"If you don't stop whingeing," I growled, "I'll make you walk the rest of the way."

Sally had spent the past hour and a half pointing out the weaknesses in Aunt Dimity's plan. Though I realized that her nitpicking arose from sheer nervousness, I was so tired of listening to her fretful chorus of what-ifs that I couldn't wait to deliver her to Willis, Sr.

I wanted to let out a shout of relief when Fairworth's front door opened mere seconds after I'd parked the car on the graveled apron. As Sally and I climbed out of the Rover, Willis, Sr., descended the front steps, flanked by the Donovans. Declan hurried forward to retrieve the suitcase, which he carried into the house, and Deirdre stayed subserviently in the background while Willis, Sr., approached Sally with open arms.

"*Bienvenida*, Lady Sarah," he said. "*Mi casa es su casa.*"

"Sorry?" said Sally uncomprehendingly.

"Welcome, Lady Sarah," Willis, Sr., translated. "My house is your house."

Sally's eyes welled with tears. "Oh, *thank you*, William. I'm so very sorry to put you to so much trouble."

"I can assure you that it is no trouble at all," said Willis, Sr. "Mrs. Donovan will show you to your suite and unpack your bag for you. When you are quite ready, you may join me for tea in the drawing room."

"Tea in the drawing room . . . ," Sally said dazedly. "It sounds like something out of a play."

"It *is* something out of a play," I muttered.

Willis, Sr., gave me a quelling look, then spoke to Sally.

"Lady Sarah is quite accustomed to taking tea in the drawing room," he told her gently. "Over tea, we will discuss your daily routine. Afterward, I will give you a tour of Fairworth. If you are to play the role of Lady Sarah convincingly, you will have to familiarize yourself with your ancestral home."

"Very true," Sally agreed, drying her eyes on her cape. "It wouldn't do to send Henrique into an airing cupboard instead of the loo."

"It would not," Willis, Sr., said gravely. "Mrs. Donovan?"

Deirdre executed a flawless bob curtsy and led a bemused Sally Pyne into Fairworth House. Willis, Sr., remained behind to confer with me.

"Did the smuggling operation proceed smoothly?" he inquired.

"Like butter," I replied. "Peggy tried to catch us out, but we slipped through her fingers."

"Mrs. Taxman is a persistent woman," he commented unnecessarily. "We will have to maintain a high degree of vigilance if we are to avoid falling into the traps she will no doubt lay for us."

"We could ask Jasper to lock her in the storeroom at the Emporium until Henrique leaves," I suggested.

"An amusing if impractical proposition," said Willis, Sr. "You will be happy to know that I have devised a more sensible solution to a problem that may surface tomorrow."

"Which problem?" I asked. "There are so many to choose from."

"It has occurred to me," he said, "that Señor Cocinero may stop in the village to ask for directions to Lady Sarah's home."

"Oh my gosh," I said, clapping a hand to my forehead. "If he goes into the Emporium, Peggy'll grill him until he squeals."

"Precisely." Willis, Sr., nodded. "Should Señor Cocinero ask for directions, *you* must be the one to give them to him. Can you devise a reasonable excuse for loitering in Finch until he appears? We have no idea when to expect him, so you may be there all day."

"Trust me," I said. "I know how to kill time in Finch. After I drop off the painting at Crabtree Cottage, I can mosey over to Bill's office, do some shopping at the Emporium, linger over a glass of lemonade at the pub, and have a snack at the tearoom. If you factor in incidental chitchat, I could spend up to eight hours loitering in Finch. I'm not sure how I'll identify Henrique, though. I don't know what he looks like."

"Señor Cocinero is a well-to-do Mexican gentleman in late middle age," Willis, Sr., reminded me. "He will, I suspect, stand out like a chili pepper in a blancmange as he drives through the village."

"Good point," I said. "If he stops in the village for any reason, I'll introduce myself to him, hop in his car, and get him away before anyone can give him the third degree."

"Excellent." Willis, Sr., consulted his pocket watch, then returned it to his waistcoat pocket. "I must leave you now, to attend to Lady Sarah's education, but I have one more question to ask before I go: Did you by any chance remove the brass compass from the billiards room?"

"No," I replied, frowning. "Why? Is it missing?"

"It is not in its usual place," Willis, Sr., acknowledged.

My frown deepened. "You don't suppose someone at the party—"

"Certainly not," Willis, Sr., cut in. "Please give my guests some credit, Lori. If there had been a thief among them, he or she would have pocketed something more valuable than the brass compass."

"Where is it, then?" I asked.

"Mrs. Donovan must have taken it to the kitchen for polishing. She is a meticulous and conscientious housekeeper." Willis, Sr., drew in a deep breath of fresh country air and rubbed his palms together vigorously. "I will bid you good evening, my dear. I must say that I am looking forward to transforming Mrs. Pyne into Lady Sarah. I feel as inspired as Professor Henry Higgins must have felt when he chanced upon Eliza Doolittle."

Whistling a jaunty tune from *My Fair Lady*, Willis, Sr., mounted the steps, leaving me to stare after him, openmouthed.

I had never before heard my father-in-law whistle.

"It's the fresh paint," I muttered. "The fumes have addled his brain."

I shook my head and returned to the Rover, feeling every bit as bemused as Sally Pyne.

Eight

"I t's the fresh paint," I repeated firmly, gazing down at the blue journal. "The fumes have addled William's brain."

The ormolu clock in the study had just finished chiming half past ten. My sons, my husband, and my husband's cat were in bed and asleep. Only Reginald was awake to keep me company while I spoke with Aunt Dimity. His black button eyes glittered attentively in the firelight as I went on.

"I'm telling you, Dimity, William is not himself," I insisted. "He jumped into hiring the Donovans, he jumped into playing Lady Sarah's American cousin, he keeps going on about sheep, and now he's *whistling*! What's next? Tap-dancing?" I shook my head worriedly. "It must be the paint. It's a proven fact that inhaling paint fumes can do funny things to a person's brain."

As I paused to chew on a thumbnail, Aunt Dimity's familiar copperplate flowed confidently across the page.

There is nothing wrong with William's brain, Lori. First of all, it's grossly inaccurate to say that he "jumped" into hiring the Donovans. You told me yourself that he reviewed their applications thoroughly before engaging them.

"He did," I acknowledged grudgingly. "But what about the rest of it?"

I would blame William's atypical behavior on retirement rather than paint fumes. Active men tend to fear retirement,

Lori. They're ill-equipped to deal with leisure time and they detest the notion of pursuing meaningless hobbies. They prefer diversions that stimulate the imagination and challenge the mind. Having finished one major project—the renovation of Fairworth House—

"Fairworth isn't finished," I interjected. "There's lots of landscaping left to do and he still has to rebuild those ruined outbuildings."

Landscaping and construction projects are absorbing in their own ways, but they can't compete with the thrill of the human drama. William is and always will be an attorney, Lori. He enjoys pitting his wits against another's.

"He drew up wills and did estate planning for rich people," I said. "How much wit-pitting does that take?"

A great deal, I promise you, especially when one is dealing with clients as fractious and exacting as William's. As I was saying . . . having finished one major project, William looked for another. Sally appeared as if by magic and served him a compelling human predicament on a plate. Is it any wonder that he "jumped" into the role of Lady Sarah's American cousin? What could possibly be more exhilarating than an attempt to pull the wool over the eyes of an entire village, not to mention those of the unsuspecting Señor Cocinero?

"William's having fun," I said, as comprehension dawned. "*That's* why he's whistling."

You have seen the light at last, Lori. William is having the time of his life refining and implementing my original plan for safeguarding Sally's reputation. I suspect that it appeals to him because of its novelty as well as its complexity. It's unlike anything he's ever done before.

"How do you explain his sheep fixation?" I asked.

I refute the word fixation. *William is simply planning ahead. Remember, Lori, Señor Cocinero will be gone by Wednesday. When the grand charade comes to an end, William will move on to his sheep project.*

"Sheep aren't part of the thrilling human drama," I objected. "If what you're saying is true, Dimity, the sheep project won't be enough to satisfy William." I groaned softly. "Will I have to engineer a never-ending series of human dramas to keep my father-in-law happy?"

I doubt it. The villagers—and the Handmaidens in particular—are more than capable of providing William with all of the human drama he requires.

I laughed. "I can't argue with you, Dimity. Life in Finch is full of drama." I glanced at the dust sheet–wrapped painting Bill had deposited in the study. "Life in Fairworth House is becoming more interesting, too, and not only because of the grand charade. It's possible that someone stole the brass compass from the billiards room."

The compass recovered from the old stables?

"That's the one," I confirmed.

Have you asked the twins if they know where it is?

"Are you accusing my sons of theft?" I asked, knowing full well that Aunt Dimity would never do such a thing.

Don't be absurd, Lori. Seven-year-old grandsons don't steal from their grandfather. They borrow. The brass compass is just the sort of gadget that would captivate a pair of intrepid little explorers like Will and Rob. If I were you, I'd ask them about it in the morning.

"I'll hold off until I speak with William," I said. "He

thinks Deirdre Donovan, the patron saint of housekeepers, took the compass to the kitchen for cleaning. I don't know why she would," I added. "I polished it myself last week and when I saw it last night, it was perfectly clean and shiny. But I guess my standards aren't as high as hers."

Do I detect a note of peevishness in your voice, my dear?

"Probably," I admitted. I drummed my fingers on the arm of the chair, then burst out, "Have you ever met someone who's good at everything, Dimity? Deirdre's a brainy, attractive neat-freak who can cook. It's enormously irritating."

Indeed it is. I'm sure you'll agree, however, that it's better for William to have a multitalented housekeeper than a useless one.

"I suppose so," I conceded. "But it's still irritating." A yawn escaped me and I glanced at the clock. "Time for me to hit the hay, Dimity. I have to be in Finch early tomorrow, to get a jump on Henrique Watch."

I wish you the best of luck, Lori, and the quickest of reflexes. You'll have to move fast to keep Peggy Taxman from flinging herself in front of Señor Cocinero's car.

I chuckled as Aunt Dimity's handwriting faded from the page, then closed the blue journal and returned it to its shelf. After saying good night to Reginald, I banked the fire, turned off the lights, and headed upstairs.

As I climbed into bed beside Bill, I made a mental note to ask Deirdre to air Fairworth House thoroughly before the week was out. Though Aunt Dimity had convinced me that Willis, Sr., was as sane as he'd ever been, I wanted to make sure he stayed that way.

*   *   *

Willis, Sr., telephoned during breakfast on Monday morning to let me know that the missing compass had, as he'd suspected, been taken to the kitchen by Deirdre Donovan, who'd subjected it to a rigorous scrubbing, using an environmentally sound polishing paste of her own invention. I suppressed the urge to hiss like a spiteful cat and asked how Lady Sarah was holding up.

"She is understandably overwhelmed by the situation," he informed me. "But I believe she will calm down by the time Señor Cocinero arrives. Mrs. Donovan is taking great pains to put her at ease, as am I, naturally."

"I'll call you as soon as I spot Henrique," I said, and hung up.

"Is Sally suffering from stage fright?" Bill asked from the kitchen table.

"Pas devant les enfants," I said, giving him a warning look.

"What's 'not in front of the children'?" Will asked brightly.

I did a double take, then demanded, "Since when do you speak French?"

"Nell's teaching us," Rob replied. *"On parle Français bien ici."*

"What's 'not in front of the children'?" Will repeated.

"What's stage fright?" Rob joined in.

"Your father will explain everything to you on the way to Anscombe Manor," I said. It was a cop-out, but a justified cop-out. Bill should have known better than to mention Sally in front of the boys.

"Is Daddy taking us to the stables?" asked Will.

"He'll drop you off on his way to work," I replied. "Mummy has to run some errands."

Before my budding francophones could come up with another way to throw me for a loop, I ordered them to put their dishes in the sink, wash their hands, and get ready for their riding lessons. Bill hung his head sheepishly after they'd left the kitchen.

"Sorry about that," he said. "I'll have to be more careful of what I say when I'm around Will and Rob. I sometimes forget how sharp they are."

"You can make up for it by putting the painting in my Mini," I said. My aged Morris Mini was too small to accomodate the boys' booster seats, but it was useful for short, child-free journeys.

"Consider it done," Bill said, getting to his feet. "What's on tap for the rest of the day?"

"I've arranged a play date with Annie Hodge," I said. "She'll bring Piero over this afternoon. I thought it would be an acceptable substitute for a trip to Grandpa's."

"Great idea," he said. "When should I expect you at the office?"

"It depends on how much time I have to kill," I replied. "And that depends on when Henrique shows up."

"I won't get any work done until he does," said Bill. "I'll be lurking near my windows all morning, looking for a stranger in a strange car."

"You and everyone else in Finch," I said. "I've said it before and I'll say it again: It'll be a miracle if we pull this off."

Bill and the boys set out in the Rover shortly after seven. I finished loading the dishwasher, then ran upstairs to select an appropriate costume. Since I was supposed to be related to the wealthy and gracious Lady Sarah Pyne, I donned a pretty lavender dress and a pair of white sandals instead of my usual T-shirt, shorts, and sneakers. After running a comb through my hair and making sure that Stanley's water bowl was full, I grabbed my shoulder bag from the hall table and headed into the village in my Mini.

As I putt-putted along the winding lane, I thought of how lucky Señor Cocinero was to be wending his way toward Fairworth House on such a perfect summer day. Small birds flitted in and out of the hedgerows, gorging themselves on seeds and berries, lambs romped in grassy pastures, and seagulls circled stands of ripe barley that rippled like golden seas in the passing breeze. It would be hot and humid later on, and thunderstorms might roll in, but the morning air was like a tonic.

I crossed the humpbacked bridge and noted that the lights were on in Wysteria Lodge, the vine-bedecked stone building that housed Bill's high-tech office. It was too early for the tearoom, the pub, the Emporium, and the greengrocer's shop to open, but curtains twitched in every cottage I passed. In Finch, it was worth inter-rupting one's breakfast to keep tabs on one's neighbors. As I approached Crabtree Cottage, I recalled its previ-ous occupant, a disagreeable woman whose curtains had never stopped twitching, and thanked heaven that Charles Bellingham and Grant Tavistock had taken her place.

The alterations Charles and Grant had made to Crabtree Cottage weren't apparent from the outside, but the interior was much changed. The front parlor, with its marvelous bay window overlooking the village green, had been converted into an office for Charles, the art appraiser, while the upstairs front bedroom had been fashioned into a well-ventilated workroom for Grant, the restoration expert. The two lived in rooms at the rear of the cottage, where they could be near the private oasis of their walled garden.

Charles, who was tall, portly, and balding, answered the doorbell clad in bedroom slippers, striped pajamas, and a lavishly embroidered black silk bathrobe, with a half-eaten piece of toast in his hand and Goya, his golden Pomeranian, cradled in the crook of his arm.

"Lori," he said, looking both sleepy and mildly surprised. "We didn't expect you to rise with the sun. Grant!" he called over his shoulder. "Lori's here!"

I heard the mingled thump of feet and patter of paws running down stairs and Grant appeared at Charles's side, accompanied by Matisse, his friendly Maltese. Grant, unlike Charles, was short and lean, with a healthy crop of salt-and-pepper hair. He was also fully dressed, in a crisp white shirt, chinos, and loafers. His smile was, as always, warm and welcoming.

"Finish your toast, Charles," he said kindly, patting his partner's arm. "I"ll look after Lori." As Charles trudged back to the kitchen, Grant continued, "Charles is an incurable night owl. He won't really be awake until noon. You're looking very bonny this morning. What's the occasion?"

The question didn't catch me unawares. I'd known that the sight of me wearing a dress on a weekday morning would intrigue my neighbors, and I'd prepared a cover story accordingly.

"William's client," I said simply. "I'm meeting him today."

"Ah, yes, the mystery man." Grant folded his arms and bent his head closer to mine, saying quietly, "You couldn't give me the tiniest hint about him, could you? I swear it won't go any farther than Charles's ear."

"No can do," I said flatly. "Believe me, you're not missing anything. He's the biggest bore ever born."

"Even so . . ." Grant read my closed expression and shrugged. "All right, I'll drop it, but I won't be the last person to pester you about Mr. Anonymous. Everyone's dying to know who he is." He looked past me at the Mini. "Is my new patient in the car? Shall I fetch it?"

"If you don't mind," I said, squatting to rub Matisse's tummy. "But be careful. The broken glass in the frame will bite you if you let it."

Grant pulled the dust sheet—swathed painting out of the Mini's backseat and suggested that I come with him to his workroom. Since the workroom's window would give me an even better view of the village than the bay window in Charles's office, I followed Grant upstairs, with Matisse pattering perkily after us.

Grant placed the painting on a large white table in the center of the room and unwrapped it. He stuffed the filthy dust sheet into a paper bag, then scrubbed the grime from his hands. After donning a pair of white cotton gloves, he switched on a high-power angle lamp and examined his "new patient" through a magnifying glass.

I stood at the window, scrutinizing the village with equal interest.

"I've seen this sort of damage before," he murmured. "The poor thing must have hung in a room with a smoky fireplace."

Score one for Deirdre, I thought sourly.

"I can't date it precisely," Grant went on, "but the frame suggests a work from the late Victorian era."

His estimated date, unsurprisingly, matched Deirdre's.

"And it's not a painting," Grant added.

"What is it?" I asked, still looking out the window.

"I'm . . . not . . . sure," he said ruminatively, bending low over the nonpainting. "I can detect small images of some sort accompanied by calligraphy. Unfortunately, I can't make out the images or the words."

"Fascinating," I said absently.

Grant straightened. "Once I remove the soot, we'll know where we stand in terms of restoration work. I'll get started on it right away and do as much as I can before Charles and I leave for London this afternoon."

I wheeled around to face him. An impromptu excursion to London merited my full attention.

"What's happening in London?" I asked.

"We've been invited to attend a gallery opening tonight," he replied, "and we'll take in a show tomorrow night. We won't be back until Wednesday. A friend is letting us use his flat while we're in town."

"Will you take Goya and Matisse with you?" I asked.

"Naturally," he said. "They adore our little jaunts to London."

"Lucky puppies," I said, and nodded at the painting. "Thanks for tackling the job, Grant. I think it's a waste of time, but William doesn't, and it's *his* masterpiece."

"You are a philistine, Lori," Grant scolded. He swept a hand over the white table. "You can't pass judgment on a work of art you can't see. My ministrations may uncover a vital link to Fairworth's past. Even if it has little or no monetary value, it should be preserved and cherished."

"If you preserve it, William will cherish it," I said, laughing, but as I turned back to the window, the laughter died in my throat.

A silver Audi was parked in front of Wysteria Lodge. No one in Finch owned a silver Audi.

"Sorry, Grant," I said, dashing toward the staircase. "Gotta run. Have a great time in London!"

"Your dust cloth!" Grant called, holding the paper bag out to me.

"Keep it!" I called over my shoulder.

Grant Tavistock was no fool. As I scurried out of the workroom, he darted to the window to find out what had caught my eye. I could feel him and many other people watching me as I hurried across the green, but it wasn't the sense of being observed that rattled me. It was the telltale jingling sound made by the sleigh bells attached to the Emporium's front door as it swung open.

Peggy Taxman had finished her breakfast.

Nine

Big ships take longer than small ones to work up a head of steam. Since Peggy Taxman outweighed me by at least a hundred pounds, she stood no chance of reaching the Audi before I did, but even I couldn't get to it as quickly as Bill. He popped out of Wysteria Lodge like a jack-in-the-box and bent to speak to the driver through the car's open window.

"*No se preocupe, Señor Cocinero,*" he was saying as I skidded to a halt next to him. "My wife will be glad to show you the way to Fairworth House."

"It is too much trouble," the driver protested in heavily accented but fluent English. "I could not ask such a favor."

"Nonsense!" I gasped and slid into the passenger's seat so fast that I nearly squashed the Panama hat that was sitting there. I snatched the hat from the seat and held it in my lap as I slammed the door. "I *insist* on guiding you. It's a courtesy we extend to all of our visitors," I went on, glancing nervously at Peggy Taxman's looming figure. "Over the bridge and first turn on the left. Let's not keep Lady Sarah waiting, Señor. "*Vámonos!*"

"*De acuerdo!*" he responded amiably and drove off before Peggy was halfway across the green. "You and your husband are most kind."

"Think nothing of it," I said, ignoring Peggy's

attempts to flag us down. "Lady Sarah is very dear to us. Any friend of hers is a friend of ours."

Señor Cocinero expressed what I assumed to be his gratitude in a string of words that meant nothing to me.

"Forgive me, Señor," I said, "but I speak very little Spanish."

"Forgive *me*," he countered. "When in England, I should speak English, no?"

"*Sí,*" I said distractedly as I watched Peggy's furious face recede in the rearview mirror. It had been a close-run thing, but Willis, Sr.'s foresight and Bill's vigilance had prevented the empress from cornering her quarry. Weak with relief, I leaned back in my seat and took a good look at Sally Pyne's amigo.

As Willis, Sr., had predicted, Henrique didn't resemble your average pink-faced Englishman. His swarthy complexion, black mustache, and black, wavy hair made me think of sunny beaches and swaying palm trees rather than hedge-lined lanes and sturdy oaks. He had a round, craggy face webbed with laugh lines, and his dark eyes twinkled genially beneath heavy black brows. His white suit was tailored to fit his short, pudgy body, his black shoes shone, and he wore a gold signet ring on the pinkie finger of his right hand. Though he would never find work as a male model, it was easy to see why Sally had found him so attractive. His voice was deep and rich and he emanated an air of old-world charm.

"You are related to Lady Sarah?" he inquired as we crossed the bridge.

"Only by marriage," I said. "My father-in-law, William Willis, is her cousin. He comes to see us every summer, but he stays with Lady Sarah because Bill and I don't have enough room for him in our cottage."

"Lady Sarah tells me that, to her neighbors, she is known as Sally of Finch," he said. "I am surprised to hear you use her title."

"The whole family does," I said, "out of respect."

"I am glad," said Henrique. "Lady Sarah, she deserves this respect. You are a close family?"

"We are," I said. "Very close."

"I like this very much," he said. "I am not as lucky as you. My wife died ten years ago and my children live far away. Life is lonely without them. You are fortunate to have those you love near you."

I was so touched by his story that I almost forgot where we were going.

"We turn here, Señor Cocinero," I said hastily.

"You must call me Henrique," he said, executing a neat left-hand turn into Willis, Sr.'s drive. "As you say, Lady Sarah's friends are my friends, and friends are not so formal."

"Then you must call me Lori," I said.

"A pretty name for a pretty señora," he said, smiling. "You are not English, I think."

"Bill and I are American," I said, "but we've lived in England for so many years that it's become our second home."

"It is good to feel at home when one lives overseas," said Henrique. "And what a beautiful home Lady Sarah has. Is this indeed Fairworth House? *Estupendo! Es un paraiso!*"

I didn't know exactly what he'd said, but I'd caught the gist. Bathed in sunlight and framed by the drive's leafy trees, Fairworth did look like a paradise. I was too preoccupied to appreciate it, however, because it had just dawned on me that I'd forgotten to warn Willis, Sr., of Henrique's imminent arrival. I could only hope that Bill had called ahead from Wysteria Lodge. If Henrique caught Lady Sarah practicing her deportment, he might wonder what was going on.

"Yes," I confirmed. "That's Fairworth House."

"The gardens have been hurt by drought, perhaps?" he said, gazing at the immature plants sprouting from mulch the landscapers had laid less than a week before the housewarming party.

"Lady Sarah is trying something new," I improvised, wondering if Sally had even noticed the gardens. "She likes to experiment with color and texture and, um, scent."

"Ah," said Henrique, nodding his understanding. "Lady Sarah has the restless spirit of a true artist."

"We never know what she'll do next," I said, with feeling.

A curtain in the attic apartment twitched as Henrique and I got out of the car, so I knew that at least one of the Donovans had noted our arrival. I hoped the lookout would use the staircase instead of the elevator to alert the others. The elevator was convenient, but slow.

I handed Henrique his hat, we climbed the steps to the front door, and I rang the bell while he stood back with a look of pleasant anticipation in his dark eyes. A moment later, Deirdre opened the door, with Declan at her side. I couldn't tell which one of them had raced down from the apartment because neither seemed flustered or short of breath. Deirdre was dressed in what seemed to be her housekeeper's uniform—a full-skirted white shirtdress and black snood—and Declan was wearing another short-sleeved shirt with a pair of khaki trousers. They both appeared to be as fresh as daisies.

Deirdre began to greet Henrique in fluent Spanish, but he held up his hand to stop her.

"Muchas gracias, Señora," he said, "but I prefer to speak English while I am here. I need the practice."

"No, you don't," I chided him. "You speak English beautifully."

"I would like to speak it better," said Henrique, "which requires practice." He smiled at Deirdre. "Please, indulge me."

"As you wish, Mr. Cocinero," she said.

"If I might have your car key, sir?" said Declan, stepping forward. "I'll see to your luggage and move your vehicle to the garage. We don't want to leave it sitting unprotected in the hot sun."

"The sun is much hotter in my country, young man," said Henrique, "but I take your point."

Henrique dropped a folded five-pound note into Declan's hand along with the car key. Declan seemed surprised by the gift, but he tucked it into his pocket and said nothing as he ran off to look after the Audi.

Having successfully delivered Henrique into Deirdre's safekeeping, I could have excused myself and returned to the village on foot to pick up the Mini, but I didn't want to spoil a lovely morning by butting heads with Peggy Taxman, who would drop whatever she was doing in order to reprimand me—loudly and publicly—for ignoring her attempts to foil our escape. Given a choice between a contentious confrontation with an irate empress and a ringside seat at the romantic reunion of Sally Pyne and her Mexican gentleman, I did not hesitate to choose the latter.

"If you'll follow me?" said Deirdre. "Lady Sarah is expecting you."

Henrique removed his hat and allowed Deirdre and me to proceed him into the entrance hall. His courtliness would, I knew, find favor with Willis, Sr., who exuded a similar brand of old-world charm. Deirdre relieved Henrique of his hat, knocked twice on the morning room door, opened it, announced us, and stood to attention just inside the doorway. When Henrique motioned for me to go ahead of him, I was treated to an unimpeded view of the opening scene in Aunt Dimity's drama.

The walls of the morning room were a delicate shade of apricot and the tall windows were hung with gold brocade drapes, which had been drawn to allow natural light to flood the room. An Aubusson carpet protected the fine parquet floors, and the ceiling was decorated with a restrained yet intricate pattern of plasterwork. A white marble fireplace faced the door to the entrance hall, and a white-painted door in the corner led to the dining room.

The furnishings were distinctly feminine, with slender cabriole legs and embroidered upholstery. The settee had, for reasons unknown to me, been shifted from its position near the center window to one nearer the fireplace. The change made the room seem slightly off balance, but the effect as a whole was still subtly sumptuous.

Sunbeams fell like spotlights on the room's occupants. Willis, Sr., stood before the inlaid rosewood writing table that held the Murano paperweights. He was dressed like a country squire, in a lightweight tweed suit and thick-soled brogues. Lady Sarah Pyne sat ramrod straight in the exact center of the settee. She was dressed like a sugary parfait.

Sally was enveloped from neck to ankle in a cloud of orange and yellow chiffon edged with rhinestones at the collar and cuffs. She wore dainty white leather slippers on her feet, which dangled a good five inches above the carpet. A small tiara glittered discreetly among her short, silvery locks and the snowflake-shaped silver pendant Henrique had given her in Mexico glinted among the soft folds of chiffon.

An old, leather-bound book lay beside her on the settee, as if she'd spent the morning improving her mind, and her plump hands were clasped tightly in her lap. She looked absolutely petrified, like an actress who'd forgotten her lines. Bill's comment about stage fright had, I thought, been spot-on.

"Lady Sarah," I said encouragingly. "Look who I found in the village."

Sally took a wavering breath and held out a trembling hand.

"H-Henrique," she stammered, in an accent that hovered precariously between the queen's and a fishmonger's. "H-how good of you to c-come."

"How good of *you* to welcome me to your splendid

home," Henrique returned. He crossed to kiss Sally's hand, then held it between both of his. "*Mil gracias por su hospitalidad,* Lady Sarah. Or, as I will say from now on: Thank you for your hospitality, Lady Sarah."

Pink patches appeared in Sally's cheeks and a girlish giggle escaped her.

"Don't be silly, Henrique," she said. "I simply *adore* it when you speak Spanish."

"I will speak it for you, *querida,* but you must allow me to speak English to everyone else," he said. He gazed down at her upturned face and stroked the back of her hand lightly with his fingertips. "How else will I learn to say all that I wish to say to you?"

Sally's lips parted and her bosom gave a discernible heave, as did mine, but Willis, Sr., ruined the moment by clearing his throat. Recalled to duty, Sally withdrew her hand from Henrique's and introduced her American cousin.

"A pleasure, sir," said Willis, Sr., coming forward.

"Also for me," said Henrique, bowing. "We are to be fellow houseguests, I am told."

"We are," said Willis, Sr. "My cousin has been kind enough to allow me to stay with her for the summer."

"Your cousin is kindness itself," said Henrique, locking eyes with Sally.

"Mrs. Donovan," said Sally, "would you please show Señor Cocinero to his room? He'll be wanting a wash after his journey."

Sally made it sound as though she expected Deirdre to scrub Henrique down with soap and water, but Henrique didn't seem to notice.

"Kindness itself," he repeated in what amounted to a purr.

"We'll have brunch in the conservatory," Sally went on. "When you've finished with Señor Cocinero, Mrs. Donovan, please meet me in the kitchen to discuss the menu."

"Very good, my lady," said Deirdre. "Will you come with me, please, Mr. Cocinero?"

Henrique gave Sally a smoldering look, then followed Deirdre out of the morning room. Willis, Sr., closed the door and a moment of silence ensued.

"Isn't he just . . . ," Sally murmured dreamily.

"He *is*," I agreed, sighing.

"Ladies," Willis, Sr., said sternly, "need I remind you that the point of this exercise is to discourage Señor Cocinero from making future visits to Fairworth House? It will be difficult for us to achieve our aim if you continue to behave like a pair of moonstruck adolescents."

Sally ducked her head guiltily.

"Sorry, William," she said, reverting to her normal accent. "It was the shock of seeing him again. I'll try to be more standoffish. The conservatory will do for brunch, though, won't it? All those ferns and things will protect us from prying eyes." She got to her feet. "If you need me, I'll be in the kitchen with Deirdre, freshening up those leftover canapés. Henrique's partial to caviar. A tot of champagne wouldn't do us any harm, either. I'll see if there's a bottle in the fridge. Champagne should be served cold, you know. Maybe I'll mix up a pitcher of mimosas. . . ."

Sally bustled through the door to the dining room in

a blur of orange and yellow, and Willis, Sr., sat down heavily on the settee.

"Tough morning?" I asked sympathetically, sitting beside him.

"The gown," he said, "was Lady Sarah's choice. Mrs. Donovan and I attempted to dissuade her from wearing such an outlandish costume, but Lady Sarah was adamant."

"It's not so bad," I said. "The colors are very, er, tropical."

"And the rhinestones?" said Willis, Sr.

"A bit twinkly for a quiet Monday morning at home," I conceded, "but not hideous."

"Lady Sarah insisted on the tiara as well," Willis, Sr., went on. "It appears that her impression of aristocratic attire has been gained entirely from comic books." He shook his head. "I cannot bring myself to discuss her accent except to say that it is strikingly original. I do not believe that it has ever been heard before on this or any other planet."

"Why did you move the settee?" I asked, hoping to distract him from Sally's myriad shortcomings.

"Has the settee been moved?" Willis, Sr., said dully.

"Yes," I said. "It was in front of the window when I spoke with you yesterday morning. Now it's closer to the fireplace."

"I failed to notice the change," Willis, Sr., admitted wearily. "I was blinded, no doubt, by Lady Sarah's rhinestones."

"Buck up, William," I said bracingly. "It'll all be over by Wednesday."

"Will it?" he retorted, raising a skeptical eyebrow. "I fear that Lady Sarah will find it more difficult to spurn her swain than I had anticipated."

"He's pretty hard to resist," I observed. "And he certainly seems to be smitten with her."

"'Still to us at twilight comes love's old sweet song,'" he murmured. "James Joyce. *Ulysses*," he added, identifying the quotation.

"I wouldn't say that Sally and Henrique are in their twilight years," I objected.

"Perhaps not," he said. "But love's old sweet song is in the air and I do not know how to silence it."

"Play it by ear," I suggested. "Henrique may be eager to leave after being cooped up here for a couple of days."

"He will no doubt find it trying to subsist on a diet of champagne and caviar," Willis, Sr., said dryly.

"Maybe the caviar's gone off," I said brightly. "Nothing gets rid of an unwanted guest faster than a good, old-fashioned case of food poisoning."

Willis, Sr., gave me a reproving glance.

"I do not wish to put Señor Cocinero in the hospital, Lori," he said. "I wish to put him on the next flight bound for Mexico City."

"Itching powder between his bed sheets?" I suggested.

Willis, Sr., smiled wanly, then peered down at the settee. "I cannot imagine why Lady Sarah felt the need to rearrange my furniture."

"You should tell her to leave everything where you put it," I said. "Otherwise you'll be tripping over chairs and bumping into bureaus every time you turn around."

An arrested expression crossed Willis, Sr.'s face.

"I barked my shin on a chair in the drawing room earlier this morning" he said. "It, too, had been moved from its original position."

"I rest my case," I said.

"I shall have a word with Lady Sarah before the day is out," Willis, Sr., said decisively, "assuming, of course, that I can get a word in edgewise."

The door to the entrance hall opened and Sally came into the morning room with Henrique following close behind her. She looked ecstatic.

"Wonderful news, everyone," she said, beaming at us. "Henrique has rearranged his travel schedule. He'll be able to stay at Fairworth for a *whole week*! Isn't it grand?"

Willis, Sr.'s mild gray eyes flashed dangerously as he rose from the settee. The prospect of expanding Henrique's visit from three days to seven clearly did not sit well with him.

"Lady Sarah," he said in clipped tones. "I have a matter of some urgency to discuss with you. Will you join me in the study? *This instant?*"

The set of his jaw as he swept Sally from the room told me that he would have no trouble getting a word in edgewise.

Ten

Willis, Sr., didn't slam the door behind him, but he closed it very firmly. Sally's expression as she left the morning room ahead of him was that of a condemned prisoner about to face a firing squad. She'd apparently realized just how bad an idea it was to announce a sudden change of plans without consulting Willis, Sr., beforehand.

I searched my mind for a way to excuse their abrupt departure, but Henrique saved me the trouble.

"Estate business," he said knowingly. "The landed gentry have a great many obligations to fulfill. Lady Sarah must not neglect her duties while I am here."

"Lady Sarah is a conscientious landowner," I said, nodding.

"Her tenants are fortunate," he commented.

"Tenants?" I said uncertainly.

"Is it not the right word?" Henrique frowned. "I refer to those estate workers who lease their cottages from Lady Sarah. She tells me of the many people who rely on her for the housing and the employment."

"Oh, *those* tenants . . . ," I said, as if his words weren't news to me. Sally had evidently given him the impression that Fairworth was a feudal estate populated by peasants who shouted "Hoorah!" as she paraded past their humble dwellings in her gilded carriage. "Yes, they're very lucky to have such a generous patroness."

"Very lucky indeed," said Henrique.

He clasped his hands behind his back and made his way slowly around the room, pausing to admire the oil paintings on the walls, the porcelain figurines on the mantel, and the cluster of colorful paperweights on the writing table.

"Fairworth is a treasure house," he said finally, with an appreciative sigh. "You will show more of its treasures to me while we wait for Lady Sarah to complete her urgent business?"

I pictured Willis, Sr., reading the riot act to Sally in his study and decided to keep as many walls as possible between him and Henrique. Although Willis, Sr., had never raised his voice in my presence, his behavior of late had been so unpredictable—and Sally had tested his patience so severely—that I didn't want to take any chances. Henrique might feel the need to defend his *querida*—possibly with dueling pistols at dawn—if he overheard Lady Sarah's American cousin hollering at her.

"I'm sure that Lady Sarah would prefer to show you the house herself," I said. "But I'll be happy to show you the grounds."

"It will be well to walk in the English countryside before brunch," he said equably. "We will work up *un apetito*."

I pressed the buzzer underneath the mantel shelf to summon Deirdre, who came in from the dining room wearing a crisply starched apron over her white shirt-dress.

"Please tell my father-in-law and Lady Sarah that Señor Cocinero and I have gone for a walk," I said.

"Mr. Cocinero will want his hat," she said promptly. "It's in the cloakroom, sir. I'll get it for you."

"Don't bother," I told her. "I'll find it."

"Brunch will be served in approximately twenty minutes," she informed me.

"We'll make it a short walk," I assured her.

Henrique and I retrieved his hat from the cloakroom and let ourselves out through the front door. I steered him into the garden in which Rainey Dawson had accosted me on the night of the housewarming party, not because it was attractive or interesting, but because it was on the opposite side of the house from the study. I pointed out the conservatory's intricate ironwork and the louvered glass panes that allowed air to flow through it, and described how the flower beds within the box hedges would look after a year's growth.

"It will be as charming as the woman who planned it," said Henrique. "Lady Sarah is truly an artist. I shall return a year from now, perhaps, to see her vision in full bloom."

"Lady Sarah won't be here next year," I said swiftly. "She'll be in America. She spends every other summer in America, with her American relatives."

"A pity. I would love to see her garden in all its glory." Henrique peered toward the stables, where Declan Donovan was forking soiled straw into a wheelbarrow. "Does Lady Sarah ride as well? But of course she does," he went on, answering his own question. "English-women of noble birth learn to ride at a young age, I think."

As far as I knew, Sally's plump foot had never come

within twenty yards of a stirrup, but if Henrique wanted to imagine her in leather boots and a velvet jacket, sailing over fences on a sleek, well-muscled hunter, who was I to disabuse him?

"A neighbor is boarding her horses at the moment," I said, to explain why the stable building and the pasture beyond it were devoid of livestock. "Lady Sarah is in the process of renovating her stables."

"Always she is improving her property," Henrique said approvingly. "Shall we walk through the meadow? The English wildflowers are very beautiful, I think."

We left the garden and strolled through the meadow behind Fairworth House, using the bridle path Willis, Sr., had laid out for Will and Rob. If we'd continued along the path, we would have ended up at the Anscombe Manor stables, but we'd walked no more than fifty paces when Henrique pulled a large white handkerchief from his breast pocket and used it to mop his sweating brow.

"As we say in my homeland, the sun grows hotter as the morning grows older." He waved his handkerchief toward the wooded corner of the estate. "Shall we seek the cool shade beneath the trees?"

I glanced at my watch. "It might be better to seek the cool shade inside the house, Henrique. Mrs. Donovan will serve brunch soon and we don't want to keep Lady Sarah waiting."

"Indeed not," he agreed fervently. "A thoughtful guest never keeps his hostess waiting."

We retraced our steps to the garden, where we were greeted by a stern-faced Willis, Sr., and a red-nosed, watery-eyed, and thoroughly chastened Sally Pyne. Deirdre Donovan looked on from the conservatory, as if awaiting her cue to enter the scene.

"Lady Sarah," said Henrique. "Your business goes well, I hope? While you work, Lori and I play. We take a small tour of your beautiful property. The garden, the meadow, the stables, the woods—they are like the pictures from a calendar."

I gave the stubby, disconnected box hedges a puzzled glance and wondered what kind of calendar would feature them.

"Thank you, Henrique," said Sally, looking everywhere but at her guest. "It's nice of you to say so."

"Now I know why you so love this place of your birth," said Henrique. "*Es un paraiso.*"

He bent to kiss her hand, but she pulled it away before his lips touched it.

"You're very kind, Henrique," she said, tucking both of her hands behind her back, "but I'm afraid I have some unpleasant news to share with you." She glanced briefly at Willis, Sr., and swallowed hard before continuing, "I'm very sorry to say it, but I was mistaken when I told you that you could stay here until next week. I'm afraid you'll have to leave Fairworth House on Thursday."

As the original plan had called for Henrique to leave on Wednesday, Sally had, it seemed, wangled one extra day out of Willis, Sr. I suspected that a bout of strategic weeping had reddened her nose and secured her a little more time with her Mexican swain.

"My cousin has brought to my attention a prior

engagement," she went on, as if she were reciting a memorized speech, "which will take both of us away from home on Thursday, when Fairworth House will be fumigated."

"Fumigated?" Henrique's bushy eyebrows shot up. "This we do in Mexico, but I did not know it was done in England."

"It is sometimes necessary," Sally said. "Fairworth has a terrible infestation of, of——"

"Deathwatch beetles," Willis, Sr., inserted.

"Deathwatch beetles," Sally repeated.

"Deathwatch beetles!" exclaimed Henrique, sounding both shocked and alarmed. "This is very bad news indeed. The deathwatch beetle is no joke, Lady Sarah. He eats the bones of the house and then——*poof!*——no more house. Fumigation is needed to stop him."

"It's needed," Sally agreed sadly. "And that's why you can't stay here, Henrique. Fairworth'll be like a gas chamber."

"If you are not here, *querida*," Henrique said softly, "why would I wish to stay? Think no more of it. I will be content to leave on Thursday."

"I'm terribly sorry for the mix-up," Sally mumbled, staring disconsolately at the ground.

"Do not apologize," said Henrique. "A lady of such importance cannot be expected to remember every small thing. This is why she has her amiable cousin." He nodded at Willis, Sr., then smiled warmly at Sally. "Life is short, Lady Sarah. We will not spoil it with regrets. We will make the most of the time we have."

"Yes," Sally murmured, and as she lifted her gaze to

meet his, her entire body swayed in his direction. "We will make the most of the time we have."

Perhaps by coincidence, the conservatory door swung open before Sally could sway all the way into Henrique's arms. She straightened with a jerk, glanced guiltily at Willis, Sr., and took a tiny step back from Henrique.

"Ladies and gentlemen," Deirdre announced, "brunch is served."

"Lady Sarah, if you will allow me?" said Willis, Sr., offering his arm to her. "Señor Cocinero will escort Lori."

I took Henrique's arm and felt an unexpected surge of pity for Willis, Sr. He could try every trick in the book to keep Henrique and Sally apart, but I knew of no power on earth that could silence love's old sweet song.

Eleven

When I thought of brunch, I thought of strawberry-stuffed french toast, Belgian waffles, fluffy omelets, eggs benedict, spinach frittatas, poached salmon with dill sauce, and baskets of homemade muffins still warm from the oven. I pictured chafing dishes arrayed in a neat row on a linen-draped sideboard, along with gleaming glass pitchers of juice, milk, and perhaps a light alcoholic beverage or two.

I was mildly confused, therefore, when I saw nothing on the teak table in the conservatory but four place settings featuring four mysterious domed plates. As Deirdre removed each dome, it became clear to me that she had, willingly or unwillingly, colluded with my father-in-law in depriving Henrique of the high-end cuisine Sally had so dearly wished to serve him. Willis, Sr., might not want Henrique to suffer the ill effects of food poisoning, but he was not above giving his unwanted guest a monumental case of heartburn.

Each plate was loaded from rim to rim with a traditional English breakfast known as a fry-up because it consisted of fried eggs, fried bacon, fried sausages, fried tomatoes, fried bread, fried mushrooms, and a puddle of tinned beans in tomato sauce. When cooked properly, a fry-up could be a tasty, if heart-attack inducing, meal, but Deirdre had evidently received orders to do her worst.

The eggs were like rubber, the sausages were burned, the tomatoes had been reduced to pulp, and the whole awful mess was awash in a slowly congealing lake of melted lard. A toast rack filled with cold, hard pieces of charred toast sat beside each place setting, and instead of mimosas or even straight champagne, Deirdre filled our cups with tea that could have—and should have—been used to stain furniture.

It must have pained Deirdre to prepare such a dreadful meal, but she maintained a neutral expression as she hovered nearby with a teapot, ready to refill our cups. Sally stared disconsolately at the unappetizing farrago on her plate, heaved a melancholy sigh, and gave Willis, Sr., a reproachful glance before turning to address Henrique.

"I hope you don't mind—," she began, but he cut her off.

"Fantastico!" he cried, grinning from ear to ear. "This is the English fry-up of which I have heard so much. You make me feel not like the visitor but like the real Englishman. It is too thoughtful of you, Lady Sarah, to welcome me in this way. *Gracias y salud!"*

Without pausing to consider the consequences, he seized his knife and fork and began wolfing down his greasy feast as if he had waited his entire life to savor such delicacies. Sally, cheered by his ebullient reaction, began to clear her own plate. Though Willis, Sr., concealed his emotions admirably, I could tell by a slight tightening of his lips that he hadn't expected his scheme to backfire so spectacularly.

While he and I toyed with our food in silence, Sally

and Henrique paused between mouthfuls to share tenderhearted reminiscences of the time they'd spent together in Mexico.

"I asked Mrs. Donovan to serve brunch in the conservatory because I thought the ferns would remind you of Mexico," Sally said to him. "Do you remember the ferns that grew along the wall near the café? And the jasmine? I can't smell jasmine now without thinking of the *arroz con pollo* we had there."

"And the walk we took after," said Henrique.

"The moonlight on the sea," said Sally.

"The moonlight in your eyes," said Henrique.

"Oh, Henrique," Sally cooed, blushing.

Willis, Sr., could have hurled mud pies at them and they would have remained lost in their own moonlit, jasmine-scented world. Recognizing defeat, he laid down his fork and turned to me.

"Were you able to transport my painting to Crabtree Cottage this morning?" he inquired.

"Signed, sealed, and delivered," I replied. "But Grant doesn't think it's a painting. He's not sure what it is, but he told me that it contains a mixture of calligraphy and painted images. He could see a few letters through the grime, but he couldn't distinguish any words."

"Calligraphy?" Willis, Sr.'s face brightened. "Most intriguing. I wonder what it could be?"

"No idea," I said, "but it piqued Grant's curiosity."

"As it has piqued mine," said Willis, Sr. "Did he estimate the amount of time he will need to complete the cleaning process?"

"He'll get started on it today," I said, "but he won't

be able to do any more work on it until he and Charles get back from London."

"How long will they remain in London?" asked Willis, Sr.

"Not long. They're taking a culture break," I explained. "You know the sort of thing—a gallery opening, a West End musical. They leave this afternoon and they'll be back in Finch on Wednesday."

"Calligraphy," Willis, Sr., said meditatively. "You must admit that it was worth saving such an unusual artifact, Lori. It will be a pleasurable challenge to answer the questions it engenders. Who created it? What message does the calligraphy convey?"

"I'm just happy it's out of your study," I said. "It probably left smudges all over the floor."

"Mrs. Donovan removed every trace." Willis, Sr., smiled at Deirdre. "One would never know that the artifact had been there."

"Delicioso," said Henrique. He mopped the last vestiges of lard from his plate with a morsel of cold toast, popped it into his mouth, and wiped his glistening lips with his grease-stained napkin. "I am enchanted by your English cuisine."

"I'm glad you like it," said Sally.

"Shall we now take the tour of your beautiful home, Lady Sarah?" he proposed, pushing his chair back from the table. "Lori tells me of your wish to be my guide. I am keen to see your treasures and to hear your many marvelous stories about the ancestors who came before you."

"M-my ancestors?" Sally stammered, looking to Willis, Sr., for help.

"The Pynes were great collectors," he said smoothly. "Señor Cocinero will, I am certain, be fascinated by the objets d'art they acquired during their many trips abroad."

"Trips abroad," Sally repeated intently, as if filing the information away for future use. A frown of concentration creased her forehead, then she turned to smile indulgently at Henrique. "I've been dying to take you round the place, Henrique. You won't believe what my ancestors got up to on their grand tours of France and Italy. All that wine, you know . . ."

Henrique rose to pull out Sally's chair, then followed her into the dining room and out of sight. Deirdre immediately began to collect their dishes, as if she were eager to erase the evidence of a meal that failed so dismally to showcase her refined culinary skills.

"Sally may not know much about objets d'art," I said to Willis, Sr., "but she knows what happens when people get squiffy. I have a feeling that she'll avoid talking about Fairworth and focus on her fictitious ancestors' drunken revels on the continent."

"Lady Sarah is a resourceful woman," said Willis, Sr. "I have no doubt that she will use her imagination to camouflage her lack of knowledge. Mrs. Donovan," he went on, "if I might speak with you for a moment?"

"Of course, sir." Deirdre stopped what she was doing and faced him.

"Thank you for preparing the meal I asked you to prepare," he said. "That it did not achieve its goal is not your fault. You did your best."

"Thank you, sir," she said. "I still think it's a good

idea to present Mr. Cocinero with substandard cuisine while he's here. We're bound to hit on something he won't be able to choke down. May I recommend pig's trotters for dinner?"

Willis, Sr., groaned softly, but nodded. "It is worth a try, Mrs. Donovan. You may serve pig's trotters for dinner."

"We'll skip afternoon tea altogether," Deirdre continued, as if she'd already mapped out her assault on Henrique's digestive system. "For breakfast tomorrow, watery porridge. Tripe for lunch and a reprise of pig's trotters for dinner. I'll have to send Declan out for the tripe and the trotters, sir. I have none on hand."

"I should hope not," murmured Willis, Sr.

"Ring Hodge Farm," I said to Deirdre. "Burt and Annie Hodge keep a few pigs. Their number's in the phone book."

"Thanks," she said. "Will there be anything else, sir?"

He gestured toward our untouched plates. "You may take these away. They have served their purpose."

Deirdre departed with the dirty dishes, but Willis, Sr., and I lingered at the table.

"I spoke with Lady Sarah about the furniture," he said. "She categorically denies rearranging the settee in the morning room and the chair in the drawing room."

"They didn't move themselves," I said. "Have you asked Deirdre if she shifted them?"

"I have not yet had the opportunity," he replied. "It took some time to convince Lady Sarah to rescind her approval of Señor Cocinero's extended stay."

"You gave him an extra day," I pointed out.

"It was all I could do to deny him *six* extra days," Willis, Sr., returned. "Lady Sarah was not cooperative." He pursed his lips. "I suppose it is possible that Mrs. Donovan is responsible for the inadvertent alteration of my rooms. She is an enthusiastic cleaner. She did not retire until the small hours last night."

"How do you know?" I asked.

"The elevator," he replied. "If I concentrate, I can hear its hum from my room. Since I had some trouble falling asleep last night, I heard Mrs. Donovan utilize the elevator to return to her quarters at two fifty-seven a.m."

"She didn't get to bed until three in the morning?" I said, astonished.

"As I said, she is an enthusiastic cleaner," said Willis, Sr.

Deirdre reappeared with two dessert plates and a cut-glass bowl filled with bunches of sweet muscat grapes, which she placed on the table.

"To cleanse the palate," she announced.

"We didn't eat anything," I reminded her.

"You inhaled the grease," she said with an apologetic smile.

"Mrs. Donovan," said Willis, Sr., helping himself to a small bunch of grapes. "Did you for some reason feel the need to rearrange my furniture last night?"

"Your furniture?" said Deirdre, looking puzzled.

"I refer to the Chippendale armchair in the drawing room," said Willis, Sr., "and to the settee in the living room. They are not where they were yesterday."

She frowned for a moment before her face cleared.

"Ah, yes, now I remember. I had to move the armchair in order to sweep the floor properly. Did I forget to put it back? I'm sorry, sir. It won't happen again."

"And the settee?" said Willis, Sr. "It *was* near the windows. It is now near the fireplace."

"Sunlight fades fabrics, sir," Deirdre replied readily. "After I opened the drapes in the morning room, I moved the settee away from the windows to protect its upholstery."

"An unnecessary precaution," Willis, Sr., said gently. "The windows throughout Fairworth have been treated with a substance that blocks the sun's harmful rays."

"I'm sorry, sir, I didn't know about the windows," said Deirdre. "I'll put everything back where it belongs."

"Thank you," said Willis, Sr. "I took great pains to arrange the rooms just so. I would prefer them to stay that way."

"Of course, sir," said Deirdre.

"Well, gang," I said, looking at my watch, "I'd like to while away the morning, nibbling on grapes, but I can't. Lunchtime approaches and I'll have to swap cars with Bill before I fetch the boys from Anscombe Manor. Bill drove the Rover this morning, so he has the twins' booster seats," I explained to Willis, Sr.

"Mr. Donovan will drive you to the village," he said.

"I can walk," I told him.

"Please allow Mr. Donovan to drive you," said Willis, Sr. "It will save time. Our inquisitive neighbors may delay your departure from the village and I do not want my grandsons to miss their midday meal. I would share it with them if I could," he added wistfully.

"He'll be gone by Thursday," I soothed.

"Declan will bring the car around in five minutes," said Deirdre, and she bustled off to speak with her mate.

"Car?" I said, after she'd gone. "What car? I thought the Donovans drove a beat-up old van."

"I have given Mr. Donovan my permission to drive my Jaguar," said Willis, Sr. "His Renault is unsafe as well as unsightly." He plucked a grape from the bunch on his plate. "I have asked my man in London to purchase a suitable utility vehicle for the Donovans."

"You're buying a car for them?" I said, taken aback.

"I am buying a car for the estate. My sedan was not designed to transport hay bales or garden manure." Willis, Sr., popped the grape into his mouth and got to his feet. "I will walk with you to the entrance hall, my dear, but I must part with you there and go in search of Lady Sarah and her guest. If I leave them alone for too long, Lady Sarah will undoubtedly forget that *she* is a fictitious character."

Twelve

D eclan was waiting for me beside the gleaming midnight-blue Jaguar when I emerged from Fairworth House. He'd exchanged his working attire for a more decorous ensemble of dark trousers, black shoes, and a clean white shirt. He snapped to attention when I came down the stairs, and opened the car's rear door for me, as if he expected me to sit in the backseat while he drove.

"I'll sit up front with you," I said, walking past him. "You're not my chauffeur and I'm not a diva."

"The true nobility sit where they wish," he said good-naturedly and ran around me to open the front door with a flourish.

I caught a faint whiff of horse as Declan took his place in the driver's seat, and recalled that when I'd last seen him, he'd been mucking out the stables. He'd evidently had enough time to change his clothes before bringing the car around, but not enough time to shower. Far from bothering me, the horsey scent made me think of my horse-loving sons and brought to mind an item I'd failed to mention to Willis, Sr.

"By the way," I said as we cruised slowly down the tree-lined drive, "I told Señor Cocinero that a neighbor is boarding Lady Sarah's horses while she finishes renovating her stables. It seemed like a good way to head off any questions he might have about why the stables are unoccupied at the moment."

"It's a plausible tale," said Declan. "I'll pass it on to Deirdre. It's best if we keep our stories straight."

"Please ask her to pass it on to William and Lady Sarah as well," I said. "I forgot to tell them, and, as you say, we should try to keep our stories straight."

"Will do," said Declan. "If you don't mind me asking, where are Mr. Willis's mounts?"

"He doesn't have any," I replied. "He doesn't even ride, but my sons are horse-crazy and William is grandson-crazy. He rebuilt the stables for them, to give them a place to keep their ponies when they ride over from Anscombe Manor."

"Anscombe Manor?" said Declan.

"The neighboring estate," I explained. "Will and Rob board their ponies there and take daily lessons from the stable master, Kit Smith. William cleared a bridle path between Anscombe Manor and Fairworth to make it easier for the boys to visit him."

"He's a greathearted man, is Mr. Willis," said Declan, running his hands over the Jaguar's custom-made wooden steering wheel. "Not every employer would loan such a fine piece of machinery to a new employee."

"My father-in-law thinks it's unfair to ask you to use your personal vehicle for estate business," I said diplomatically.

Declan laughed. "You mean, he's afraid the van'll fall to bits before it gets to the end of the drive. I can't argue with him. The van's not the most reliable of vehicles, but it has its uses."

"Such as?" I said.

"It got us here, didn't it?" Declan said lightly.

Eventually, I thought, remembering the Donovans' late arrival.

"I'll tell you this for nothing, though," he went on. "If I'd known how often the old Renault would break down, I'd've studied engine repair instead of music theory."

"Music theory?" I said, interested. "Are you an Oxford scholar, like Deirdre?"

"I am," he said. "That's where we met and that's where we hatched our mad scheme to open a guesthouse."

"Why 'mad'?" I asked.

"Degrees in art history and music theory make for grand conversations around the dinner table, but they're not the best preparation for the down-and-dirty work of running a guesthouse," said Declan. "Ah, well, we wanted an adventure and we had one. It was fun while it lasted." He turned out of the drive and immediately stomped on the brakes. "Heavens above, Lori, will you look at *that*?"

"I'm looking," I said tersely. "Don't move."

"Yes, ma'am," he said.

While the car idled, I snatched my cell phone out of my purse and speed-dialed Willis, Sr.'s number. The moment he answered I said urgently, "*Keep Sally in the house. Elspeth Binney is standing on the bridge with a telescope.*"

"You jest," he said.

"I do *not* jest," I assured him.

"Where did Mrs. Binney obtain a telescope?" he asked.

"How should I know?" I retorted. "She used to be a schoolteacher. Maybe she taught astronomy. All I can tell you is that she's on the bridge with a telescope pointed in your direction. I don't think she's searching for a new planet."

"We have, it seems, an aspiring paparazzo in the village," observed Willis, Sr.

"I don't see a camera," I told him, "but an eyewitness report of a Sally-sighting would be enough to set tongues wagging."

"Indeed it would," Willis, Sr., agreed.

"I'll try to budge her," I said. "In the meantime, ask Deirdre to draw the drapes in every room, and for pity's sake, don't let Sally put so much as a *toe* outside the house."

"I shall batten down the hatches," he declared. "Thank you for alerting me to the situation, Lori."

"No problem." I cut the connection, dropped the phone into my purse, and signaled for Declan to drive ahead. When we were abreast of Elspeth, I asked him to stop.

"Elspeth," I said, lowering my window, "what are you doing?"

"Bird-watching," she replied with a straight face.

"Bird-watching," I repeated. "In that case, I owe you an apology."

"For what?" she asked.

"It had crossed my mind that you might be spying on William's guest," I replied. "I should have known that a woman with your integrity, your sense of decency, and your respect for other people's privacy would never stoop so low. I should have realized that a former school-teacher, a woman who taught innocent children the value of living virtuous lives, a woman who plays the organ in church every Sunday, that you, of all people, would never behave like a vile, vulgar, immoral, money-grubbing member of the gutter press." I paused to let my words have their desired effect before concluding humbly, "Forgive me, Elspeth. I was mistaken."

"I, uh, yes, naturally, I, uh, forgive you," she faltered, blushing to her roots. "I can understand your suspicions—some of our neighbors are intolerably intrusive—but I've observed nothing but birds, I promise you." She looked at her wristwatch. "Dear me, is that the time? I'm afraid I must dash. I have to jot down some ideas for the flower arrangements at St. George's. It's my turn to do them next week."

"I've always loved your flower arrangements," I said solemnly. "They remind me of purity and piety. Be careful as you step down from the bridge, Elspeth," I added. "It can be a slippery slope."

Declan drove on and I watched in the rearview mirror as Elspeth fumbled with the tripod supporting her telescope, tucked the whole contraption under her arm, and walked speedily toward her cottage, her flaming face averted from the Jaguar.

"That'll teach her to snoop in broad daylight," I muttered. "Bird-watching, my foot."

"You have the gift of the gab, Lori," Declan declared. "I've seldom heard a more comprehensive put-down. The poor woman looked ready to shrivel up for shame."

"Serves her right," I said waspishly, and motioned for him to park at Wysteria Lodge. "Here's where I leave you. Thanks for the lift."

"It was my pleasure," said Declan. "And it's on my way. I'm off to Hodge Farm next, to pick up miscellaneous pig parts. Will you be joining us for dinner?"

"Not if I can help it," I said, laughing. "I'll swap cars with Bill, fetch the boys, and enjoy a decent meal with them at home."

"I can ferry Bill to your car," he offered.

"You needn't bother." I pointed across the village green to the Mini. "It's right over there, in front of Crabtree Cottage. I had to leave it behind after I delivered William's painting this morning because I hitched a ride to Fairworth with Señor Cocinero."

"I believe your husband will be able to manage the journey on his own two feet," Declan said with mock gravity.

"Do you know the way to Hodge Farm?" I asked.

"Mr. Willis drew a map for me," he replied.

"Please tell Annie that I'll expect her at half past one," I said as I got out of the car. "She's bringing her son over to play with Will and Rob."

"Will do," he said. "Cheerio!"

Once I was sure he was driving in the right direction, I strode into Wysteria Lodge, where I found my husband perusing a sheaf of legal documents. He instantly set them aside and came around his desk to give me a comprehensive kiss.

"Tell me all about everything," he said, half sitting on his desk and pulling me into his arms.

"Sally would like Henrique to stay forever," I began. "They're a match made in heaven, Bill—short, round, middle-aged, and incurably romantic."

"Sounds as though Father has his work cut out for him," said Bill.

"He may need a rest cure when it's all over," I said. "And Deirdre's not helping matters. She rearranged some of William's furniture without asking his permission. You know how touchy he is about his stuff."

"I do know," Bill said, giving a low whistle. "Did he blow a fuse?"

"He kept his temper," I said, "but he straightened her out. He also put his foot down when Sally tried to tack a few extra days on to Henrique's visit."

"Bully for him," said Bill. "Anything else?"

"He came up with a cunning plan to discourage repeat visits from Henrique," I said. "Deirdre's under orders to cook nothing but the most god-awful swill until Henrique leaves."

"What will Father eat for the duration?" Bill asked.

"Whatever slop Deirdre plunks in front of him," I said. "He's not too happy about it."

"Hoist by his own petard," said Bill, chuckling. "He'll survive. It's only until Wednesday."

"Thursday," I corrected him. "Sally's tears gained her an extra twenty-four hours with her amigo."

"Maybe you can smuggle something edible to Father between now and then," said Bill. "I can't imagine him dining on—"

"Tripe and trotters," I interjected.

"—until Thursday," Bill finished. He frowned at the

ceiling. "On second thought, I can't imagine Father *ever* dining on tripe and trotters."

"Nor can I," I said. "I'll see what I can arrange in the way of emergency food drops." I glanced toward the window. "I don't mean to be critical, Bill, but I have to point out that you've fallen down on the job. I just chased Elspeth Binney off the bridge. She's been surveilling Fairworth with a telescope. You must have seen her. Why didn't you stop her?"

"I *didn't* see her," Bill protested. "I haven't gotten much work done this morning, but I've managed to squeeze in the odd five minutes here and there. Elspeth must have made her move during one of those rare moments of peace."

"What's kept you from working?" I asked.

"What do you think?" Bill retorted. "I've had half the village in here since you left, quizzing me about Father's anonymous client. They're convinced that Henrique stopped here to consult with me before driving on to Fairworth."

"Why *did* he stop here?" I asked.

"To ask for directions," said Bill. "The only reason he chose Wysteria Lodge was because my lights were on." He turned his head to peer through the window. "Here comes Rainey. Looks as though she's had a lively morning, too."

Bill relinquished his hold on me as Rainey Dawson let herself in through the front door. She looked as though she'd been in the midst of a bakery explosion. Her long nose was smudged with flour and her flowered apron was streaked with jam, dotted with chocolate, and sprinkled with powdered sugar. Her auburn hair hung down her back in a pair of tidy braids, but her hands were damp, as if she'd just finished washing them.

"How's Gran?" she asked anxiously.

"Your grandmother is fine," I told her. "Completely and totally fine. Who's minding the tearoom?"

"Bree," Rainey replied. "She's been brilliant. She showed up before I opened the shop this morning and volunteered to help me run it until Gran comes back. She even braided my hair for me, to keep it clear of the baking tins."

"Bree's a great kid," said Bill.

"She's *brilliant*," Rainey repeated fervently. "Mrs. Taxman was after me to give her Great-aunt Judith's telephone number. She *said* she wanted to find out how Gran was doing, but I reckoned she was trying to get the goods on Gran. Well, she shouldn't have tried it while Bree was there. Do you know what Bree said to her?"

"Do tell," I said.

"She pointed at the Emporium and told Mrs. Taxman to mind her own business!" Rainey's hazel eyes were filled with awe. "After Mrs. Taxman stormed out, Bree *laughed*. She said she wouldn't allow the old cat to harass me *or* Great-aunt Judith while Gran was so ill. Then she told me to ring Great-aunt Judith and warn her that a crazy woman in the village was making *crank phone calls* and that she should *hang up* if someone rang her asking about Gran. And that's exactly what I did," she finished triumphantly.

"Wow," I said, deeply impressed. "Bree's a born schemer."

"She's also a loyal friend," said Bill.

"Don't I know it," Rainey said earnestly. "Mrs. Taxman is the only one who seems suspicious about Gran. Everyone else is just worried about her. It makes me feel a bit guilty."

"Me, too," I said consolingly. "But it'll all be over by Thursday."

"*Thursday?*" Rainey cried. "What happened to Wednesday?"

"There's been a minor change of plans." I hesitated, then asked, "Has your grandmother ever spoken with you about Henrique?"

"I know she's daft about him, if that's what you mean," said Rainey, blushing. "You should have seen her scrambling around to find the right dresses and the right shoes and the right jewelry. You'd've thought she was *my* age!"

"She does seem to be very fond of Henrique," I said, "which will make it hard for her to say good-bye to him a second time. She'll need a lot of comforting after this is all over."

"I can't look that far ahead," said Rainey, shaking her head. "I have to finish a batch of jam doughnuts and make sure the summer pudding is setting up and whip cream for the cream cakes. Oh, Lord," she said, glancing through the window. "Here come Mrs. Taylor, Miss Buxton, and Miss Scroggins. They'll probably ask me for Great-aunt Judith's phone number, too."

"Run along," said Bill. "Lori and I will deal with them."

"Thanks," said Rainey, and sprinted back to the tea-room.

The three Handmaidens arrived a minute later, sweeping into Bill's office as if it were a regular stop on their daily rounds. Opal Taylor and Millicent Scroggins were dressed in serviceable tweed skirts, white blouses, and sensible shoes, but Selena Buxton, a former wedding planner, wore a pale blue linen skirt with a matching blazer and a pair of beige peep-toe heels.

"Good morning, Lori," said Opal. "Lovely day, isn't it?"

"Lovely," I agreed.

"We hoped you'd be able to tell us if William's housekeeper has made any decisions about hiring daily help," said Millicent.

"It can't be easy for her to care for the house *and* William's special guest," said Selena.

"Mrs. Donovan is managing quite well," I said. "She's a remarkable woman—experienced, professional, and in tiptop physical condition."

Their faces fell.

"How nice for William," murmured Opal.

"Delightful news," mumbled Millicent.

"Most reassuring," muttered Selena.

"If she changes her mind, she'll post a notice on the schoolhouse board," I informed them.

All five of us jumped in alarm as the front door banged open and Peggy Taxman sailed into the room.

"Lori!" she thundered. "What's going on? I went to the trouble of finding Judith Crosby's telephone number in the Chipping Norton directory, but when I rang her, she hung up on me!"

"She was probably tending to Sally," I said.

"It takes time and energy to nurse a woman in Sally's state," Opal reasoned. "I'm sure that Judith doesn't have a moment to spare for *frivolous* telephone calls."

"Her patient's welfare must come first," Millicent agreed primly.

"If I were her," said Selena, "I certainly wouldn't put up with people pestering me."

"I wasn't *pestering* her," Peggy bellowed, her eyes flashing dangerously behind her pointy glasses. "I rang to ask if Sally was feeling better."

"She was at death's door yesterday," said Opal. "I sincerely doubt that there's been any change in her condition since then."

Peggy muttered something under her breath, then turned her wrath on me again.

"Didn't you see me waving at you this morning?" she demanded.

"I saw you," I admitted. "But I couldn't do anything about it. William's client refused to stop."

"Shame on you, Peggy," Opal said crossly. "You had no business waving at William's client."

"None at all," said Selena. "You were there when William asked us to respect his guest's privacy."

Peggy scowled. "William's guest looks foreign to me. *Mexican.*"

"Does he?" Millicent asked avidly. She gave me a guilty, sidelong glance, then glowered at Peggy. "A notion you should keep to yourself, Peggy Taxman."

"Someone's been paying a little too much attention to Sally's endless tales about her trip," said Selena, looking down her nose at Peggy. "For all we know, William's client could be Spanish or Peruvian or something else altogether."

"It's a pity Sally isn't here," said Millicent. "She'd be able to tell us whether he's Mexican or not."

"Ladies," Opal said reprovingly, "William's client is none of our business. I agree with Millicent. We should keep our opinions about him to ourselves. If his identity is leaked to the press, goodness knows what might happen."

"We don't want the pub overrun by reporters," said Millicent, "and we certainly don't want lorry-loads of photographers pointing their long lenses at Fairworth."

"In that case, you should be having it out with Elspeth Binney, not me," Peggy boomed. "*She* was the one on the bridge with the *telescope*."

Opal gasped. "A telescope?"

"As if you didn't know," Peggy said scornfully.

"How could we?" Selena protested. "We've only just got back from Upper Deeping."

"Monday's our painting class," said Opal. "En plein air with Mr. Shuttleworth, remember? Such a nice man and so talented. He says I have a gift for——"

"Did Elspeth *really* have a telescope?" Selena broke in impatiently.

"Did she *see* anything?" asked Millicent.

"Birds," I put in. "She was bird-watching."

The four women eyed me with naked incredulity, then made for the door.

"I wish I could stay and chat, but my garden needs weeding," said Opal.

"I have to clean my paintbrushes," said Millicent.

"I have a letter to write," said Selena.

"I have to get back to the Emporium," Peggy roared.

They bustled out of Wysteria Lodge and across the green diagonally, picking up Mr. Barlow, George Wetherhead, Christine Peacock, and Miranda Morrow along the way. Bill strode to the window to survey their progress.

"Uh-huh," he said, nodding. "Their trajectory will place them at Dove Cottage in less than thirty seconds."

"Dove Cottage," I said, wholly unsurprised. "Elspeth Binney's house."

"I hope Elspeth has a big pot of tea ready," said Bill. "She's about to receive eight extremely chatty visitors. Wouldn't you love to be a fly on the wall?"

"If they keep fighting among themselves, they'll never figure out who Henrique really is." I glanced at my watch. "William guessed that our neighbors would slow me down. It's past time for me to pick up the boys. Kit and Nell won't let them starve, but a mother should make lunch for her own children, don't you think? Will you join us?"

"I'll grab a bite to eat at the pub," said Bill, "after which I will close my curtains and pile my filing cabinets against the door. It's the only way I'll get any work done today."

My husband and I exchanged kisses as well as keys and I took off in the Rover, leaving an electrified gaggle of villagers in my wake.

Thirteen

I called Willis, Sr., on my way to Anscombe Manor to let him know that I'd routed Elspeth Binney from her observation post.

"Thank you," he said. "I will maintain a state of heightened vigilance nonetheless. Individuals who own binoculars may be inspired to imitate the observant Mrs. Binney." He paused before saying meditatively, "I begin to think we were wrong to emphasize my client's need for anonymity. The mystery surrounding him has done nothing but stimulate the villagers' curiosity."

"It doesn't take much to stimulate the villagers' curiosity," I said dryly, "but you're right. We'd have been better off if we'd told them that your client is"—I picked a name out of thin air—"Tim Thomson, a taxidermist from Topeka. Even they couldn't get excited about a guy who stuffs dead animals for a living."

"Perhaps you could drop a few hints to that effect?" Willis, Sr., suggested.

"I could," I said, "but it doesn't really jibe with the story we've already established. Why would a taxidermist from Topeka insist on anonymity?"

Willis, Sr., answered without a moment's hesitation. "Mr. Thomson has chosen to revise his last will and testament in a private and remote setting because he does not want his adult children—two wastrel sons and an ungrateful daughter——to learn that he has disinherited them. Will that do?"

"Absolutely," I said, bedazzled by his inventiveness. "You have a knack for improvisation, William."

"I have, alas, handled many similar cases in my time," said Willis, Sr. "It required very little imagination to superimpose them on our taxidermist."

"Where are Sally and Henrique?" I asked. "Since you're speaking freely, I assume they're not with you."

"Lady Sarah and Señor Cocinero are enjoying a friendly game of billiards," he replied, "but I believe they will retire shortly for a siesta." He heaved an exasperated sigh. "I am not entirely convinced that they will retire to separate rooms."

"They will," I said reassuringly. "It's been a tiring day for both of them, and there comes a time in everyone's life when napping is more important than canoodling."

"I hope devoutly that you are correct," he said. "I beg your pardon, Lori, but I am required elsewhere. Mrs. Donovan wishes to discuss the dinner menu with me. Such as it is."

The thought of *not* having to partake in a meal consisting of badly cooked pig parts cheered me greatly as I turned into Anscombe Manor's curving drive.

Rob and Will were blissfully unaware of my tardiness when I pulled up to the stables, and Nell and Kit were refreshingly incurious about the happenings at Fairworth House. Emma Harris, whom I hadn't seen since the night of the housewarming party, turned out to be the toughest challenge I faced at Anscombe Manor.

"Lori," she said, as I strapped Rob into his booster seat. "I've been hearing the most bizarre rumors about William's houseguest."

"What else is new?" I said with a nonchalant shrug.

"Is it true that he's a Colombian drug lord working out a secret deal with the CIA?" she asked. "Or is he a Brazilian movie star in the midst of a messy divorce from his fifth wife? Or could he possibly be an Argentinean football player negotiating a new contract behind his coach's back?"

I straightened so abruptly that I banged my head on the car roof. Years of experience with the village grapevine had failed to prepare me for such a prodigious outpouring of utter rubbish.

"He's none of the above," I said indignantly, rubbing my battered head. "Listen, Emma, you're my best friend, so I won't lie to you. I'm not at liberty to tell you who William's guest is, but you can take it from me that he isn't a crime lord, an actor, or an athlete."

"Okay," she said equably. "Will you ever reveal the truth to me?"

"I don't know," I said. "It's not my secret to reveal."

"Fair enough." She leaned closer, her blue-gray eyes twinkling. "I can't wait to hear what the villagers come up with next."

"I can't imagine anything more outrageous than a Colombian drug lord," I said.

"Ah, but *they* can," she said happily.

I rolled my eyes in response, called good-bye to Kit and Nell, and climbed into the Rover, wondering how many other ludicrous rumors would surface before I could squelch them with the taxidermist story.

I changed into a cotton blouse, a pair of shorts, and my good old grubby sneakers as soon as we reached the cottage, then tossed the boys into the tub for a bubbly scrub before I helped them to dress in clean clothes. I could tolerate a whiff of horse, but after their riding lessons, my sons tended to smell like a whole herd.

While I prepared a simple, wholesome, and grease-free lunch, Will and Rob regaled me with a blow-by-blow account of a morning spent mastering the emergency dismount maneuver. Though images of my precious babes tumbling repeatedly from their saddles would haunt me for days to come, I did my maternal duty and concealed my abject terror with a show of enthusiasm.

I helped myself to a grilled chicken burger and some creamy cucumber salad and watched contentedly as the twins devoured theirs. I would never be a gourmet chef of Deirdre Donovan's caliber, but it was comforting to know that my family thought my cooking was first-rate.

"Can we go to Grandpa's after lunch?" Will asked.

"We cannot," I replied. "Grandpa has company and you will, too. Don't you remember? Piero Hodge is coming over to play."

"I like Piero," Rob said, with a judicious nod. "He ate a worm once."

"Not a *whole* worm," Will temporized. "Just a bite."

"Why?" I asked, grimacing.

"Clive Pickle dared him to," Rob explained.

"Poor worm," I said sadly.

"It's okay, Mummy," said Will. "The worm was dead."

"You console me," I said, stifling an urge to gag. "Does Clive Pickle dare you to do silly things?"

"All the time," said Rob. "But we ignore him."

"Daddy says Clive Pickle isn't worth listening to," Will declared.

"Clever Daddy," I said and got to my feet. It is a truth universally acknowledged that small boys will tell revolting tales, but I tried not to encourage the habit, especially during mealtimes. "Dishes in the sink, please, and teeth brushed. Piero will be here in two ticks."

While Rob and Will were upstairs staging sword fights with their toothbrushes, I slipped into the study and read the application forms Davina Trent had faxed to me on Saturday morning. I then picked up the telephone and called Mrs. Trent.

"How thoroughly did you vet the Donovans?" I asked, after we'd exchanged the usual pleasantries.

"Quite thoroughly," she replied. "I conducted personal interviews with their university tutors and with more than a dozen people who stayed at their guesthouse in the west of Ireland. No one had a bad word to say about them. Indeed, I was left with the impression that the Donovans are intelligent, hardworking, and eager to please."

"Why did they sell the guesthouse?" I asked.

"The building developed structural flaws they couldn't afford to repair," Mrs. Trent replied. "When they realized they were in over their heads, they cut their losses and started afresh. I spoke with the estate agent who handled the sale for them. It was quite straightforward and aboveboard. Why do you ask, Ms. Shepherd? Has there been a problem?"

"No," I said. "They just seem a tad overqualified for their positions."

"In these difficult times, many people have been forced to take jobs they would normally pass up," said Mrs. Trent, "but I can assure you that the Donovans haven't settled for second best. They specifically requested placement in a country house such as your father-in-law's. In fact, it was the only type of employment they would consider."

"I see," I said.

"Mr. Willis expressed his complete satisfaction with the Donovans in his telephone call to me," Mrs. Trent went on, "but if you've discovered some fault—"

"I haven't," I said quickly. "I'm sorry. I didn't mean to pick holes in the Donovans. I have no reason to complain about them. I guess I'm just being an overprotective daughter-in-law."

"I understand," she said. "It's a perfectly natural reaction. Is there anything else I can help you with, Ms. Shepherd?"

I told her there wasn't, thanked her, and hung up, feeling strangely dissatisfied.

"Davina Trent and William may adore the Donovans," I said to Reginald, "but I choose to reserve judgment. Oxford scholars don't jump at the chance to clean toilets and stables for anyone but themselves. They just don't."

My pink bunny said nothing, but I could tell by the tilt of his ears that he agreed with me.

I would have liked to discuss the matter with Aunt Dimity, but there was no time. I'd scarcely finished speaking to Reginald when the doorbell summoned me to the front hall to welcome Annie Hodge and her worm-eating son. Will and Rob promptly thundered downstairs and proposed an expedition to the narrow stream that ran along the bottom of our meadow. After securing parental permission, they whisked Piero to the garden shed, to arm him and themselves with nets and buckets, then galloped through the garden and across the flower-strewn meadow to the brook. Annie and I followed at a more sedate pace.

"I see three wet boys in our future," I proclaimed portentously.

"No prizes for that prediction," she said, smiling. "It's such a hot day, I may wade in with them."

"I'll join you," I said. "Nothing says summer like a good splash in the brook."

We walked through the sweet-smelling grasses in companionable silence, serenaded by birds and bees and the shouts of intrepid explorers. I marveled inwardly at Annie's self-restraint, because I was certain that she, like everyone else within twenty miles of Finch, was bursting to ask me about William's mysterious guest.

"William's gardener came by the farm today," she said. "He seems a nice young man."

"He does, doesn't he?" I said noncommittally.

"He picked up the tripe and the pig's trotters William's housekeeper ordered," she went on. "I must admit that I was a bit surprised by her selection of meats. I had William pegged as a filet mignon man, not as a tripe lover."

"If it were up to him, he'd have the filet," I said, "but his client prefers less choice cuts and you know what they say—the customer's always right."

"Fancy that." Annie frowned reflectively. "I'd have expected a dictator to ask for posh things like caviar and foie gras."

"A dictator?" I said, eyeing her with some trepidation.

Annie glanced over her shoulder, as though to make sure we were alone, then lowered her voice to a confidential murmur.

"I know you're sworn to secrecy, Lori, so I won't ask you to say a word about it one way or the other," she said, "but Opal Taylor has it on good authority that William's client is a South American dictator seeking asylum in Great Britain after his long-suffering but courageous people finally gave him the heave-ho." Annie paused to catch her breath before adding with a faint air of disillusionment, "You'd expect a man like that to fancy filet, wouldn't you?"

"I suppose you would," I said, my mind reeling, "but Opal Taylor has bats in her cotton-picking belfry if she thinks that my father-in-law would have anything to do with a dictator."

"Has the wrong end of the stick, does she?" Annie asked, in a tone of voice that was much too casual.

"She has the wrong stick altogether," I stated firmly, coming to a halt. "I shouldn't tell you this, Annie, but between you and me . . ."

Annie's lips parted and her eyes narrowed intently as I gave her the inside story on Tim Thomson, Topeka's most successful taxidermist. The more softly I spoke, the more confident I was that my words would soon be heard far and wide.

I could almost feel the village grapevine quiver.

Fourteen

What seemed like the longest Monday in recorded history was finally drawing to a close. Rob and Will were in bed and asleep, Bill was dozing in his favorite armchair in the living room, and Stanley was dozing in Bill's lap. While my family slumbered, I sat at the old oak desk in the study, scouring a stack of magazines for new recipes. When the telephone rang, I snatched it up, to keep the noise from disturbing my menfolk. I wondered fleetingly if it would be Peggy Taxman, badgering me about the new rumor that had drifted her way, and felt a sweet sense of relief when the caller turned out to be Willis, Sr.

"The man of the moment," I said cheerfully. "Are you alone?"

"Lady Sarah and Señor Cocinero have retired for the evening," he informed me. "I have taken refuge in my study. Why, may I ask, am I the man of the moment?"

"Because you've created such a stir in Finch," I replied. "Are you aware that you're harboring either a drug lord, a famous actor, a soccer player, or a fugitive dictator with a taste for peasant food?"

"You are, of course, referring to the stories that have surfaced concerning Señor Cocinero," he said dryly.

"Have they reached your ears already?" I asked, mildly surprised.

"Indirectly," he said. "Mr. Donovan was treated to

an assortment of colorful tales when he stopped at the pub on his way back from Hodge Farm. He refused to comment on any of them, of course, but he felt duty-bound to report them to me. He seemed to find them highly entertaining."

"It's helpful to maintain a sense of humor in the face of adversity," I said.

"The firm of Willis & Willis does not consort with criminals or with so-called celebrities," he declared vehemently. "Such rumors are bound to damage my reputation among the villagers."

"Not a chance," I said. "They'll enhance your glamor."

"I do not wish to be considered glamorous," he protested.

"Then you can relax," I said placatingly. "I told Annie Hodge about Tim Thomson from Topeka. If I know Annie, everyone in Finch will have heard about Tim by daybreak. I can almost guarantee that no one, not even Peggy Taxman, will be able to make a big deal out of a taxidermist."

"Would that it were true. . . ." Willis, Sr., paused, as though to compose himself, then continued in a more temperate manner, "The purpose of my call is to share a rather interesting tidbit of news with you. Mr. Tavistock telephoned me a short time ago."

"Grant called you from London?" I said. "Why?"

"I believe Mr. Tavistock wished to impress me with his professionalism," Willis, Sr., answered. "Concerned that I might accuse him of neglecting my commission, he telephoned from London to present me with the results of the work he accomplished today."

"Well done, Grant," I said appreciatively. "Did he figure out what the thing is?"

"It seems that Mr. Tavistock has uncovered an illuminated family tree," Willis, Sr., announced with quiet exultation.

"Illuminated?" I said.

"Illustrated," Willis, Sr., clarified. "The names on the family tree appear to be accompanied by miniature portraits."

"Whose family tree is it?" I asked.

"It appears to record succeeding generations of the Fairworthy family," said Willis, Sr. "I consider it a discovery of inestimable value because, as you know, the Fairworthys built Fairworth House and lived in it for over a century."

"You were right and I was wrong, William," I conceded. "A family tree, however grubby, is an undeniable treasure. It's a window into Fairworth's past."

"Indeed it is," said Willis, Sr. "Mr. Tavistock was able to discern the name Frederick Fairworthy beside one of the portraits," he went on. "A gentleman with the same name wrote *Notes on Sheep*, the book that kindled my desire to restore a flock of Cotswold Lions to the estate."

"*Oh,*" I said as the penny dropped. "It's *his* fault."

"Fault?" said Willis, Sr., sharply. "Do you disapprove of my ambition?"

"No," I said, backtracking hastily. "I think it's a terrific idea. I just didn't know where it came from."

"I will lend you the book," he said coolly. "You will, no doubt, find it instructive."

"No doubt," I said, making a wry face at Reginald. *Notes on Sheep* didn't strike me as a compelling read.

"Thank you, Mrs. Donovan," Willis, Sr., said in an aside. "Yes, please place it on the desk. As I was unable to do anything with my dinner but gaze disconsolately at it," he explained, for my benefit, "Mrs. Donovan has prepared a chop for me, a simple, succulent chop accompanied by freshly made applesauce, roast potatoes, and some extraordinarily attractive brussels sprouts. I believe there will be a lemon syllabub to follow."

"How nice for you," I said, in exactly the same tone of voice Opal Taylor had used when I'd informed her of Deirdre's manifold virtues. "How'd the trotters go down with Henrique?"

"He requested a second helping," Willis, Sr., replied stoically. "The poor man claimed that it reminded him of a dish his *madre* used to make for him. Yes, Mrs. Donovan," he said to Deirdre, "the Shiraz is an excellent choice and a Riesling will go well with the syllabub. Forgive me, Lori," he continued, "but as you can imagine, I am eager to appease my appetite with the splendid viands Mrs. Donovan has so kindly provided. I will speak with you again tomorrow."

"Enjoy your dinner," I told him.

I put the phone down and looked askance at the pages I'd torn from the magazines. Not one included a recipe for lemon syllabub.

"You know what, Reginald?" I said through gritted teeth. "I'm beginning to *loathe* Deirdre Donovan."

"That's a shame, because Father thinks very highly of her."

I was fairly certain that Reginald couldn't talk and I was absolutely certain that he wouldn't refer to Willis, Sr., as "Father," so I addressed my next remarks to Bill, who stood in the doorway with Stanley draped over his shoulder.

"I wish I could like her," I said plaintively, "and maybe I will someday, but right now I have my doubts about her. I can't explain it, but——"

"I can," Bill interrupted. He smiled sleepily and stroked Stanley's gleaming black back. "You'd have doubts about anyone Father hired, Lori. In your eyes, no one will ever be good enough to look after him, and I love you for it. Was that him on the phone just now?"

I nodded. "He wanted to let me know that his dirty picture is a Fairworthy family tree."

"He must be delighted," Bill said. "I am, too. It'll give him something pleasant to dwell on while he's engulfed in Sally's soap opera. How'd Henrique like his trotters?"

"He gobbled them down," I said. "Maybe they should try serving him worm tartare. I'm sure Deirdre had a recipe for it."

Bill chuckled, set Stanley on the floor, and came over to cup my chin in his hand.

"You'll have to get over your dislike of Deirdre Donovan," he said gently. "Unless I'm very much mistaken, she and her husband are here to stay." He looked at the mantel clock as it began to chime. "Half past nine? It's too early to turn in, but I'm turning in anyway. I'll have to put in a long shift at work tomorrow to make up for slacking off today. But don't you fret, my sugar lump——

I'll take the boys to Anscombe Manor in the morning. I want you to be free to ride to Father's rescue at a moment's notice."

"I'll be at the ready, sword drawn and steed saddled," I promised. "Kiss Stanley good night for me."

"I always do." Bill bent to press his lips lingeringly to mine, then left the study, yawning, with Stanley padding worshipfully at his heels.

I gave the magazine pages another dark look, then shook off my crotchety mood, slid the blue journal from its shelf, and curled up with it in the tall leather armchair before the hearth. After pausing to collect my thoughts, I opened the journal and gazed at it expectantly.

"Dimity?" I said.

I smiled as the familiar lines of royal-blue ink flowed sinuously across the blank page.

Good evening, Lori. I'd hoped to hear from you sooner.

My smile faded. I glanced at the desk and realized with a twinge of guilt that the time I'd spent searching for recipes would have been better spent chatting with Aunt Dimity. She had every reason to expect a prompt update on the scheme she'd so cleverly devised.

"I'm sorry," I said. "I've been a little distracted this evening."

Apology accepted. Now, will you please get on with it? I'm dying, so to speak, to hear about Lady Sarah's adventures at Fairworth House!

Determined to make amends for my blunder, I launched into an exhaustive description of everything that had happened since I'd last spoken with her, from my early arrival at Crabtree Cottage to Willis, Sr.'s most recent telephone call. Aunt Dimity's initial response to my long and complex narrative made me gurgle with laughter.

Orange and yellow chiffon? With rhinestones? My word.

"Sally looked very pretty," I said staunchly. "Henrique thought she was gorgeous."

Is he color-blind?

"If love is blind," I said, "then Henrique's eyesight is definitely impaired."

His hearing must be impaired as well, if he failed to note the incongruities in Sally's speech.

"He's Mexican," I said, shrugging. "Maybe all Englishwomen sound alike to him. I can't tell an upper-class Spanish accent from a lower-class one. Why would I expect him to be an expert on English accents?"

As a well-to-do man of the world, Señor Cocinero must encounter authentic English aristocrats on a regular basis. It should be easy for him to recognize the differences between them and Sally Pyne.

"Men of the world don't necessarily hang out with aristocrats," I said. "If Henrique pulled himself up by his own bootstraps, he may be more comfortable around regular folk."

A humble beginning would explain his fondness for fry-ups and trotters. Oh, dear, Lori . . . I begin to suspect that Señor Cocinero would have fallen for Sally regardless of her position in society. If she'd been honest with him from the start, she might have found the man of her dreams—and kept him. Instead, she's created an absurdly difficult situation for herself.

"If she tells him the truth, he *may* leave," I said, "but if she continues to lie to him, he *will* leave."

She is, regrettably, wedged firmly between a rock and a hard place. *I wonder if we should go on aiding and abetting her in her attempt to deceive Señor Cocinero? Perhaps it would be kinder to persuade her to present herself to him as she is, not as she pretends to be.*

"You seem to forget," I said, "that Sally was prepared to leave Finch forever in order to *avoid* revealing her real self to Henrique."

So she was. Poor, dear, foolish Sally. She will, I fear, come to regret letting Señor Cocinero slip from her grasp.

"If she can go through with it," I said cautiously.

Do you believe she will hesitate?

"She may change her mind completely. She's *bonkers* about Henrique." I stretched my legs out on the ottoman and gazed bemusedly at the journal. "To tell you the truth, Dimity, I didn't expect the two of them to generate so much . . . heat."

Because they're middle-aged?

"Partly," I admitted. "Sally's always been so feisty and self-reliant that it's still hard for me to imagine her going all soppy and weak-kneed over a man. And, yes, I suppose I had the quaint notion that at a certain age the, um, embers would, er, burn low."

Bill would be disappointed to hear you say so. Come now, Lori. Any firefighter will tell you that it takes but a single glowing ember to start a conflagration. Señor Cocinero clearly knows how to fan the flames.

"You can say that again," I confirmed. "He may not be the handsomest *hombre* on earth, Dimity, but he has a seriously sensual way with words. He positively purrs every time he locks eyes with his *querida*. If I were Sally, I wouldn't be able to let him go."

Her heart may overrule her head or it may not. I doubt that even Sally knows what she will do on Thursday.

"It would be a crime to let all that passion go to waste," I declared. "I hope she swallows her pride, throws caution to the wind, and bares her soul to Henrique, come what may."

You have a penchant for drama, my dear. I expect William will have had his fill of drama by the time Señor Cocinero leaves. Still, he's kept a remarkably cool head, given the circumstances. Tim the taxidermist was a stroke of genius.

"It should put a spoke in the rumor mill," I agreed.

Everything is going according to plan, then. Good. There was a pause. *I can't help but notice that you've been unusually tight-lipped about the Donovans, Lori. After our last talk, I expected to be treated to a litany of their shortcomings.*

"I don't want to be accused of being peevish," I said, "or jealous or overprotective or possessive, so the only thing you'll hear me say about the Donovans from now on is that they're . . . perfect."

I'd rather you be critical than hypocritical, Lori. It's as plain as the nose on your face that the Donovans still make you uneasy. What is it about them that troubles you?

"Let me put it this way," I said, glad of the chance to vent my pent-up frustration. "If it was your first day on the job and your new boss asked you to join in an elaborate scheme to hoodwink some poor schnook, would you do it? If you were a gifted chef, would you jump at the opportunity to sling hash and dish up swill? Would you stay up until three in the morning to clean a house that doesn't need cleaning? I mean, it's not as if we left the place in a shambles after the housewarming party." I shifted my shoulders irritably. "The only mistake Deirdre's made so far was to mess around with William's furniture and even that was a result of overzealousness."

She moved the settee to protect it from the sun and she moved the chair in order to sweep behind it.

My brow furrowed as Aunt Dimity's words triggered another memory.

"And . . . I don't know how to describe it, Dimity," I said hesitantly, "but Deirdre reacted . . . strangely . . . when William asked her about the chair in the drawing room. His question seemed to take her by surprise. She had to think about her answer before she gave it."

She had a lot on her mind at the time.

"Yes, but it wasn't as if she'd forgotten that *she'd* moved the chair," I said in a rush. "It was as if she couldn't figure out who *had* moved it. I don't know. . . ." I slumped in my chair, discouraged. "Maybe Declan walks in his sleep. Maybe Deirdre was covering for him. Maybe I'm making mountains out of molehills. It wouldn't be the first time."

I don't believe you are. Making mountains out of molehills, that is.

"You don't?" I said, taken aback.

Far be it from me to dismiss intuition. I don't know what to make of Deirdre's reaction to the chair-moving incident, but if you sensed something off-kilter about it, I'm willing to believe that there's more to it than meets the eye.

"You are?" I said, sitting upright.

If something seems too good to be true, Lori, it usually is, and the Donovans seem much too good to be true. They're too accommodating, too helpful, too eager to please. They should never have agreed so readily to participate in my scheme. There was no need to spend half the night cleaning a clean house. A good cook would rather lose her job than produce inedible meals. They are, as you say, perfect, and you and I both know that no human being is perfect.

"I am flabbergasted," I said slowly, staring at the journal in disbelief. "I'm dazed and amazed. I never in a million years thought you'd *agree* with me, Dimity. You're always telling me not to jump to conclusions."

Have you jumped to any conclusions?

"Not yet," I said proudly. "Have you?"

I haven't reached a conclusion, but I can think of one possible explanation for the Donovans' curious behavior. I will gladly share it with you if you will promise not to overreact.

"I promise," I said before the final word was fully formed on the page. I was so relieved to have Aunt Dimity on my side that I would have promised to hop around the cottage on one foot if she'd asked me to.

I offer nothing more than a theory, Lori. I may be wrong from start to finish.

"Disclaimer noted," I said impatiently. "What's your theory?"

Servants have been known to lull their masters into a false sense of security. Perhaps the Donovans intend to gain William's trust in order to betray him.

My heart began to beat a little faster. "How would they betray him?"

I would remind you of the brass compass.

"The one Deirdre polished," I said, after a moment's thought, "even though it didn't need to be polished."

Deirdre created certain expectations when she took the

compass to the kitchen for cleaning. When other, more valuable objects vanish, William will assume that they, too, are
being cleaned. By the time he realizes that the missing objects
have been missing for some time, the Donovans will be long
gone—with the tidy sum of cash they earned by fencing stolen
property.

"They're going to rob him!" I exclaimed, thumping
the armrest with my fist. "That's it, Dimity! The Donovans plan to pick William's pocket while he's looking
the other way. That's why they want to work at places
like Fairworth. Their grand plan is to mosey from country house to country house seducing the owners while
they scoop up trinkets to sell to the highest bidder. I'm
sure you're right!"

I'm not. Calm down, Lori.

"How can I calm down?" I demanded. "You've just
told me that William's at the mercy of two no-good,
underhanded crooks!"

*I've told you nothing of the sort. I've merely set forth a
theory. You will need to gather hard evidence of wrongdoing
before you level any accusations at the Donovans.*

"I'll keep an eye on them," I said grimly. "I'll watch
their every move. They're bound to slip up eventually,
and when they do, I'll catch them."

*Of that I have no doubt. If there's a nest of vipers in Fair-
worth House, you will be the one to cast it out. But I would urge
you to make sure of the vipers before you do the casting out.*

"I won't call the police unless I catch either Deirdre
or Declan red-handed," I said.

*A sound policy. You've done well today, Lori. Without you,
my scheme would have been scuppered first thing this morning*

by Peggy Taxman and later, by Elspeth Binney. I hope you'll be equally successful in fending them off tomorrow.

"I shall be as a bulwark against snoopy villagers," I vowed, "and sneak-thieves."

Your primary concern should be to see William through until Thursday. Then you may focus your full attention on the Donovans. The next few days should be very interesting indeed. I look forward to hearing about them—in a timely fashion. Sleep well, my dear.

"I will," I said with a sheepish grin. "Good night, Dimity."

I waited until the lines of fine copperplate had faded from the page, then closed the journal and returned it to its shelf. For a moment I stood stock-still, pondering my next move. Though I was determined to do what was best for Willis, Sr., I wasn't sure he would thank me for it.

"William will be glad to see the backs of Lady Sarah and Henrique," I said to Reginald, "but he won't let go of the Donovans so easily."

My bunny's steadfast gaze bolstered my resolve. Instead of going to bed, I sat at the desk, shoved the magazines aside, and began to compile a room-by-room inventory of Fairworth's priceless, portable, and potentially threatened treasures.

Fifteen

Bill took off with Will and Rob at eight o'clock the following morning. I waved good-bye to them from the doorstep, then retreated to the kitchen with Stanley. As I loaded the dishwasher, I toyed with the idea of heading into the village as soon as the shops were open and laying claim to one of the tearoom's window seats.

It was, in my humble opinion, a stellar plan. Rainey would be pleased to have me on hand to shield her from Peggy Taxman; the tearoom's chatty patrons would let me know whether or not the taxidermist story had taken hold; and I would be perfectly placed to spring into action if I spotted a Handmaiden with binoculars making a beeline for the bridge. If I had to disguise my vigil's true purpose by indulging in a tasty pastry or two, so be it.

"Sacrifices must be made," I said to Stanley, who eyed me quizzically, then went back to washing his face.

I was debating the relative merits of cream cakes and jam doughnuts when the telephone rang.

"Lori?" Willis, Sr., said without preamble. "Would you please come to Fairworth House immediately? There has been a disturbing development."

"Already?" I said, my eyes widening. "What's missing?"

"Missing?" Willis, Sr., echoed. "Nothing is missing.

To the contrary, my home has become overcrowded. The workmen have arrived to put the finishing touches on the library, the billiards room, and the conservatory."

"Oh, no," I groaned, putting a hand to my forehead. "Didn't you tell them to come next week?"

"Had I done so, they would not be here today," he replied somewhat testily. "Unfortunately, it is a detail I overlooked. I require your assistance, Lori," he went on. "I can do many things, but I cannot juggle Lady Sarah, Señor Cocinero, and a houseful of manual laborers."

"Don't worry," I said. "I'll be over in twenty minutes."

"No sooner?" he asked piteously.

"Not unless you want me to prance around in my pajamas," I said. "I didn't sign up for dawn patrol."

"Come as soon as you can," he said, and hung up.

I saw no evidence of workmen when I reached Fairworth, presumably because they'd parked their vehicles around the back, but I detected their presence as soon as I stepped into the entrance hall. A chorus of bangs, thuds, taps, squeaks, and shouted conversations led me first to the library, where the carpenter and his assistant were finishing the crown molding on the massive bookshelves, then to the billiards room, where the plasterer and his assistant were touching up the sconce medallions, and finally to the conservatory, where the glazier and his assistant were discussing with Willis, Sr., the adjustments they needed to make to the louvered windows.

I waited for an opportune moment, then pulled Willis, Sr., into the dining room and shut the door. He was dressed meticulously in a lightweight tweed suit, but his face was flushed and his snowy hair was mussed, as if he'd run his hand through it instead of a comb.

"Private Shepherd, reporting for duty," I said, snapping off a salute.

"As you were," said Willis, Sr., smiling weakly at my attempt to lighten his mood.

"You don't look so good, William," I said with a sympathetic moue. "Have you had breakfast?"

"I have," he replied, and his expression brightened slightly. "Mrs. Donovan served breakfast to each of us in our rooms this morning. It was an inspired notion, since it enabled her to prepare individual meals. Mine was epicurean, but Lady Sarah and Señor Cocinero were treated to watery porridge."

"Which Henrique loved, of course," I said.

Willis, Sr., shrugged helplessly. "It reminded him of the porridge his *madre* used to make."

"Where are the Donovans?" I asked.

"Mr. Donovan has gone to Upper Deeping to take delivery of a shipment of tawny port I ordered some months ago," Willis, Sr., informed me. "Mrs. Donovan is attending to the bedrooms."

"And the lovebirds?" I asked. "Where are they?"

"Lady Sarah and her friend are in my study, playing backgammon," said Willis, Sr. "I would like them to stay there until the laborers leave."

"Why?" I asked. "The workmen won't recognize Sally. She never came to Fairworth during the renovation and they never went to the tearoom. As I recall, they rocketed straight through Finch without stopping, to avoid further contact with the Handmaidens."

"I wish you would refrain from using that term," said Willis, Sr., frowning. "I realize that you and my son find it amusing, but I consider it unkind and inappropriate."

"Sorry," I said, "but my point is—"

"I understand your point," Willis, Sr., broke in, "but I do not accept it. The workmen may decide, against their better judgment, to visit Peacock's pub after they leave Fairworth today. It will not help our cause if Mr. and Mrs. Peacock overhear the men chatting about Lady Sarah and Señor Cocinero." He shook his head. "It is a risk I am unwilling to take."

"What do you want me to do?" I asked.

"I would like you to keep my guests segregated from the workmen," he replied fretfully. "I cannot be everywhere at once."

"You don't have to be," I soothed. "I'm here."

"Thank you, Lori." He took a calming breath. "I also rely on you to keep Lady Sarah from giving away all of my earthly possessions."

"What are you talking about?" I asked.

"Lady Sarah pleaded with me to allow her to present Señor Cocinero with one of the snuffboxes found in the ruined stables," Willis, Sr., explained. "Her desire to bestow a memento upon her friend is laudable, but an eighteenth-century Meissen snuffbox is rather an expensive souvenir."

"Is it?" I said. "I didn't realize that the snuffboxes were valuable."

"The entire collection has been appraised at two hundred thousand pounds," Willis, Sr., said, lowering his voice. "The Meissen alone is worth thirty thousand pounds."

"Are you *kidding* me?" I exclaimed. "You never said——"

"The collection's monetary worth is irrelevant," Willis, Sr., interrupted. "The snuffboxes are fragments of Fairworth's history. I do not intend to part with any of them on a whim, especially when the whim is not my own. Now, if you will excuse me, I must try once more to make myself clear to the glazier."

Willis, Sr., smoothed his hair, straightened his tie, and reentered the conservatory, looking marginally less frantic.

I stood with my mouth agape, staring into the middle distance in stunned silence. How, I asked myself, had a collection of snuffboxes worth two hundred thousand pounds found its way into the rubble of the old stables? More importantly, how could Willis, Sr., be so foolish as to display it in an unlocked glass case in the drawing room?

I hadn't even included the snuffboxes in my inventory of small treasures because I'd been under the impression that they were nothing more than decorative gewgaws. An Oxford scholar with a degree in art history might know better. I made a mental note to count the snuffboxes carefully before the day was through, then set out for the study.

I found Sally and Henrique seated at a gate-leg games table that had been filched from the billiards room.

Henrique wore a loose-fitting muslin shirt, white trousers, and huaraches. Sally was dressed in sparkly flip-flops and a flowing white caftan with a colorfully embroidered yoke. Her tiara was firmly in place and the snowflake-shaped pendant glittered at her breast.

"Lori!" Henrique exclaimed jovially. "How lovely you are today, all in yellow, like *el botón de oro*—the buttercup, I think you say."

"Thanks, Henrique," I said, smoothing my silk dress and pulling a chair up to the table. "You're looking good, too. How's the game going?"

"Lady Sarah wins two times in a row," he replied, bowing to Sally. "She is the backgammon queen."

"I'm nothing of the sort," said Sally, blushing. "It's all a matter of luck."

"And concentration," said Henrique. "The workers, they make a racket, but Lady Sarah does not notice."

"Cousin William forgot to tell me that they were coming." Sally gave me a meaningful look, then twirled a hand in the air and said blithely, "As a rule, I don't pay much attention to repairs and maintenance and suchlike. I leave all the mucky jobs to dear Cousin William."

"It is good to have a man in the house," Henrique purred.

As he caught and held Sally's gaze, I could almost feel the glowing ember's heat rise between them. I cleared my throat to keep the glow from bursting into flames and they turned to peer at me politely.

"Did you sleep well?" I asked, grasping at the first question that came to mind.

"Like the contented baby," Henrique replied. "The soft music does not disturb me at all."

"Soft music?" I said blankly.

"Henrique told me just now that he heard music coming through his bedroom ceiling late last night," Sally said indignantly. "I'll have a thing or two to say to the Donovans about their stereo, I can tell you."

"Please do not speak to the Donovans," said Henrique. "I like this big band music."

"Big band music?" I echoed stupidly.

"Benny Goodman," he clarified. "*Mi madre*, she adored Benny Goodman, and I, too, like him very much. The music is soft, it comes and goes very quickly. It is no trouble."

"In that case, I won't say a word about it," Sally said, with a gracious nod.

"You will permit us to continue our game?" Henrique asked me, gesturing to the backgammon board.

"Play on," I said.

While they rolled the dice and moved the checkers, I leaned back in my chair and slowly lifted my gaze to the ceiling. Neither Willis, Sr., nor Sally had complained about a late-night concert, which meant that the Donovans' sound system had to be located directly above Henrique's bed. How the couple could work all day, then listen to Benny Goodman's blazing clarinet all night was beyond me. They were beginning to seem superhuman.

There was nothing remotely superhuman about Sally and Henrique. As the game progressed, Sally stopped simpering, became openly competitive, and began to lose her bizarre accent. Henrique seemed to relish everything she said and did, and the more delightful he found her, the more delightfully herself she became. It was a touching, very human scene, and I found myself wishing that Sally could see it through my eyes.

In the midst of their fifth hotly contested game—Sally had won the previous four—the study door opened and the carpenter put his head into the room.

"Beg pardon, ma'am," he said to Sally. "But Liam and I are pining for a cuppa. It's gone eleven and we're parched."

"I'll put the kettle on," said Sally. She caught herself, then added loftily, "Since my cook is busy elsewhere."

"Always so thoughtful," Henrique murmured. He turned to the carpenter and said solemnly, "It is a great pity that your work will be eaten by the deathwatch beetle."

"Eh?" said the carpenter, looking startled.

"Tea!" I said, jumping to my feet. "Lady Sarah, take Henrique to the kitchen with you. I'm sure he'll enjoy seeing your, er, appliances."

"Come along, Henrique," she said, and hustled him past the carpenter and out of the room.

"What's all this about deathwatch beetles?" the carpenter demanded. "It's the first I've heard of them."

"You'll have to forgive William's guest," I told him. "He seems to think that every house in England is infested with deathwatch beetles. If he mentions it again, just smile and nod."

"Right, then," said the carpenter, mollified. "I'll get back to work."

I chewed my lower lip worriedly. I wasn't sure how

I would keep the workmen away from Sally if she served tea to them. While I was pondering my options, my cell phone rang. I pulled it from my purse, wondering what new emergency had cropped up while I'd been sequestered in the study.

"Lori?" said Willis, Sr. "Would you please join me in the drawing room? Something rather odd has happened to my snuffboxes."

"I'm on my way," I said tersely.

I shoved the phone into my shoulder bag and high-tailed it for the drawing room. I was so certain that the snuffboxes had been stolen that I shouted "Aha!" when I saw the empty display cabinet.

"Aha?" said Willis, Sr.

"That's right," I said, nodding vigorously. *"Aha!* That's what you say when you uncover a crime."

"I do not know what book you are reading at the moment," said Willis, Sr., "but if it is a detective novel, I suggest that you put it aside for a while. It has clearly inflamed your imagination. No crime has been committed, Lori."

"Then where are your snuffboxes?" I demanded.

"There," he said, pointing over my shoulder.

I wheeled around and saw that the snuffboxes had been arranged in a neat circle on the low table beside the infamous Chippendale armchair.

"What are they doing there?" I asked.

"I do not know," said Willis, Sr. "Would I be correct in assuming that you did not put them there?"

"Of course I didn't put them there," I said, turning to face him. "Did you?"

"I did not." Willis, Sr., rubbed his chin. "It seems far-fetched to believe that one of the laborers was seized by an uncontrollable impulse to redecorate my drawing room, and Lady Sarah denies all knowledge of the prank. Since Fairworth is, to my knowledge, untroubled by polter-geists, I have summoned Mrs. Donovan, in hopes that she will provide us with a rational explanation for this as well as one other anomaly."

"What other anomaly?" I asked.

"The brass compass has been removed from the bil-liards room," he replied. "It now resides on the map case in the library. Ah, Mrs. Donovan," he continued as Deirdre entered the drawing room. "I apologize for interrupting your morning routine, but I wonder if you can explain . . . this." He gestured first at the display cabinet, then at the low table. "As you can see, my snuff-boxes are not in their usual place."

Deirdre's eyes shifted from the table to the cabinet, then focused on Willis, Sr. For a split second I had the distinct impression that she was as puzzled as we were, but she answered readily enough.

"I'm so sorry, sir," she said. "I took the snuffboxes out of the cabinet this morning because I wanted to dust the shelves. When the workmen arrived, I must have been so flustered that I forgot to put them back."

"And the compass?" asked Willis, Sr.

"The compass, sir?" she said.

"The compass that was once in the billiards room," said Willis, Sr., "is now on the map case in the library."

"If you'll forgive me, sir," she said, "it makes more

sense to display a compass near maps than near a billiards table."

"As it happens, I agree with you," said Willis, Sr., "and for that reason I will leave the compass where you have placed it. I must insist once again, however, that you consult with me before you make even the slightest alteration to my decor."

"Yes, sir," said Deirdre.

I watched her beadily as she transferred each snuffbox from the table to the display case. I couldn't accuse her of theft because she hadn't stolen anything, and I couldn't tell Willis, Sr., that she was preparing the ground for a future robbery because I would only sound paranoid. The one thing I could do was to let her know, in a subtle way, that I had my eye on her.

"I count ten boxes," I observed as she closed the cabinet door. "Ten boxes. Not *eight*. Not *nine*. *Ten*."

"Your arithmetical skill has been noted," said Willis, Sr., eyeing me with mild curiosity. "That there are ten snuffboxes in the collection cannot be disputed. Why you should feel the need to state the obvious is——" He broke off suddenly and cocked his head to one side. "Do I hear . . . *singing*?"

I held my breath and listened.

"Yes," I said. "I hear it, too. Benny Goodman didn't sing, did he?"

"Benny Goodman?" said Willis, Sr., raising his eyebrows.

"It's coming from the billiards room," said Deirdre.

"Let us investigate," said Willis, Sr.

My father-in-law gave me a perplexed, sidelong look, then led the way up the main corridor and through the library to the billiards room, where evidence of my failure to keep the workmen segregated from Sally and Henrique was on full display.

Henrique sat on the edge of a tapestry wing chair at the far end of the room, strumming a guitar and singing a soulful Mexican ditty before an appreciative audience composed of the plasterer, the glazier, the carpenter, their assistants, and Sally. Henrique had a wonderful singing voice and an even better stage presence. His listeners were clearly entranced by his performance and when he finished, they gave him a big round of applause and called for another song. He happily obliged.

Willis, Sr., motioned abruptly for Deirdre and me to retreat with him to the library. We complied, closing the door behind us.

"Where did the guitar come from?" I asked.

"It must belong to one of the laborers," said Deirdre. "Mr. Cocinero didn't have a guitar case in his baggage."

"We are not here to discuss guitars," said Willis, Sr., with a touch of asperity. "We have a much greater problem to resolve. The workmen must not be allowed to visit Peacock's pub."

"How can we stop them?" I asked.

"Feed them lunch?" Deirdre suggested. "If they're well fed when they leave here, they'll be less tempted to stop in Finch for pub grub and a pint. I can whip up bangers and mash in a trice."

"Sausages and mashed potatoes," I translated. I was

fairly certain that Willis, Sr., had never in his life encountered a dish as plebeian as bangers and mash.

"If I hurry," Deirdre continued, "I may be able to reach Declan while he's still in Upper Deeping. He can bring a case of lager back with him."

"We cannot send the men home inebriated," Willis, Sr., protested.

"I'll limit them to one bottle apiece," said Deirdre, "and I'll fill them up with starchy food. If they work for another hour or so after lunch, they'll have no trouble driving home."

Willis, Sr., contemplated the plan briefly, then nodded.

"Make it so," he said to Deirdre.

A roar of laughter exploded in the billiards room as Deirdre raced to the kitchen, cell phone in hand. I opened the door a crack and saw Henrique juggling billiard balls.

"Henrique's the life of the party," I murmured. "And Sally's his biggest fan."

"Has she no sense of self-preservation?" Willis, Sr., asked wistfully.

"I'm afraid not," I said, smiling. "She's a woman in love."

Sixteen

A blanket of blessed silence descended on Fairworth House when the workmen called it quits at three o'clock. They'd completed the finishing touches in good spirits, heartened by the meal Deirdre had provided and energized by the entertainment Henrique had supplied. Henrique and Sally, worn out by the festivities, had repaired to their rooms for naps once they'd finished waving good-bye to their new best friends.

I sat with Willis, Sr., in the drawing room, awaiting the arrival of a pot of chamomile tea and a few easily digested nibbles. Though the bangers and mash had looked appetizing—Henrique had cooed over each bite—neither Willis, Sr., nor I had sampled more than a forkful. Willis, Sr., had been too agitated to eat and I'd been too busy keeping the party from getting out of hand.

"Will and Rob," said Willis, Sr., as if he'd just remembered their existence. "Who is caring for my grandsons?"

"Kit Smith," I told him. "I called Anscombe Manor around noon and asked Kit to feed them. He said he'd take them on a trail ride afterward. Trust me, they're happy campers."

"They are fond of their ponies," Willis, Sr., agreed. He sank more deeply into his chair and rested his clasped hands on his waistcoat. "Thank you for staying here with me, Lori. Thank you for preventing the carpenter from performing his clog dance on the dining room table."

"No problem," I said.

"Thank you for rescuing my spoons from the plasterer when he threatened to play a tune on them," Willis, Sr., continued.

"You don't have to keep thanking me, William," I said, embarrassed.

"Ah, but I do," he returned. "Without you to steady me, I would have lost my temper when Señor Cocinero began to do magic tricks with my Victorian salt and pepper shakers. Having resurrected them from the depths of old stables, I was understandably reluctant to see them disappear again."

Bill would have laughed like a hyena at the thought of his panic-prone wife steadying his unflappable father, but I felt that I'd earned the accolade. Every time I'd sensed a spike in Willis, Sr.'s blood pressure during lunch, I'd reminded him, sotto voce, that it was better to have the men lunching with us than gossiping at Peacock's pub. Although he'd muttered "We can still send them there" at one point, my influence had, on the whole, been a calming one.

"Your little flock of silver sheep is intact," I assured him. "I counted them after Henrique finished pulling them out of people's ears."

"You counted my snuffboxes, too," Willis, Sr., commented idly. "Why?"

I had no wish to burden my father-in-law with a

fresh set of worries, so I said lightly, "It never hurts to keep track of things."

"True," said Willis, Sr. "Very true."

Deirdre appeared with the tea tray, which she placed on the low table at my elbow. While I poured the tea and cut generous wedges from the rather plain-looking cake she'd baked, she turned to address Willis, Sr.

"I have good news to report, sir," she said. "The workmen bypassed the pub on their way through Finch."

"How do you know?" asked Willis, Sr., sitting upright.

"Declan," she said. "He parked himself on the war memorial bench about thirty minutes ago, to keep an eye on Peacock's pub. As soon as he sat down, four women converged on him to ask if I'd made any decisions about hiring extra help, then stuck around to quiz him about the state of things at Fairworth. Declan said that when the workmen saw the four women, they rolled up their windows and raced out of Finch as if the hounds of hell were nipping at their heels."

It was, I thought, a fair description of the Handmaidens.

"All's well that ends well, sir," Deirdre concluded.

"You and your husband are marvelous," said Willis, Sr., in an almost awed voice. "Simply marvelous. I am grateful to both of you for——"

"Deirdre," I broke in, peering curiously at the cake. Its single layer was round, unfrosted, and oddly familiar. "Is this seedcake?"

"Yes," she said. "You requested something simple."

I passed a piece of cake to Willis, Sr., and bit into my own.

In an instant I was transported back to a sunny afternoon nearly a decade earlier, when I'd invited the late Ruth and Louise Pym to tea at the cottage. I'd baked a seedcake for them then, using a recipe I'd found in an old, dog-eared cookbook that had belonged to Aunt Dimity. *It is so difficult these days,* Ruth had said, *to find* real *seedcake.*

Ruth wouldn't have hesitated to classify the cake Deirdre had baked as *real* seedcake. It was virtually identical in size, color, texture, aroma, and flavor to the cake I'd served to the Pym sisters.

"Where did you get the recipe?" I asked, when the unsettling wave of déjà vu had passed.

"I'm afraid I don't remember," Deirdre said. "I've collected so many recipes over the years that it's difficult to recall where each one came from."

"Your seedcake resembles one my daughter-in-law makes from time to time," Willis, Sr., explained.

"I see," said Deirdre, nodding. "Perhaps we own the same cookbook."

"Perhaps," I said.

"While we're on the subject of books," said Willis, Sr., "would you be so kind as to retrieve a book from the desk in my study and bring it to me, Mrs. Donovan? It is entitled *Notes on Sheep.* My daughter-in-law wishes to borrow it."

I gave him a furtive glance, wondering if he'd decided to punish me for interrupting his praise of the Donovans.

"Of course, sir," said Deirdre. "Will there be anything else?"

"Dare I ask about the dinner menu?" said Willis, Sr., with a delicate wince.

"Since Mr. Cocinero enjoyed the trotters, sir, I thought I'd try mushy peas and burnt beef burgers tonight," said Deirdre. "I've never met a foreigner who likes mushy peas."

Willis, Sr., shrugged philosophically. "I will bear up under the strain if you will prepare something palatable for me after my guests have gone to their rooms. Last night's chop was delectable."

"I'm already working on it, sir," said Deirdre, and she left the drawing room, smiling.

"Mrs. Donovan is a treasure," murmured Willis, Sr., easing himself back into his chair.

I finished my tea in thoughtful silence.

I left Fairworth a half hour later, with *Notes on Sheep* in my hand and a host of unanswered questions tumbling through my head. After swapping cars with Bill, I brought Will and Rob home from Anscombe Manor, bathed them, dressed them in clean clothes, threatened them with grievous bodily harm if they played in the dirt before dinner, and began to throw a meal together.

The boys settled at the kitchen table with crayons and drawing paper to record their afternoon's adventure for posterity. I was too preoccupied to listen closely as they described their trail ride with Kit, but maternal instinct enabled me to *ooh* and *aah* in all the right places, and when I asked the boys to help me set the table, they were content to move their drawings to the desk in the study.

Bill was equally preoccupied when he came home from work. One of his favorite clients, a Bavarian art collector named Karla Schniering, had suffered a massive stroke from which she was unlikely to recover.

"There's bound to be a family squabble when Frau Schniering dies," he told me over dinner. "I may have to leave for Munich at a moment's notice, to make sure that no one reinterprets her will."

"I'll pack a bag for you tonight," I said. I was accustomed to Bill's sudden departures. As an estate attorney with an international clientele, he was always on call.

"Are you going away, Daddy?" Will asked.

"Not tonight," said Bill. "But I may have to take a trip tomorrow."

"Why?" asked Rob.

"Because a very nice old lady is about to die." Bill didn't believe in sugarcoating the facts of life, but he did believe in framing them in terms that made sense to his children. "When she does, I'll have to make sure that her toys go to the right people."

"Does she have little boys?" Will asked interestedly.

"She has four grown-up sons," said Bill. "And they don't get along very well."

"Oh," said Rob, with an air of enlightenment. "They'll fight over the toys."

"If they fight too much," Will said, after a meditative pause, "you can take the toys away."

"And bring them to us," said Rob.

"We won't fight over them," Will promised.

"I'll bear that in mind," Bill said gravely.

"Who wants blackberry crumble?" I asked, and

blackberry-picking swiftly replaced death as the prime topic of conversation.

The thunderstorm began after dinner. While I cleared the kitchen, Bill and the boys hunkered down on the window seat in the living room to count the seconds between flashes and booms. At half past seven, Bill took the boys up to bed, as he always did on the night before a journey.

He spent the rest of the evening in his armchair, monitoring Frau Schniering's declining health via the telephone and his laptop. Stanley, as if sensing the gravity of the situation, rubbed his head against Bill's leg, then curled up in a gleaming black ball on the window seat.

I didn't want to distract Bill with my unanswered questions, so I stretched out on the sofa and read *Notes on Sheep*. I'd expected the book to be a dry-as-dust instructional manual on sheep rearing, but it turned out to be a well-crafted meditation on the importance of sheep to the Cotswolds. I was so pleasantly surprised that I couldn't keep myself from sharing a few fun facts with Bill.

"Did you know that the Romans introduced the longwool sheep breeds to Britain?" I asked.

"Mmm-hmm," said Bill, tapping away at his keyboard.

"Did you know that the word *Cotswolds* comes from 'cote,' meaning a sheep enclosure, and 'wolds,' meaning rolling, treeless hills?" I asked.

"Mmm-hmm," said Bill.

"Did you know that Cotswold Sheep used to have bat wings and venomous fangs?" I asked.

"Mmm-hmm," said Bill.

I closed *Notes on Sheep* and got to my feet.

"If you need me, I'll be in the study," I said.

"Venomous fangs," Bill said without glancing up from his computer. "See? I'm listening."

"You're an amazing multitasker," I said, "but you should focus on Frau Schniering right now. She needs your attention more than I do."

I gently ruffled his hair and left him to his sad vigil.

Windswept rain washed in waves against the diamond-paned windows above the old oak desk in the study. I lit a fire in the hearth to chase away the chill in the storm-cooled air and touched a finger to Reginald's snout.

"It's a good night to be indoors, Reg," I said. "Especially if you're made of flannel."

Smiling, I pulled the blue journal from its shelf and snuggled up with it in the tall leather armchair before the fire.

"Dimity?" I said as I opened the journal. "I'm here earlier than I was last night. Do I get a gold star on my report card?"

I chuckled as Aunt Dimity's elegant copperplate curled and looped across the page.

Two gold stars, my dear, and a silver moon. Tell me quickly: Has Sally been unmasked?

"No," I said. "The Lady Sarah charade continues, but something strange is definitely going on at Fairworth."

Something stranger than the charade?

"A whole lot stranger," I confirmed. "But I'd better start at the beginning. I don't want to leave anything out."

I'm all ears. Metaphorically speaking.

"Okay," I said. "My day began with a phone call from William. . . ."

I spoke steadily while the fire snapped and crackled and the rain continued to fall, recounting everything that had happened at Fairworth from the moment I'd arrived to the moment I'd left. I told Aunt Dimity about the workmen, the Benny Goodman music, the impromptu hootenanny in the billiards room, the bangers and mash luncheon, the Handmaidens' unwitting role in protecting Sally's secret, and the eerily familiar seedcake. I gave particular emphasis to the snuffboxes' monetary value and to Deirdre's confession that she had moved them as well as the brass compass, just as she'd moved the settee and the Chippendale armchair. When I finished, I felt more confused than ever.

"The snuffboxes and the compass fit into your theft theory," I said, "but I don't see how they relate to the music Henrique heard in his bedroom last night or to the seedcake."

Must everything be related?

The question brought me up short. I'd assumed that Aunt Dimity would connect the dots for me. Instead, she'd underscored a fatal flaw in my reasoning.

"I suppose not," I said, feeling a bit deflated.

If anything, the Benny Goodman music points to the Donovans' innocence. If they were intent on lulling William into a false sense of security, why would they draw attention to themselves by playing loud music?

"What about the seedcake?" I asked. "Don't you find it a little odd that it was so similar to yours?"

I didn't invent seedcake, Lori. It's been around since the Middle Ages. I'm quite sure that many people have recipes similar to my own.

"And the snuffboxes?" I went on a little desperately. "And the compass? Deirdre keeps moving stuff, just as you predicted. Have you changed your mind about her?"

No, I haven't. I still suspect her and her husband of masterminding a forthcoming robbery, which is why you mustn't allow yourself to be distracted by music and cake. Concentrate on collecting relevant evidence, Lori, or you'll find yourself mired in a morass of extraneous details.

"But you just told me that the Benny Goodman music points to the Donovans' innocence," I protested.

I'm willing to keep an open mind about the Donovans, which is more than I can say for you. I may suspect them of foul play, but you are already convinced of their guilt. Your prejudice is clouding your judgment. What will catch your eye next? Will you try to persuade me that Declan's red hair and the prominent mole on Deirdre's face are signs of corruption?

"Of course not," I said, abashed.

I cherish your passionate nature, Lori, but you must learn to harness it. You must learn to separate the trivial from the significant. Don't dwell on trifling incidents. Focus instead on Deirdre's sleight of hand with William's possessions.

"At least his precious book was where he left it," I mumbled.

What book?

"*Notes on Sheep*," I said, "by Frederick Fairworthy. It's one of the books the builders unearthed when the old stables were torn down. William loaned it to me, to help me to understand his obsession with sheep. And it did help. I think it'd be wonderful to see a flock of Cotswold Lions grazing Fairworth's pastures."

They wouldn't be the first Cotswold Lions to graze there. Sheep were the foundation of the Fairworthy family fortune, as indeed, they were the foundation of England's wealth. Wool production fueled a significant portion of England's economy for several centuries. Did you know that the Lord Chancellor sits on a sack stuffed with wool in the House of Lords?

"As a matter of fact, I did," I said smugly. "According to *Notes on Sheep*, the Lord Chancellor's woolsack symbolizes the importance of sheep to England."

Did Notes on Sheep *also discuss their role in shaping the Cotswolds? The exquisite churches found in modest towns like Fairford and Northleach were built by wealthy wool merchants. The merchants took such pride in their profession that their gravestones were sometimes carved to resemble woolsacks.*

"The woolsack tombs," I said, nodding. "Bill and I saw them in Burford."

There are some very fine examples of woolsack tombs in Burford, mementos of prosperous days gone by. When the price of wool plummeted in the early nineteenth century, the entire region was engulfed in a great depression. Since no one could afford to renovate or to replace old structures, villages like Finch retained their quirkiness and their sublime architecture. To understand the Cotswolds, one must first understand the rise and fall of sheep.

"Did the Fairworthy family rise and fall with them, too?" I asked.

Naturally. Fairworth wasn't the family's principal residence, you know. They lived in Worth Hall, a much grander edifice on the outskirts of Gloucester. They built Fairworth House as a country retreat. Sadly, Worth Hall was pulled down during the rather depressing period between the wars when we lost so many of our stately homes.

"What happened between the wars?" I asked.

Taxation, inflation, stagnation. . . . Many of our older families could no longer afford to maintain their ancestral residences. The National Trust attempted to preserve historic houses for posterity, but a great many were razed to the ground before laws were enacted to protect them.

"How did Fairworth House manage to survive?" I asked.

The last Fairworthys to live there sold it to a bank some fifty years ago. It was then sold to a succession of owners who didn't have the wherewithal to maintain the property but who weren't permitted to tear it down. It languished, unloved and unlived-in for more than a decade, until a certain American gentleman decided to establish a residence near his grandsons in England. William brought Fairworth to life again after many long years of neglect. I do like happy endings, don't you?

"I'm a sucker for them," I said, grinning. "I hope William goes ahead with his plan to buy some Cotswold Lions. They'll put the true finishing touch on Fairworth's restoration."

I hope so, too. In the meantime, however, we must continue to do what we can to insure that Sally Pyne's story has a happy ending. Whether it will be with Señor Cocinero or without him remains to be seen.

"I also have to make sure that the Donovans keep their greedy paws off of William's things," I said. "Which means that I'd better get some shut-eye. Heaven knows what tomorrow will bring."

Sleep well, my dear.

"I always sleep well when it's raining," I said. "Good night, Dimity."

The curving lines of royal-blue ink slowly faded from the page. I closed the journal, returned it to its shelf, banked the fire, and gave Reginald a pat between the ears. I was about to leave the study when Bill's figure loomed in the doorway.

"Frau Schniering died ten minutes ago," he said with a heavy sigh. "I'll leave for Munich first thing in the morning."

Bill would have been a basket case if he'd taken the loss of every client to heart, but he'd been extremely fond of Karla Schniering, and her death, though not unexpected, had clearly hit him hard.

I put my arms around him in silent sympathy. At that moment, Sally Pyne's charade and the Donovans' misdeeds seemed very trivial indeed.

Seventeen

Will, Rob, and I watched Bill drive away in his Mercedes on Wednesday morning, finished breakfast, and headed for Anscombe Manor in the Rover. The storm had blown itself out in the night, leaving a rain-washed landscape glistening beneath a clear blue sky. Silvery rivulets crisscrossed the lane, and the droplet-strewn hedgerows looked as though they'd been draped in diamonds.

Fortunately, the riding ring had an excellent drainage system, so the twins' lessons could proceed as scheduled. I thanked Kit again for treating the boys to a trail ride the previous afternoon, watched them go through their warm-up exercises with Nell, chatted with Emma, and fed a few apples to Toby, the oldest and sweetest pony in the stable, before returning to the cottage, where I busied myself with household chores. I checked each of my telephones periodically throughout the morning, but since they were in good working order, I was forced to conclude that Willis, Sr., was managing to survive without me.

I was pleased, of course, that Willis, Sr., didn't need my help, but when my cell phone rang just before noon, I slapped it to my ear so eagerly that I nearly concussed myself.

"*Guten Morgen, mein Liebling,*" said Bill.

I felt momentarily disoriented when I heard my husband's voice instead of my father-in-law's, a state of mind exacerbated by his unusual greeting.

"Hi," I said, pulling myself together. "I forgot that you speak German as well as Spanish."

"I dabble," he said modestly. "I'm in a limo on the Autobahn, en route to the Schniering estate, so I thought I'd touch base. What's happening at Fairworth?"

"Smooth sailing," I replied brightly. "Your father hasn't called, which is fantastic because it means that everything's hunky-dory at Fairworth and since yesterday was so stressful, I'm happy that today is going so well. I'm very happy for William. Very, very happy."

"It's good to be happy," said Bill.

"I couldn't be happier," I gushed. "Did you have a nice flight?"

"Pretty routine," he replied. "It wasn't nearly as happy as your happy morning at home, but——"

"Oh, shut up," I said without rancor. Bill could always see right through me, possibly because I wasn't terribly opaque. "You'd think William would've called by now," I grumbled, giving vent to my true feelings, "if only to tell me that he's okay."

"Maybe he hasn't had a chance," said Bill. "Maybe he's caught up in a killer game of backgam——"

"Bill!" I broke in excitedly. "My phone just beeped. I'd better take it. It may be your father."

"Talk to you later," said Bill.

"Good luck with the Schniering brothers," I said, and switched over to the incoming call.

"William?" I said. "What's wrong?"

"It's not *William*, it's *Charles*," said Charles Bellingham.

"Back from London already?" I said, my excitement ebbing. "How time flies when you're——"

"Stop *gibbering*," Charles snapped. He sounded upset. "Oh, Lori, you have to get over here right away, and I do mean *tout de suite*. The constable's come and gone, Grant's having a full-blown anxiety attack, and I have absolutely no idea how to break the news to William."

"Break the news about what?" I asked, bewildered.

"The burglary!" he cried. "Crabtree Cottage has been pillaged, plundered, ransacked—we've been robbed! No time to talk now, Grant needs me. Just hop in that sad little car of yours and stomp on the gas pedal, will you? Coming, Grant!" he called and cut the connection.

My brain spun wildly for a moment before it kicked into gear. I called Kit and asked him to keep the twins at Anscombe Manor until further notice, then grabbed my shoulder bag and ran for the Rover. My Mini was an unquestionably sad little car, but I could burn up the road in the Rover.

I simply couldn't believe that Crabtree Cottage had been burgled. Finch was virtually crime-free. Local teenagers occasionally left a few beer bottles on the village green, but their parents always marched them back the next day to clean up after themselves. Local adults might fling unpleasant words at each other from time to time, but once they'd cleared the air they reverted to civilized behavior.

Yet it seemed equally unlikely that a non-local had broken into Crabtree Cottage. Finch was the exact opposite of a tourist mecca. It was so far off the beaten track that few outsiders were aware of its existence.

Unless, of course, one counted the outsiders who'd recently moved into Fairworth House. I recalled Aunt Dimity's cautionary words and ordered myself to keep an open mind about the Donovans, but as I sped past Willis, Sr.'s drive I couldn't help remembering that he'd heard someone use the elevator in Fairworth House at the curiously early hour of 2:57 a.m. on Tuesday.

"Grant and Charles left for London on Monday and returned on Wednesday," I murmured as I crossed the humpbacked bridge. "Crabtree Cottage was burgled sometime between Monday and Wednesday. Someone at Fairworth used the elevator in the wee hours of Tuesday morning. No prejudice here, Dimity. Just a recitation of cold, hard facts."

A sizable crowd of villagers had already gathered in front of Crabtree Cottage by the time I arrived. Under normal circumstances I would have plunged straight into the gossip fest, but Charles's needs were greater than my own, so I pushed my way politely past my neighbors and through the cottage's front door.

"Charles?" I called, peering down the narrow hallway that led to the living quarters at the back of the cottage.

Charles Bellingham appeared at the far end of the hall and beckoned frantically to me. I detected no signs of ransacking as I hurried toward him. His office was as neat as a pin, the dining room chairs were upright, and the framed watercolors that lined the hallway seemed undisturbed, but Charles was a bundle of nerves, wringing his hands and shifting anxiously from foot to foot. When I reached him, he put an arm around my shoulders and spoke in the hushed tones of an intensive care nurse.

"Grant's in the garden with Goya and Matisse," he said. "The dogs have calmed him down, but he's still in a state of shock. You must convince him that none of this is his fault."

"None of what?" I asked. "Forgive me, Charles, but I don't know what's going on."

"I'll let Grant explain," he said. "He believes in talk therapy, but I've thrown in a whacking great gin and tonic to help the process along. May I offer you a drink?"

"No, thanks," I said. "Best to keep a clear head."

"'When all about you are losing theirs,'" he quoted feelingly. "Kipling understood trauma. I regard him as one of England's most underrated poets. Modern critics may dismiss his poems as doggerel, but in *my* opinion—"

"Charles?" I interrupted gently. "Grant?"

"Sorry," he said, and pressed the heel of his hand to his forehead. "Focus, Charles, focus." He breathed in through his nostrils and out through his mouth, then dropped his hand. "There. I'm back again. Let's go."

Charles led the way through the kitchen and into the most charming garden in Finch. It was overcrowded and untidy and it would never win a prize for originality, but I loved every square inch of it, from the old-fashioned morning glories gracing the stone walls to the unruly clumps of thyme edging the rosy brick paving.

An ancient oak table and four wobbly, mismatched chairs usually occupied a spot in the center of the garden, but two of the chairs had been placed next to the bamboo chaise longue in which Grant reclined, shaded by the leafy boughs of the gnarled crabapple tree that had given Crabtree Cottage its name. His whacking great gin and tonic rested on a small wrought-iron table at his elbow.

Grant's eyes were closed, but the dogs sharing the chaise longue with him were alert and thrilled to have company. They jumped down from their perch and bounded over to welcome me as soon as I stepped out of the kitchen. While I bent to scratch their ears, Charles crept forward to hover solicitously over his partner.

"Grant?" he said softly. "Lori's here."

Grant opened his eyes to peer first at Charles, then at me. He looked away for a moment, then shrugged resignedly and motioned for me to take the chair closest to the wrought-iron table. Charles helped Grant to sip his drink, then sank onto the second chair, which wobbled alarmingly until he shifted it to a more stable position on the bricks. Goya and Matisse trotted off to explore a thicket of fern fronds.

"I don't know what to say," Grant began, in a trembling voice. "One expects this sort of thing to happen in London, but not in Finch, *never* in Finch. That's why I . . . I . . ." His words trailed off and he shook his head, as if he couldn't go on.

Patience is a virtue I don't have. I wasn't about to spend half the day coaxing crumbs of information from

Grant, so I decided to add a dose of shock therapy to the mix.

"You're in no condition to talk, my friend," I said, getting to my feet. "When you are, give me a buzz. You have my number."

Grant lunged for my hand, crying, "You *can't* go!"

"Then tell me what happened," I said sternly, "without the theatrics."

"All right," he said grudgingly, "but sit down. I'll get a stiff neck if I talk with you looming over me."

I sat.

"You're worse than the constable," Grant muttered, but when he spoke again, his voice was quite steady. "Charles and I returned from London at nine this morning. We took Matisse and Goya for a run on the green, unpacked our bags, sorted through the mail—we did the usual things one does after a trip. At approximately half past nine, I went to my studio to resume work on the family tree. It was then that I discovered that my studio had been turned over." He took a long pull on his G and T, without Charles's assistance, and dabbed the corners of his mouth with a fingertip. "I don't wish to become emotional," he continued, "so I won't describe the scene in great detail. Suffice it to say that my studio was a complete shambles."

"I heard a heartrending shriek," said Charles, "and dashed upstairs to find Grant on the verge of collapse. I brought him out here to recover from the initial shock— the garden is so soothing—then rang the police station in Upper Deeping. A constable arrived at half past ten. He wasn't entirely sympathetic when Grant admitted—"

"It's my fault," Grant murmured, bowing his head. "It's my fault and no other's. You see, Lori, when Charles and I left for London, I . . . I *didn't lock our doors.*"

"So what?" I said. "I never lock my doors. I don't think there's a locked door in the village, except maybe at Fairworth House and that's only because William's new here. Finch isn't a locked-door kind of place."

"That's what we thought," Grant said mournfully. "Until today."

"Today's an aberration. Don't let it destroy your peace of mind." I put a comforting hand on his arm. "Did the constable discover any clues?"

"Not a sausage," said Grant. "I expected him to find footprints or fingerprints or both, but the thunderstorm must have washed away the footprints and the burglar must have worn gloves because the constable didn't find a thing."

"Did he question the villagers?" I asked.

"He did," Charles answered. "But after they bombarded him with stories about a drug lord, a film star, a footballer, a dictator with a taste for trotters, and a taxidermist named Tim Thomson, he concluded that they weren't reliable witnesses."

I groaned softly and buried my face in my hands.

"Before he left, the constable suggested that I compile a complete inventory of the studio's contents and bring it to him in Upper Deeping," said Grant. "At the time, we couldn't tell if anything had been stolen."

"The studio was such a mess, you see," said Charles.

"I felt that I owed it to my customers to clarify the situation as quickly as possible," said Grant, "so I set my shattered feelings aside and reentered the studio. After I returned everything to its proper place, I saw——"

"——beyond a shadow of a doubt," Charles inserted.

"——that something *was* missing," Grant finished dramatically. "It gave me such a turn that Charles had to help me back into the garden before he rang you."

My head came up. "Why did you ring me?"

"You tell her, Charles," said Grant, turning his face away from me. "I simply can't bear to be the bearer of such terrible news."

"I rang you," Charles said somberly, "because the burglar took only one item from Grant's studio: the Fairworthy family tree."

I stared at him in disbelief. "You're joking."

"I wish I were," said Charles.

"But he isn't," Grant chimed in mournfully.

"Why in the world would anyone steal someone else's family tree?" I asked.

"There's a market for everything, Lori," said Grant. "For all we know, there may be a collector out there who salivates at the mere mention of a Victorian illuminated family tree."

"But why would a collector want something so . . . grubby?" I asked, wrinkling my nose.

"Some works of art are more valuable in their original state," Grant replied. "Finicky collectors won't touch items that have been restored by an expert they haven't hired."

"I still don't get it," I said. "How would a collector 'out there' know that the Fairworthy family tree was in your studio?"

Grant studied his fingernails. "I may have mentioned it in the Emporium before we left on Monday, when I picked up a packet of travel tissues." He lifted his eyes to mine. "I couldn't help myself. It was such an exciting find!"

"Word could have spread from the Emporium to the ends of the earth," said Charles. "You know how the villagers talk."

"Have you reported the theft to the police?" I asked.

"Not yet," said Grant. "I wanted to speak with you first, to tell you how dreadfully sorry I am for betraying your trust. I shouldn't have left William's property in an unsecured location."

"Stop it," I chided him. "If you need to blame someone, blame the burglar. If you'd locked your front door, he probably would have jimmied it. We can't live in concrete bunkers because we're terrified that some fool will break a window. I'd rather risk a break-in and see sunlight than live safely in the dark."

"I hope William will feel the same way," Grant said mournfully. "I haven't spoken with him yet, either. I thought you might want to deliver the crushing news to him yourself. It might be less painful, coming from you."

I gazed absently at a cluster of scarlet poppies while I considered the best course of action to take. My first impulse was to race over to Fairworth House and point an accusing finger at the Donovans, but I didn't think such a display would sit well with my father-in-law. He, like Aunt Dimity, would demand that I produce hard evidence to support my accusation, and I didn't have a speck of evidence to connect the Donovans to the theft.

The sound of Peggy Taxman's voice boomed over the garden wall and I glanced toward the front of the cottage, where the villagers were assembled. If I could find someone who'd seen one or both of the Donovans sneaking through Finch in the wee hours of Tuesday morning, Willis, Sr.—and Aunt Dimity—would be more inclined to listen to me. What I needed was an eyewitness.

"Let's hold off on telling William about the burglary," I said. "He's at a critical stage in the negotiations he's conducting for his client and he won't welcome the distraction. And please don't report the theft to the police until you hear from me. William may not want to involve them."

"I understand," said Grant, looking immensely relieved. "Mum's the word until you tell us otherwise."

"Our lips are sealed," said Charles, drawing a finger across his mouth.

"Thanks. I'll be in touch." I stood. "I'm really sorry that you two had such a rotten homecoming."

"We'll get over it," said Grant. "The studio may have been a mess, but nothing was damaged or defaced. After another G and T, I may forget the whole sorry incident." He cocked his head to one side. "I liked your sermon about living in sunlight."

"Is there any other way to live?" I said, smiling.

Charles, Matisse, and Goya walked me to the front door, but Charles hesitated before opening it.

"Brace yourself," he cautioned. "The village paparazzi are about to ambush you."

"I'm counting on it," I said. "If I ask the right questions, I may learn a thing or two your constable overlooked."

"I believe you could give the detective chief inspector himself a run for his money," said Charles.

"We'll see," I said.

I gave Matisse and Goya farewell pats, lifted my chin, and stepped fearlessly into the waiting maelstrom.

Eighteen

"Did Grant have a heart attack?"

"Did the burglar daub foul language on the walls?"

"Did he smash up the furniture?"

"Is Crabtree Cottage *cursed*?"

"No, no, no, and I very much doubt it," I said, wading into the knot of hard-core busybodies who'd resisted the urge to return to their own homes and businesses. "Grant's shaken but he'll be fine, there's no graffiti on the walls, nothing was smashed, and Crabtree Cottage is too beautiful to be cursed."

"I don't know," Mr. Barlow temporized, pursing his lips. "There was that woman who died there a few years ago, and now there's been a burglary. It makes you think."

"It makes me think that life is full of surprises," I said, raising my voice to be heard over the welling murmurs of agreement. "There's not a house in Finch that hasn't had a death associated with it at one time or another."

"Maybe a long time ago," Mr. Barlow allowed, "but not recently."

"In a hundred years, *now* will be a long time ago," I said. "And a burglary can happen anywhere."

"It's unusual for one to happen here," Christine Peacock pointed out.

"I agree," I said. "But what's more unusual is that none of you saw any suspicious activity on the night of the burglary." I surveyed my neighbors' faces. "Come on, people. You know as well as I do that nothing goes unnoticed in Finch. The break-in took place between Monday afternoon and nine o'clock this morning. Think back. One of you must have seen something, and I'm talking about something *real*, not something you made up or heard about secondhand."

Heads turned and feet shuffled and finally George Wetherhead stepped forward. It couldn't have been easy for him. Mr. Wetherhead was the most timid man in Finch.

"I may have seen someone acting suspiciously on Monday night," he admitted, fixing his gaze resolutely on the ground. "Well, on Tuesday morning, really. I got up a little after midnight to fill my hot water bottle because my hip was aching. It always aches when a storm's coming."

The villagers nodded. Most of them could predict the weather by referring to aches and pains in various body parts.

"While I was up," George went on, "I thought I saw someone walking back and forth on the bridge. It was dark, though, and the bridge is at the far end of the green from my house, so I may have imagined it."

"Did you tell the policeman what you saw?" asked Mr. Barlow.

"No," George replied. "Didn't get a chance to, with the rest of you mobbing him. And, like I said, I may have imagined it."

"You're coming with me, George," Mr. Barlow said firmly. "I'm taking you straight to Upper Deeping. You need to make a statement to the investigating officer."

"I don't want to be a pest," George mumbled.

"It's your civic duty to be a pest," said Mr. Barlow. "Come along, now. Best to get it over and done with."

"Um," said Elspeth Binney, raising her hand.

"Yes?" I said, peering intently at her.

"Before you make any statements to the police, George," she said to Mr. Wetherhead, "I should tell you that I went for a stroll on Monday night. Well, on Tuesday morning, really. I was too restless to sleep—I always get restless when a storm's coming—so I thought I'd stretch my legs. It may have been me you saw on the bridge."

Peggy Taxman rounded on her. "What in blazes were you doing, wandering around in the middle of the night, Elspeth Binney? Is your telescope equipped with night vision?"

"I wasn't the only one who was out and about," Elspeth retorted, firing up at once. "And I didn't need a telescope to see who *else* was up late. Ask Millicent what *she* was doing, lurking behind the war memorial."

"I was keeping an eye on *you*," Millicent Scroggins exclaimed. "I got up for a drink of water and saw you sneaking past my cottage. I wanted to find out what you were up to, so I put on my dressing gown and—"

"I wasn't up to anything," Elspeth broke in. "But Opal may have been. *She* was skulking in the doorway of the Emporium."

"I beg your pardon?" said Opal Taylor, blushing

crimson. "I'm sure I don't know what you're talking about."

"Oh, yes, you do," Selena Buxton said heatedly. "I heard your front door open and close at half past twelve, so I got up to make sure nothing was amiss. When I saw you walking toward the bridge, I went after you, to keep you from breaking our agreement."

"What agreement?" asked Mr. Barlow.

"Our agreement to stay away from Fairworth House," said Selena, staring hard at Opal. "If Elspeth hadn't been on the bridge, Opal wouldn't have stopped at the Emporium. She would have sneaked right up to Fairworth and peeked through the windows."

"How *dare* you?" Opal cried melodramatically, clapping a hand to her breast. "I'm not a Peeping Tom!"

"Maybe not," Selena conceded, her eyes narrowing, "but you've been dying to find out if William's new housekeeper is up to snuff. A look through the windows would have told you whether or not she's doing the dusting."

"If you weren't going to Fairworth," Elspeth said to Opal, "where *were* you going?"

"I was following *you*," Opal exploded, bristling. "I thought *you* were going to Fairworth. After your stunt with the telescope, I wouldn't put anything past you."

"Nor would *I* put anything past *you*!" Elspeth swept her arm in an arc that encompassed Selena and Millicent as well as Opal. "The only reason I blocked the bridge in the first place was to protect William from *you*!"

"*Protect William?*" Serena, Millicent, and Opal chorused ferociously, closing in on Elspeth.

I backed away from the battlefield and climbed into the Rover. For one brief, shining moment I'd thought I'd struck gold, but Mr. Wetherhead's lead had turned to lead. He'd evidently seen Elspeth Binney standing on the bridge on Tuesday morning, and the Handmaidens had seen no one but one another. I had no doubt whatsoever that the ladies had rattled off stories about drug lords and dictators in order to divert the constable's attention away from their own nocturnal activities, none of which had had anything to do with the burglary.

I returned to the cottage, deep in thought. Though I had neither an eyewitness report nor a scrap of evidence linking the Donovans to the crime, I had a well-reasoned argument that pointed to the possibility of their guilt. Since my well-reasoned arguments had been known to fizzle ignominiously on past occasions, however, it seemed like a good idea to rehearse this one with Aunt Dimity before presenting it to Willis, Sr.

I dropped my shoulder bag on the hall table, called a greeting to Stanley, who was sleeping in Bill's chair, and went to the study. The ivy covering the windows above the old oak desk glowed like stained glass in the bright sunshine and cast dappled shadows on the drawings Will and Rob had made of their trail ride with Kit.

"I may be jumping to conclusions," I said to Reginald as I slid the blue journal from its shelf, "but I don't think so."

I was too wound up to sit, so I cradled the open journal in my hands as I paced back and forth from desk to doorway.

"Dimity?" I said. "There's been a development."

A development? Shifting shadows swam across the page as Aunt Dimity's handwriting appeared. *Can you be more specific?*

"A burglar broke in to Crabtree Cottage," I said, "and stole the Fairworthy family tree."

Oh, dear. William must be devastated.

"William doesn't know about it yet," I said.

Why ever not?

"Because I asked Grant Tavistock and Charles Bellingham to keep it to themselves until I've had a chance to look into it," I said.

Surely they notified the police.

"The police know about the break-in, but not about the theft," I explained. "If my suspicions pan out, William will want to inform the police himself."

What do you suspect?

"I *know* that Crabtree Cottage was burgled while Grant and Charles were in London," I said. "They left on Monday afternoon and returned at nine o'clock this morning."

Ergo, we have a time frame for the crime.

"We also have a peculiar incident that took place within our time frame," I said. "William heard someone use the elevator at Fairworth House at 2:57 on Tuesday morning."

Yes, I recall the elevator incident. You and William assumed that Deirdre Donovan had used it to reach the attic apartment after staying up half the night, cleaning.

"What if William and I were wrong? What if the Donovans used the elevator to transport the family tree to their apartment? Bear with me, Dimity," I said, before she could lodge a protest. "I've pieced this together very carefully."

If you bring up Declan's red hair or Deirdre's beauty spot, I'll refuse to listen to you.

"I'm offering supposition, not superstition," I assured her.

In that case, you may proceed.

"On Monday, during brunch," I began, "I told William that I'd delivered his grubby masterpiece to a local art restorer named Grant, who lived and worked in a place called Crabtree Cottage. I also told William that Grant and Charles would leave for London on Monday and return to Finch on Wednesday. Deirdre was manning the teapot during brunch. She could have heard the entire conversation."

Go on.

"I identified Crabtree Cottage for Declan by pointing it out to him on Monday, when he dropped me off at Bill's office," I said.

Declan, therefore, knew where to find the so-called masterpiece.

"Exactly," I said. "And on Monday evening, Deirdre could have overheard the most significant tidbit of all."

Did she glean the tidbit from you? You seem to have been instrumental in dispensing vital information to the Donovans.

"William dispensed it this time," I said, "though he didn't realize it. He telephoned me from his study on Monday evening, to tell me that his grimy masterpiece was, in fact, a Victorian illuminated family tree."

Did he catch Deirdre eavesdropping at the study door?

"Nope," I said. "She was *in the study*, serving William a late dinner. By listening to our brunch conversation as well as our telephone conversation, Deirdre could have learned that a Victorian illuminated family tree would be sitting in an unoccupied Crabtree Cottage from Monday to Wednesday."

And in the small hours of Tuesday morning, someone used the elevator at Fairworth House.

"Supposing that my suppositions hold water," I said, choosing my words with great care, "I would *suggest* that Declan carried out the actual robbery. Deirdre would stay behind at Fairworth, in case William rang for a midnight snack or something."

A sensible precaution.

"I *allege*," I continued, "that Declan slipped out of Fairworth, crept into Finch, let himself into Crabtree Cottage, stole the family tree, and returned with it to the attic apartment at 2:57 a.m., using the elevator."

Someone in the village would have seen him.

"You'd think so, wouldn't you?" I said. "Unfortunately, the Handmaidens chose the wee hours of Tuesday morning to play hide-and-seek on the village green."

Were they instituting a new village tradition?

"No," I said, smiling, "they were practicing an ancient one. In other words: They were spying on one another. Each suspected the others of sneaking off to Fairworth in the middle of the night to assess Deirdre's housekeeping skills."

How did they expect to assess Deirdre's housekeeping skills in the middle of the night?

"By pressing their noses to William's windows," I said.

Good grief.

"It wouldn't have worked," I went on, "because Deirdre closes the draperies at night. Even if the Handmaidens had reached Fairworth—which they didn't, because Elspeth Binney was guarding the bridge—they wouldn't have seen anything but yards and yards of fabric."

How disappointing it would have been for them.

"I'm sure they would have consoled themselves by criticizing the drapes," I said dryly. "In any case, the Handmaidens were too busy watching one another to pay attention to anyone else who might have been sneaking around the village."

Declan could have avoided the Handmaidens by wading the river at the shallow spot west of the bridge and taking the back way to Crabtree Cottage. He'd have no trouble climbing the garden wall and letting himself in through the kitchen, assuming the door was unlocked.

"An extremely safe assumption," I confirmed. "Apart from that, Grant and Charles took their dogs with them to London. Since they have no other alarm system, Crabtree Cottage was ripe for the picking." I hesitated. "So . . . what do you think? Have I hit a home run or am I way off base?"

Baseball terminology has never been my forte, Lori, but I can make a rough translation. I'm afraid you haven't quite hit a home run, my dear. You've constructed a persuasive argument, with one glaring omission: Motivation. Why would the Donovans steal something as arcane as a family tree?

"Money," I said bluntly. "According to Grant, there's a market for everything, even Victorian illuminated family trees. Maybe Deirdre got to know a few unscrupulous collectors when she was studying art history at Oxford—the sort of people who won't ask questions when she sells the family tree on the black market."

But why steal it now? Why not wait until the restoration work is complete?

"Grant says that some collectors don't like restored items," I said. "They won't buy a work of art unless it's in its original condition."

Congratulations, Lori, on successfully defending your wicket. You've persuaded me that the Donovans are likely suspects. Will you tell William what you've told me?

"Not yet," I said. "He won't accept a persuasive argument, Dimity. I have to catch the Donovans with their hands in the cookie jar."

William won't allow you to search their apartment, Lori. He would consider it an unwarranted invasion of privacy.

"Then I'll just have to—" I stopped short as the telephone rang. "I'll be right back, Dimity. It may be Bill on the phone."

Take your time, my dear. I'm not going anywhere.

I placed the journal face-up and open upon the desk and picked up the phone. This time, I was surprised to hear my father-in-law's voice instead of my husband's.

"Good afternoon, Lori," said Willis, Sr. "Have you been enjoying your day off?"

"I have," I said. "How's life at Fairworth?"

"Effortless," he replied. "I spent the morning with Lady Sarah and Señor Cocinero in the drawing room, looking at the photographs Lady Sarah took during her trip to Mexico. She took copious photographs and each one prompted a lengthy reminiscence."

"I can imagine," I said, rolling my eyes.

"After a thoroughly nauseating lunch," Willis, Sr., continued, "which Señor Cocinero consumed with evident relish, Lady Sarah and I were treated to a concert of Mexican ballads sung a cappella by none other than Señor Cocinero. Very little has been required of me."

"Or of me," I said ruefully.

"I have need of you now," said Willis, Sr., "but only to answer a few questions."

"Fire away," I said, wondering if he'd heard about the theft.

"My guests retired for their afternoon siestas a short time ago," said Willis, Sr. "I retreated to the study to catch up on some correspondence, but when I approached my desk, I found that my chair was already occupied." He paused. "Did you discuss *Notes on Sheep* with my son?"

"I quoted a few items from it," I said. "I wouldn't really call it a discussion."

"Did you tell him of my interest in Cotswold Lions?" he asked.

"I may have mentioned it to him in passing," I replied. "Why? What has Bill done?"

"Bill visited Fairworth on his way to Heathrow this morning to inform me of Frau Schniering's passing,"

Willis, Sr., explained. "He must have decided that I was in need of a diversion because he played a practical joke on me. He placed a lamb on my chair."

"A lamb?" I said doubtfully.

"It is not alive," said Willis, Sr.

"Bill put a *dead* lamb on your chair?" I exclaimed.

"It is neither living nor dead," Willis, Sr., stated firmly. "It is a *toy*, a somewhat tattered stuffed animal with a faded green ribbon around its neck. It upset Mrs. Donovan considerably."

"Why?" I asked, relieved to know that Bill's famous sense of humor hadn't taken a turn for the ghoulish. "It's just a toy."

"She considers it unsanitary," Willis, Sr., replied. "She wished to dispose of it, but I prevented her. The lamb may be old and worn, but he was well loved once. It would be a pity to consign him to the rubbish bin. No, I will keep him as a symbol of lambs to come."

I smiled when Willis, Sr., ceased referring to the lamb as "it" and couldn't resist asking, "Have you named him?"

"I believe I shall call him Frederick," Willis, Sr., replied thoughtfully, "in honor of the man who wrote *Notes on Sheep*, the work that inspired me to protect a breed that might otherwise vanish from the face of the earth."

"An excellent choice," I replied. "I'm sorry that Bill's prank upset Deirdre, but I'm glad you've had an otherwise peaceful day."

"Tomorrow is Thursday," said Willis, Sr. "After Señor Cocinero departs and Lady Sarah returns to her tearoom, I anticipate an unending succession of peaceful days. I will telephone you when the time comes for you to smuggle Mrs. Pyne out of Fairworth."

"I'll take the booster seats out of the Rover," I said, "and put the king-sized quilt in the backseat." I touched the oak desk for luck. "I don't want to get ahead of myself, William, but I do believe we've managed to fool the entire village."

"I expect the truth to come out at some point," Willis, Sr., said fatalistically. "Until then, I believe we may take credit for perpetrating a successful hoax."

"Was it worth it?" I asked.

"Was it worth enduring a few minor and temporary inconveniences in order to prevent Mrs. Pyne from fleeing Finch in disgrace?" said Willis, Sr. "Yes."

We said good-bye and I hung up, wondering where Bill had obtained the lamb. Will and Rob had a veritable zoo of stuffed animals, but none of them was sheep-shaped.

"He must have borrowed it from a villager," I said to Reginald. "I hope whoever gave it to him doesn't want it back. William has a definite soft spot for his little Frederick."

Reginald's eyes glimmered with quiet amusement in the shadowy room, but I knew that he agreed with me completely.

I put a hand out for the journal, but as I did so, my gaze fell on one of the drawings Will and Rob had made of their trail ride. The drawing depicted a man standing in front of a dense growth of trees. The man wore brown shorts and a short-sleeved white shirt and his head was covered with a flaming shock of bright orange hair.

I stared at the orange-haired man, dumbstruck, while a sparkling new possibility danced across my mind. As I grabbed the telephone and speed-dialed Kit Smith's number, I vowed that I would never again be too self-absorbed to listen to my sons.

Nineteen

"**K**it?" I said as soon as Kit Smith answered his phone. "What trail did you and the boys take yesterday afternoon?"

"Hello, Lori," Kit said mildly. "How are you? I hope you're having a pleasant day."

"I'm having a fantastic day," I said impatiently. "Now, please, for the love of all that's holy, answer my question!"

"We took the new trail," he said. "The one that leads from Anscombe Manor to Fairworth House. Rob and Will were keen to give it a go."

"Did you see Declan Donovan while you were out?" I asked.

"Yes, now that you mention it, we did," he said. "Rob spotted him coming out of William's woods. Will told me who he was and we all waved to him."

"Was he carrying anything?" I asked.

"Nothing," said Kit. "When I first noticed him, he was brushing his hands together, as if he'd gotten them dirty. When he raised his right hand to wave back at us, his palm seemed a bit grubby. It looked to me as though he'd been doing some digging."

I clutched the phone and grimaced with frustration. If I'd listened to the twins' stories about their trail ride or paused to admire their drawings before they'd taken them from the kitchen to the study, I would have known about Declan's jaunt in the woods much sooner. I had no trouble imagining what he'd buried there.

"Lori?" said Kit.

"I'm still here. Listen, Kit," I said urgently. "Would you and Nell do me the most enormous favor? Would you keep the boys with you overnight? Bill's in Germany and there's something I need to do tonight. I'll be out very late, possibly past midnight." I was on the verge of inventing a nocturnal errand, but I could no more lie to Kit Smith than I could to Emma Harris. "I can't explain why right now, but——"

"You don't have to," Kit said gently. "Nell and I will be happy to look after the twins. We'll have a campfire and tell horse stories and make up beds for them in the hayloft."

"They won't want to come home," I said, laughing. "Honestly, you guys are the best honorary aunt and uncle two little boys could ever have. I'll call you as soon as I can in the morning."

"Lori," said Kit, with a trace of worry in his voice. "I don't know what you're about to do and I don't have to know, but if you need someone to watch your back——"

"I'll be fine," I assured him. "But thanks for the offer. And thanks hugely for taking care of Will and Rob. Kiss them good night for me and tell them I'll see them in the morning." I hung up the phone, leaned both hands on the desk, and peered down at the blue journal. "Dimity? What if the Donovans are too clever to keep the family tree in their apartment? What if they've hidden it somewhere else?"

In their van, perhaps?

"Too close to home," I said, shaking my head. "If William or the police suspected them of the burglary, the apartment and the van would be the first places they'd search."

Where, then?

"How about the little forest on William's property?" I asked. "Will, Rob, and Kit saw Declan coming out of the woods yesterday afternoon. He was brushing dirt—or possibly soot—off his hands. I'll bet you anything that he'd just finished stashing the family tree in there."

It would be a safe place to cache a stolen item while negotiating a deal with a potential buyer.

"Which is why I'm going there tonight," I said.

Alone? Is that advisable?

"I'm not going to make a citizen's arrest," I said. "I won't do anything foolish. I'll just watch from a safe distance and wait for the Donovans to incriminate themselves."

But why must you go at night?

"Because a lot of strange things are happening at Fairworth House," I said, "and almost all of them take place at night."

Twilight seems to linger forever in summer months. I had to wait until half past eight for the sun to go down, then wait another hour for true darkness to set in. To keep myself from fidgeting, I prepared the Rover for Thursday's smuggling operation, cleaned the cottage from top to bottom, did four loads of laundry, made three freezable casseroles, fed and watered Stanley, and chatted with Bill about the squabbles that had arisen over the fair division of the farm animals Frau Schniering had kept as pets on her country estate.

I decided to let his father have it out with him about Frederick the lamb, but when Bill asked to speak with Will and Rob, I told him straightforwardly that they were spending the night at Anscombe Manor.

"Why?" he asked.

"I'll be spending the evening at Fairworth," I replied.

"See?" he said, as if he were consoling a weepy five-year-old. "Father can't get along without you."

I didn't contradict him but I didn't tell him that Willis, Sr., would be unaware of my presence, either. Bill could sometimes be a tad overprotective and I didn't want him to fret unnecessarily.

As soon as it was dark enough, I rolled my bicycle into the lane and pedaled it toward the village. I was dressed in a black, hooded sweatshirt, black jeans, and black boots, in part to ward off the evening chill, but also to make myself less visible to prying eyes. I carried a flashlight in the wicker basket strapped to my handlebars and a cell phone in my jeans pocket, programmed with the telephone number of the Upper Deeping police station.

Though the moon shone brightly in the puddles that still dotted the lane, I wasn't overly concerned about being seen by the villagers. After the hide-and-seek fiasco, I was confident that my neighbors, and the Handmaidens in particular, would be too embarrassed to leave their homes at night. The Donovans, on the other hand, might have a very good reason to be out and about in the wee hours, and I didn't wish to be seen by them.

When I reached the mouth of Willis, Sr.'s drive, I concealed the bicycle in a clump of bushes and went the rest of the way on foot, walking on the grass verge instead of the gravel and pointing the flashlight downward. As soon as Fairworth came into view, I switched off the flashlight and crept stealthily to the stables.

I hunted around for a patch of dry ground, then sat with my back against an exterior wall and scanned the open pasture that lay between the house and the woods. If Declan took anything into the dense stand of trees or retrieved anything from it, I would see him.

I couldn't see into the house, but the lamplit drapes on the ground floor indicated that those within hadn't yet gone upstairs to bed. I envisioned Willis, Sr., sitting patiently through another barrage of Mexican ballads while his mind drifted contentedly to the moment when he would finally have his new house all to himself.

My heart twinged a little when I remembered that this might be Sally's last evening with Henrique, and my back twinged even more when it recalled the amount of scrubbing and polishing I'd done before leaving the cottage. I vowed to reward myself with a steamy bubble bath when my task was done, then pulled my hood over my head, nestled my cold hands in my sweatshirt pockets, and settled in for the long haul.

I woke with a start some time later, with an unfamiliar hand clamped over my mouth.

"It's Kit," Kit Smith said quietly and removed his hand.

I collapsed against the wall, panting with terror, while my heart tried to pound its way through my rib-cage. Then I whacked Kit on the shoulder.

"For Pete's sake," I said in a furious whisper. "You scared me half to death! Between you and Rainey, I'll be lucky to survive the summer! What are you *doing* here?"

"Nell sent me," he replied, sitting next to me.

"How did Nell know . . ." My words trailed off. Kit's wife had always had a fey quality to her, even as a young child. It wasn't entirely absurd to imagine that Nell's uncanny sixth sense had guided Kit to my location. "Did Nell have a . . . a *premonition* that I would be here?"

"Yes," Kit said solemnly. "After the break-in at Crab-tree Cottage this morning, you called in a panic, asking if I'd seen Declan Donovan carrying something near William's woods and telling me that you'd be out late for some mysterious reason. Nell's psychic powers enabled her to connect the break-in to Declan and the woods and to surmise that you might be spending the night somewhere in the vicinity of Fairworth House."

"Okay, so I'm not opaque," I acknowledged ruefully.

"You're as transparent as glass," Kit concurred. "Nell and I both hear alarm bells whenever you use the phrase 'I'll be fine,' so she sent me to watch your back whether you want me to or not. I drove to the cottage first, to make sure you'd gone, then followed your tire tracks to Fairworth."

"I left tracks?" I said, surprised.

"Between puddles," said Kit. "I wouldn't have noticed if I hadn't been looking for them. I left the pickup at the mouth of the drive and walked in. I've been combing the woods for the past hour, looking for you. When I didn't find you there, I circled the house until I heard someone snoring."

"I don't snore," I stated firmly.

"I heard someone purring," Kit corrected himself, his teeth showing white in the moonlight as he grinned. "And found you, dressed like a cat burglar and sleeping like a kitten. I'm sorry I startled you, but you wouldn't have thanked me if I'd let you scream."

"I wouldn't have," I admitted.

Kit, too, was dressed in dark clothing, though he'd used a black stocking cap instead of a hood to conceal his gray hair. As he settled his long, lean body more comfortably against the stable's stone wall, he placed an unlit flashlight on the ground between us. He gave me a friendly look, folded his hands in his lap, and peered up at the stars.

"Lovely evening," he said.

"It's half past twelve," I said, glancing at my watch. "Technically, it's a lovely morning."

"Looks as though everyone's gone to bed," he said, nodding at the house.

I studied the darkened windows and murmured, "No all-night cleaning binge for Deirdre. She must be slacking off. Or," I added ominously, "she has a more important job to pull off tonight."

Kit turned his face to the stars again.

"Don't you want to know what I'm talking about?" I said, willing him to ask.

"I'm no psychic," Kit said, tilting his head to one

side, "but deductive reasoning suggests that you're staking out the house because you believe the Donovans had something to do with the break-in."

"I do," I said quickly. "I'm convinced that they burgled Crabtree Cottage because . . ."

For the next twenty minutes I luxuriated in depicting Deirdre and Declan Donovan as a pair of charming con artists who'd gone to extreme lengths to gain Willis, Sr.'s trust in order to set him up for a robbery. It was such a relief to unburden myself that I went through the whole of my persuasive argument in a rush, scarcely pausing to take a breath. I didn't say a word about Sally Pyne or Henrique, but I said quite a few about the Donovans.

I explained to Kit that Deirdre had moved the settee, the Chippendale armchair, the brass compass, and the snuffboxes in order to make it difficult for Willis, Sr., to keep track of items she and her husband planned to steal. I recounted the revealing conversations I'd had with Willis, Sr., concerning the family tree and pointed out that Deirdre had been on hand to overhear both of them. I mentioned the elevator and Deirdre's degree in art history and finished with a flourish, telling Kit without demur that Declan had stolen the family tree from Crabtree Cottage and stashed it in the woods.

"And that's why I'm here," I concluded. "If Declan leaves the house and makes for the woods, I'll follow him. If I'm lucky, I'll catch him red-handed with his ill-gotten gains."

Kit pursed his lips. "I don't suppose it crossed your mind that Declan might object to being caught red-handed. I don't suppose it even occurred to you that you might be putting yourself in danger."

I pulled my cell phone from my pocket and waggled it in Kit's face. "I have the police station's phone number on speed dial."

"I feel much better now," said Kit, smiling wryly, "considering that it will take the Upper Deeping police at least twenty minutes to get here—probably longer, since it's the middle of the night and they'll be half asleep when you ring them. While you're waiting for them to arrive, you can discuss Declan's future with him. I'm sure he'll be eager to chat with you about prison life."

"I'm not a complete idiot," I retorted. "I won't pounce on Declan. I'll hang back, call the police, and keep him under observation until—"

"Lori," Kit said, gripping my arm. "Look."

I followed his gaze and saw someone fling open a set of draperies in the drawing room. I leaned forward, straining to see, and felt a shiver trickle down my spine as the moonlight illuminated the gaunt, hollow-eyed features of an elderly woman. She wore an old-fashioned white nightdress with beribboned sleeves and a high, frilled collar and her gleaming white hair fell in rippling waves almost to her waist. Her ribbons fluttered and her long hair seemed to float behind her as she moved from window to window, opening drapes, then drifted, wraithlike, into the shadows.

"Deirdre?" Kit asked.

"Definitely not," I replied. "Deirdre's in her thirties and she has chestnut hair. I have no idea who—"

"Lori!" Kit cried.

He jumped to his feet and hauled me to mine, pointing at a rear window in the attic apartment. I watched, horrorstruck, as a cloud of smoke billowed out of the window and rose lazily toward the night sky.

Fairworth was on fire.

Twenty

"Fire!" I bellowed, racing for the front door. "Get up! Get out! Fire!"

"Call the police!" Kit shouted as he sped past me. "They'll call the fire department."

"Keys," I hollered, pulling mine from my pocket and tossing them to Kit, who swung around, caught them deftly in one hand, and kept running.

I punched the speed-dial as I ran and spoke with a placid constable who snapped out of his lethargy when I screamed in his ear. He promised to rouse the Upper Deeping fire brigade immediately and to send it to Fairworth House.

I shoved the phone in my pocket and hurled myself up the front steps to find Kit trying each of the keys in turn while pounding on the front door and shouting. I snatched the keys from him, thrust the correct one into the lock, and let both of us into the entrance hall.

"Find the old woman," I said, pelting toward the main staircase. "I'll get the others."

I took the stairs three at a time, yelling as I went. When I reached the second floor corridor, Willis, Sr., Sally, and Henrique were emerging from their respective suites, pulling robes over their nightclothes.

"Fire!" I wheezed, clutching a stitch in my side. "Get out!"

Henrique hustled Sally downstairs, but when I

turned to dash upstairs, Willis, Sr., called for me to stop.

"Wait," he said, putting a hand to his ear. "Listen."

I thumped the bannister in frustration as the elevator's unmistakable hum came to us from the rear of the house.

"For pity's sake," I roared, exasperated. "Don't the Donovans know they're not supposed to use an elevator during a fire?"

"Apparently not," Willis, Sr., said calmly. "Come along, Lori. Let us evacuate in an orderly fashion."

Willis, Sr., descended the staircase expeditiously but with dignity and I followed after him, wondering if it would be the last time I'd walk down Fairworth's gleaming marble stairs. When we reached the entrance hall, I was dismayed to see Sally, Henrique, and Kit standing in a half circle before the old woman, pleading with her to come with them. Though the woman was painfully thin, she was tall enough to look Kit in the eye and she didn't seem to be budging.

"Leave the house?" she said, in a refined, upper-class drawl. "Don't be ridiculous. Why should I leave the house?"

"A fire has broken out upstairs," Kit explained.

"I know where the fire is, young man," the woman said tartly. "I lit it."

"You . . . lit it?" Kit said hesitantly.

"Naturally," said the woman. She lifted the hem of her nightdress and wiggled her bony toes. "My feet were cold."

"I beg your pardon, madam," said Willis, Sr., stepping forward. "I do not wish to seem intrusive, but would you be so kind as to tell me who you—"

At that moment, Deirdre and Declan burst into the entrance hall and skidded to a halt next to Willis, Sr.

"Aunt Augusta!" Deirdre cried.

"Aunt Augusta?" said Willis, Sr.

"Aunt Augusta," Declan said, with a weary sigh.

"Now that you know *my* name, young man," said the old woman, pointing her long, thin nose at Willis, Sr. "I should very much like to know *yours*."

"Can we postpone the meet-and-greet?" I said, glancing nervously up the staircase. "There's a fire—"

"There's no fire," Declan interrupted.

"We saw smoke," Kit and I chorused.

"Where there's smoke, there's not always fire," said Declan. "Aunt Augusta forgot to open the flue in her fireplace. I've taken care of it."

"But I've already called out the fire brigade," I protested. "They're on their way."

"Call them again," said Willis, Sr. "Inform them, with my apologies, that their services will not be required this evening. Mr. Donovan, please fetch a wrap and some slippers for your aunt, then light a fire in the drawing room. Mrs. Donovan, tea, please, as quick as you can. Madam," he said, making a courtly bow to the old woman, "would you do me the honor of accompanying me to the drawing room?"

"You have a take-charge attitude, young man." Aunt Augusta eyed Willis, Sr., with gruff admiration. "You remind me of my cousin Ernest—he was killed in Burma, you know—but you don't sound like him. You have an

American accent. A soldier, are you? An officer, I'll wager. I know all about American officers." She twinkled coquettishly at Willis, Sr., raised a frail, liver-spotted hand, and pinched his blushing cheek. "Rascals, every one. Don't look so shocked, Deirdre," she added haughtily as Willis, Sr., escorted her into the drawing room. "A woman without a past is like a fruitcake without brandy—insipid!"

Deirdre didn't seem shocked. She seemed crestfallen. She bowed her head, took her lower lip between her teeth, and went to the kitchen without meeting anyone's eye. I turned to herd Sally and Henrique back upstairs and into their rooms, but I was too late. Sally had already pulled Henrique into the drawing room, spurred on by her unquenchable thirst for tittle-tattle. I looked at Kit.

"Sally's looking well," he observed.

"She's in disguise," I told him. "It's top secret."

"She didn't seem to mind being seen by me," he said.

"She knows her secret is safe with you," I said. "You don't gossip."

"Ah." He nodded. "And Aunt Augusta? Is she top secret, too?"

"Your guess is as good as mine," I replied. I reached for my cell phone and waved him into the drawing room. "Go ahead, join the gang. I'll be in as soon as I've pacified Constable Sleepyhead."

The constable was none too pleased to learn that I'd ruined his otherwise tranquil night shift with a false alarm.

"The men'll be all the way to Hodge Farm by now," he complained.

"Can you bring them back?" I asked meekly.

"Oh, I can bring them back all right," he allowed grudgingly. "But they won't like it. All that adrenaline pumping through their veins for nothing? It's a waste of resources, that's what it is."

I soothed his ruffled feelings by pledging a substantial sum to the firemen's charitable fund, said good-bye, and walked into what had to be the strangest pajama party in Fairworth's history.

Moonlight streamed through the windows to mingle with firelight and the warm glow of several lamps. Everyone but the Donovans and the mysterious Aunt Augusta sat with their backs to the windows, facing the center of the room. Kit and I alone were fully dressed. The others wore a mixed bag of night attire.

Willis, Sr., who'd seated himself in the Chippendale armchair, was resplendent in a paisley silk dressing gown, neatly pressed pajamas, and slippers made of supple Italian leather. Sally, perched hip-to-hip with Henrique on a Regency chaise longue, looked like a little girl playing dress-up in her sparkly tiara, her baby-blue quilted bathrobe, and her feathery white mules. Henrique, the traveler, wore packable slippers and a lightweight robe over loose-fitting, coffee-colored pajamas.

Deirdre's chestnut hair fell down her back in a tangle of disordered curls, but she and Declan were dressed almost identically, in cheap velour bathrobes, baggy striped pajamas, and nondescript brown slippers. They sat directly across from Willis, Sr., in a pair of Chippendale side chairs, but their eyes were fixed on the floor.

Aunt Augusta sat rigidly upright in a Gainsborough

chair that had been placed near the marble hearth, gazing vacantly into the flames. She'd donned a pair of bulky knitted bed socks and enfolded herself in a voluminous white duvet. Kit had stationed himself on a footstool beside Aunt Augusta, as if he were keeping watch over her.

It was odd enough to see a group of silent, pajama-clad adults sipping tea before a roaring fire in the small hours of the morning. Odder still was the tableau that captured my attention the moment I entered the room. In the center of the Aubusson carpet, a fluffy, cream-colored toy lamb with a faded green ribbon around his neck sat at the head of a line of small, silver sheep, as if he were waiting for a shepherd to open the gate to the next pasture.

"Frederick?" I inquired, looking from the sheep to Willis, Sr.

"Good name," Aunt Augusta said abruptly. "I never gave him a proper name. Called him Lamby. Frederick's much better. He'll be called Frederick from now on, after Grandpapa."

"Aunt Augusta presented her lamb to me anonymously, as a gift," Willis, Sr., explained to me. "She placed him in my study while the rest of us were asleep."

"Deirdre tells me you're bringing sheep back to Fairworth, young man," said Aunt Augusta. "Excellent notion. They'll keep the pastures nice and tidy."

"What's Frederick doing with your salt and pepper shakers?" I asked, sinking into the chair next to Willis, Sr.'s.

"Playing," Aunt Augusta answered in a softer, less

snappish voice. "Mama lets me play with the sheep and Papa lets me play with his snuffboxes. Pretty things. Shiny."

"And the brass compass?" Willis, Sr., asked gently. "Does Papa let you play with it, too?"

"The compass isn't a toy, young man," Aunt Augusta said sternly, shaking her head. "Papa brought it home with him from the war. We keep it with the maps, of course." She sipped her tea and lapsed into silence.

Sally and Henrique exchanged meaningful looks, Kit gazed compassionately at Aunt Augusta, and the Donovans stared at their slippers. Willis, Sr., placed his cup and saucer on the table at his elbow, tented his fingers over his paisley dressing gown, and gazed at the young couple.

"I have, it seems," he said quietly, "been the unwitting host of an unacknowledged guest."

"I didn't invite her," said Aunt Augusta, glancing over her shoulder at Sally. "Why is she wearing a tiara at this time of night? Is it her birthday? And who is that man next to her? Reminds me of the Spanish ambassador I met in Adelaide. Wonderful dancer. Did you invite them, Ernest?"

"Yes, madam," said Willis, Sr. "They are friends of mine."

"Aunt Augusta," said Declan. "Perhaps we should let Deirdre talk for a while."

"I'm not stopping her, am I?" said Aunt Augusta, and resumed her contemplation of the fire.

"Mrs. Donovan," said Willis, Sr., "you have our undivided attention."

Deirdre straightened her shoulders, folded her hands in her lap, and faced Willis, Sr., squarely.

"Before I start," she said, "please allow me to apologize for taking advantage of your kindness and for concealing the truth from you. I wouldn't have done things differently, but I'm sorry nonetheless."

"I accept your apology," said Willis, Sr., "and I look forward to hearing why it was made."

"My maiden name is Deirdre Augusta Fairworthy," Deirdre began, "but I'm only distantly related to Aunt Augusta. Technically, she's a cousin rather than an aunt."

"Did she grow up here?" asked Willis, Sr.

"She was born in Fairworth House," Deirdre replied, "and she lived here until the age of ten, when she was sent off to boarding school. She never spent any length of time at Fairworth after that. After boarding school came finishing school in Switzerland, then a secretarial job in London, then the war."

"In 1940, Fairworth was requisitioned by the army," said Declan, "to be used as a convalescent home. By the time it was released, Aunt Augusta's parents could no longer afford to live in it, so they sold it."

"At the end of the war," Deirdre continued, "Aunt Augusta married an Australian soldier and moved with him to his country. They had no children, so after her husband died, she came back to England to share a small house in Bromley with her sister. When her sister died, she was passed from one relative to another until she ended up with my parents." A defensive note entered her voice as she continued, "My mother and father are busy professionals—"

"They put her in a nursing home," Declan interjected bitterly.

"And we took her out," said Deirdre, lifting her chin. "Aunt Augusta came to live with us in Ireland a year after we purchased the guesthouse."

"Family's family," Declan declared, "for better and for worse. We were making good money and we worked at home, so it was no trouble keeping her with us. And, truth be told, she wasn't quite as far gone as she is now."

"Do you know what's wrong with her?" I asked.

"She was diagnosed with senile dementia when she was in her early seventies," Deirdre replied. "I don't know what the diagnosis would be today and I don't really care. It may sound freakish to you, but I've grown to love her just as she is."

"It is not freakish, Señora," Henrique said gravely. "To love someone as she is, this is the very essence of love."

Sally looked up at him with a glimmer of hope in her eyes and Deirdre acknowledged his words with a gracious nod.

"Her state of mind is unpredictable," Declan admitted. "One moment she's anchored in the here and now, and the next she's time-traveling. It can be disconcerting if you're not used to it."

"Time-traveling?" Aunt Augusta's chuckle was surprisingly deep and hearty. "Why don't you come straight out with it, boy? Tell them I'm gaga and have done with it."

"She's gaga," said Declan, winking at her. "Round the bend."

"Loopy," Aunt Augusta murmured and turned her smiling face to the fire.

Deirdre entwined her hand in Declan's and resumed her tale.

"You know what happened next," she said. "Our dream fell apart. During the last year, when we were struggling to keep the guesthouse afloat, Aunt Augusta became restive. She pleaded with us to take her home to Fairworth."

"We told her it was impossible," said Declan. "As the months passed, she grew quieter and quieter and finally stopped talking altogether. She became so feeble that we had to get a wheelchair for her. It was as if she'd given up."

"Is that why you bought the Renault van?" I asked. "To accommodate the wheelchair?"

Declan nodded. "With the guesthouse eating up our savings, it was the best we could afford."

"In May, shortly after we'd sold the guesthouse, my mother mentioned that an American gentleman had purchased Fairworth," said Deirdre. "And Declan came up with a . . . a madcap scheme."

"Our dream had failed," said Declan, "but I thought we might be able to make Aunt Augusta's dream come true."

"We made a few inquiries," Deirdre went on, "and we found out that Fairworth's new owner was looking for live-in help. We registered with Davina Trent's agency, making it clear that we would work only in a country house that had separate staff accommodations. She sent us to you."

"Your late arrival was intentional, I presume," said Willis, Sr.

"We intended to arrive after dark, yes, but not after midnight," said Declan, rolling his eyes. "We didn't have to invent the story about the Renault breaking down. It breaks down with spectacular regularity."

"But you hoped to convey Aunt Augusta from the van to the house under cover of darkness," Willis, Sr., clarified.

"We didn't think you'd hire us if we wheeled her into the study," said Declan.

I snapped my fingers and pointed at the Donovans. "That's why you wouldn't let Bill help you to unload the van. He thought you felt awkward, asking the boss's son to carry your stuff, but you were just getting him out of the way so you could move Aunt Augusta without being seen."

"Bingo," said Declan.

"What would you have done had I not hired you?" asked Willis, Sr.

"The possibility never crossed our minds." Declan smiled wryly. "There are two things you learn when you run a guesthouse: You learn to read people and you learn to please people. With all due respect, sir, we had you pegged within five minutes of meeting you."

"Apart from that," Deirdre said, elbowing her husband in the ribs, "we'd been coached very thoroughly by Davina Trent. Forgive me for saying so, sir, but you'd rejected so many applicants by then that she was at the end of her tether. She was desperate for us to make a good impression, so she made quite sure that we understood what would be expected of us."

"Mrs. Trent could not have prepared you for the"—
Willis, Sr., gave Sally and Henrique a sidelong glance—
"additional duties that would be thrust upon you."

"We came here expecting to look after a single gentleman," said Deirdre, "and we found ourselves looking
after three people with, um, special dietary require-
ments. I've lost count of the number of meals I've cooked
since Mr. Cocinero arrived, on top of doing the housework to your high standards and checking in on Aunt
Augusta. To be perfectly honest, sir, I've never been so
exhausted in my life. When I went to bed, I slept as if I'd
been drugged."

"I've had to do the weeding, the mowing, the raking, the trimming, and the sweeping single-handedly,"
said Declan, "in between running errands and conducting the wildflower survey."

"What wildflower survey?" I asked.

"Your father-in-law asked me to map the wildflowers growing in the stand of trees at the northeast corner
of the estate," Declan replied. "I hunted around in there
on Tuesday afternoon, sir, and I found the orchids you
mentioned."

"They are exquisite, are they not?" said Willis, Sr.

"That they are, sir," said Declan.

I caught Kit's eye and conceded with a small shrug
that I'd been wrong. Declan hadn't been hiding anything in the woods on Tuesday. He'd been searching for
wild orchids.

"We're not complaining, sir," Deirdre was saying.
"We're explaining why we've slept so soundly for the past
few nights. We weren't aware of what was going on

around us at night, which is why it took us a while to realize that Aunt Augusta had regained the use of her legs."

"Deirdre and I were dead to the world," said Declan, "when she came downstairs on Sunday night and rearranged some of your furniture."

"The settee and the armchair," I said, gazing at Deirdre with fresh understanding. "Now I know why you looked so confused when William asked you if you'd moved the furniture."

"I was gobsmacked," Deirdre confirmed. "I had to come up with a believable story on the fly, then run upstairs to have a chat with Aunt Augusta. She admitted quite readily that she could walk."

"She claims that being back at Fairworth has healed her," Declan put in. "And why not? Happiness is good for your health."

"We were delighted by her recovery, of course," said Deirdre, "but it did complicate matters. She startled us awake on Monday night by cranking up the volume on our sound system."

"Benny Goodman," I said.

"She's Benny's biggest fan," said Declan.

"The King of Swing," murmured Aunt Augusta, tapping her foot to a melody only she could hear.

"We unplugged the machine," said Deirdre, "and fell back into bed. As soon as we were asleep, she came downstairs to play with the snuffboxes and to move the brass compass from the billiards room to the map case in the library."

"Where it belongs," Aunt Augusta muttered. "What sort of fool puts a compass in a billiards room?"

"I found her playing choo-choo trains with the snuff-boxes at three o'clock in the morning," said Declan. "I put her back to bed with strict orders to stay put for the rest of the night."

"Pish tush," Aunt Augusta said, waving her hand dismissively. "I'll do as I please in my own home."

"You have always done as you pleased in your home, have you not, Augusta?" said Willis, Sr., eyeing her shrewdly. "I believe you did as you pleased a long time ago, when you were a little girl, before you left for boarding school."

I caught Kit's eye and shrugged, mystified. Though I sensed that Willis, Sr., was leading the witness, I had no idea where he was taking her.

"Would you like to tell us, Augusta?" said Willis, Sr. "Would you like to tell us what you did with your mama's shiny silver sheep and your papa's pretty snuff-boxes?"

"I hid them," Aunt Augusta said proudly. "I hid them with Grandpapa's book and Papa's compass and the family tree Mama painted." Her expression clouded over. "There was talk of selling Fairworth, of auctioning its contents to pay death duties—what utter nonsense!—so I hid my treasures in the stables." She sighed. "I meant to come back for them, but I never did. Life moves so fast, so very fast, and we're swept along like dried leaves in the wind."

Silence fell, save for the snap and crackle of the burning logs. Kit reached up to pull the duvet more closely around Aunt Augusta's spare shoulders. Deirdre refilled everyone's cups. Declan went to stir the fire.

Willis, Sr., contemplated his tented fingers. Sally looked thoughtful and a slight frown creased Henrique's forehead.

"We're very sorry, sir," Deirdre murmured, resuming her seat.

"You apologized at the beginning of your remarkable testimony," Willis, Sr., observed. "Does your second apology signal its conclusion? If so, I feel compelled to point out that your confession is woefully incomplete. You, Mr. Donovan, have failed to answer an indisputably significant question."

"What question would that be, sir?" said Declan.

"Why," Willis, Sr., said calmly, "did you break into Crabtree Cottage and steal the Fairworthy family tree?"

Twenty-One

I jumped as if scalded.

"How did you find out about the robbery?" I demanded, rounding on Willis, Sr.

He gave me a look that was almost pitying. "Need you ask? You have told me on countless occasions that secrets do not remain secret for very long in Finch. You of all people should have known better than to try to keep one from me."

"Grant spilled the beans, didn't he?" I said, my eyes narrowing.

"Mr. Tavistock is in a fragile emotional state," Willis, Sr., acknowledged. "When I telephoned him after dinner to ask for a progress report, he lost his composure completely and insisted on giving me an unexpurgated account of the unfortunate events that transpired at Crabtree Cottage while he and Mr. Bellingham were in London."

"I wonder how many gin and tonics he'd tossed back before you called," I grumbled.

"In vino veritas," Willis, Sr., said loftily, and turned his attention to the Donovans. "I note that you do not deny embarking on a sordid life of crime. Am I to assume, therefore, that you are guilty as charged?"

"Please excuse me, sir," Deirdre said abruptly. "I have something to show you. I'll be right back."

She stood and left the room, her brown robe swirling behind her. A moment later I heard the distant hum of the elevator.

"The break-in, Mr. Donovan?" prompted Willis, Sr.

"It . . . it wasn't a break-in," Declan temporized. "It was more of a walk-in. Doesn't anyone lock their doors around here?"

"No," Sally and I said simultaneously.

"I do," said Willis, Sr.

"The exception that proves the rule," I pronounced, and Sally nodded her agreement.

"I didn't damage anything," Declan went on. "I wanted to delay a full-on police investigation, so I made it look as though Mr. Tavistock's studio had been properly turned over. I figured that, if the studio was in disarray, it'd take him longer to figure out what had gone missing. But I didn't break so much as a pencil point."

"Your respect for Mr. Tavistock's property will no doubt count in your favor," Willis, Sr., said dryly, "but there is still the small matter of the theft."

"What a nightmare." Declan leaned his head in his hands. "I thought it'd be a doddle to sneak through the village at two o'clock in the morning, but the entire place was crawling with women. I had to wade the river to avoid the short, skinny one marching back and forth on the bridge, and after that it was like being inside a pinball machine. Every time I turned around, there was another woman creeping from pillar to post. It was all I could do to avoid bumping into them!" He raised his head and looked around the room imploringly. "Is it like that every night?"

I opened my mouth to speak, but Sally Pyne cut me off.

"Depends on the weather," she said knowledgeably. "On a fine summer night, you'll usually find someone out taking the air. Village folk aren't afraid to wander about after dark, the way city folk are. We, er"—she glanced self-consciously at Henrique—"I mean to say, *they* take an interest in things, too. The villagers know what Finch sounds like and if they hear something out of the ordinary, they get up to investigate."

"Interfering pack of busybodies," Aunt Augusta said with a contemptuous sniff. "Can't adjust one's garter without it making the rounds."

Kit raised a hand to his mouth to cover his smile.

"I did take the family tree, Mr. Willis," said Declan, "because—"

"He took it because I panicked," Deirdre stated firmly. She stood framed by the doorway for a moment, then marched into the room, carrying the grubby masterpiece that had once soiled Willis, Sr.'s pristine study. "I asked Declan to steal the family tree, sir. I believe you'll understand why after you've seen it."

I winced when she placed the painting on the white marble mantel shelf, but realized at once that my fears were groundless. The worst of the soot had been removed, as had the broken glass. The gilt frame was far from immaculate, but I could detect a muted gleam of gold through the residual grime, and the calligraphy as well as the painted images could be seen as if through a fine layer of darkened lacquer.

The Fairworthy family tree wasn't a conventional

chart recording the names and relationships of succeeding generations in minute detail. It was a true work of art. An ancient oak tree in full leaf stood tall against a pale sky, with the tops of lesser trees just visible on the horizon. Miniature portraits labeled in flowing calligraphy hung like glimmering oval ornaments along the oak's twisted branches or stood solidly among its gnarled roots.

Deirdre backed away from the hearth, but Willis, Sr., and I rose as one and approached it, drawn to the extraordinary artifact like moths to a flame. The names Augusta and Frederick were repeated in every generation, but I was less interested in the names than in the faces. There weren't enough portraits to account for the entire Fairworthy family. The artist had chosen instead to commemorate a select group of men and women who had, I imagined, made the most meaningful contributions to the family's good fortune.

"Our rise in the world began in the fourteenth century, during the reign of Edward the Third," Aunt Augusta informed us. "Sheep made us. We raised them, sheared them, and spun the finest wool from their fleeces. We built mills and exported fabrics to more countries than I can name. We didn't sit on our backsides like the lazy, grab-all aristocracy. We were the hardworking merchants who made England a force to be reckoned with."

"Marvelous," Willis, Sr., murmured, peering closely at a miniature identified as "Frederick Frances Fairworthy, Author of *Notes on Sheep.*"

I stood on tiptoe to drink in the wealth of details in

the women's portraits. The artist had taken great pains to depict the fashions of each period accurately. The elaborate head wrappings, bejeweled hairnets, seed pearl headdresses, and powdered wigs adorning early generations of Fairworthy women stood in stark contrast to the severe and sober hairstyle worn by the Victorian matron whose image hung from the tree's tallest branch.

Though the women's fashions reflected different eras, their features were strikingly similar. The artist had elected to paint all the faces from the same angle, as if to underscore the resemblance. Each woman had high cheekbones, a strong, straight nose, shapely lips, and almond-shaped eyes, and each had a prominent mole near the corner of her right eye.

"Mama painted it," Aunt Augusta said, gazing affectionately at the family tree. "She wrote the names as well. It was the sort of thing women did in those days—needlework and painting and calligraphy. Busy hands are happy hands, she used to say."

"Your mother was a gifted artist," said Willis, Sr., with heartfelt sincerity.

"Papa used to tease her," said Aunt Augusta. "He scolded her for putting her own face into every portrait. But Fairworthy women have always looked alike. It's what comes of inbreeding." She chuckled heartily and looked from image to image, as if she were reacquainting herself with old friends.

I studied her upturned face in the firelight. Though her skin had lost its luster, her bone structure all but shouted her allegiance to the Fairworthy clan, and when she tilted her head to one side, I discerned a faded mole half hidden in the wrinkles near her right eye.

Deirdre crossed to stand beside Willis, Sr.

"I know from old family photographs Aunt Augusta brought with her that I look almost exactly as she did when she was my age," she said. "When Aunt Augusta told me that the faces in the family tree looked like hers, I panicked, because it meant that those faces would also look like mine."

"Deirdre was afraid," said Declan, leaving his chair to put a protective arm around his wife. "She was afraid that, when you saw the resemblance, you'd realize that she was a Fairworthy."

"Once you made the connection," said Deirdre, "you'd be bound to wonder why I'd returned to Fairworth without declaring my true identity, and you'd suspect me of having ulterior motives."

"Which you had," Willis, Sr., pointed out.

Deirdre clasped her hands together pleadingly. "Yes, but we never meant—"

"Please forgive the intrusion," Henrique broke in. His slight frown deepened to a scowl as he got to his feet and strode over to plant himself, arms akimbo, before Deirdre and Declan. "I am a guest in this house and I do not wish to interfere, but I can no longer hold my tongue. I must ask you: Why do you speak only to Señor Willis? Why do you make no apology to Lady Sarah? It is she who employs you, no? It is her trust you have betrayed."

"Never mind, Henrique," Sally said lightly. "I leave all of my staffing problems to Cousin William."

She darted over and began to tug her gallant defender back with her to the chaise longue, but she'd taken no more than a step when she looked up, gave a horrified squeal, and spun in a queer little pirouette that left her huddling behind Henrique.

I scanned the room to see what had frightened her and beheld a vision that made my blood run cold.

Peggy Taxman and the four Handmaidens stood shoulder-to-shoulder, their arms folded and their faces like thunder, peering beadily through the window at Sally Pyne.

"Oh, dear," said Willis, Sr. "The jig, it seems, is up."

Twenty-Two

"**G**ood God, what's gotten into the woman?" Aunt Augusta turned her head to leer saucily at Henrique. "Pinch her bottom, did you, Señor?"

Henrique looked affronted. "Señora, I would never—"

"Shall I answer the door, sir?" asked Deirdre.

"No, thank you, Mrs. Donovan. I shall attend to it. Mr. Donovan? Christopher?" Willis, Sr., always used Kit's given name rather than his nickname. "Please bring five chairs from the dining room and arrange them in a row at a right angle to my daughter-in-law's chair. Mrs. Donovan? I believe we shall need a larger pot of tea. Please, Mrs. Pyne, have a seat and attempt to control your emotions. Lori, close your mouth. I shall return in due course."

He flicked an index finger at the apparitions in the window to indicate that he would meet them at the front door, then left the room. Kit and Declan went in search of chairs and Deirdre went to the kitchen. Henrique coaxed Sally to return with him to the chaise longue. I closed my mouth and stumbled dejectedly to my chair.

It's over, I thought numbly. The fantasy world we'd constructed to safeguard Sally's reputation was about to be reduced to rubble. The web of lies we'd woven would be ripped to shreds, Sally would be exposed as a fraud, and Henrique would realize that the woman he loved had deceived him. Sally's heart would be broken beyond repair. She would leave Finch in disgrace, taking her jam doughnuts and her delightful granddaughter with her. One more day, I told myself, and we would have been home-free. Aunt Dimity's absurd and glorious scheme, the greatest act of deception ever perpetrated on the good people of Finch, had come painfully close to succeeding, but it had in the end crashed and burned.

I was only distantly aware of movement as Kit and Declan arranged the five dining room chairs as per Willis, Sr.'s instructions, then resumed their seats. Some time later, Deirdre returned, pushing a tea trolley laden with an ornate silver tea urn and five additional cups and saucers. For a while, no one spoke. Then Aunt Augusta shifted restlessly in her chair and craned her neck to search the room.

"Where's Ernest?" she asked querulously. "Gone to bed, has he? Party pooper."

I, too, began to wonder what was keeping Willis, Sr., but before I could voice my concerns, the door to the entrance hall opened and the four Handmaidens shuffled in, followed by Peggy Taxman. Bringing up the rear, like a shepherd chivying a flock of recalcitrant ewes, was Willis, Sr. He gestured wordlessly for the newcomers to be seated in the dining room chairs, then crossed to stand with his back to the fireplace, facing them. His night attire did nothing to diminish his air of authority.

Though they eyed Frederick, the family tree, Henrique, and Aunt Augusta with undisguised curiosity, Elspeth, Opal, Selena, and Millicent seemed strangely subdued, almost cowed, and Peggy's lips were clenched so tightly that she might have had lockjaw. They accepted their cups of tea with soft words of thanks, then subsided into what was, to my knowledge, a wholly unprecedented silence.

Willis, Sr.'s gaze never wavered from their faces as he began, "Most of you are familiar with Mrs. Hodge of Hodge Farm."

Kit and I exchanged puzzled glances. Like him, I couldn't imagine what Annie Hodge had to do with anything.

"You may not be aware of the fact that Mrs. Hodge's brother-in-law is a member of the Upper Deeping fire brigade," Willis, Sr., continued. "When the brigade was recalled earlier this evening, Mrs. Hodge's relative stopped at Hodge Farm to inform her and her husband that the fire at Fairworth House had, mercifully, been a false alarm. Mrs. Hodge then used the telephone to relay the essential points of their conversation to Mrs. Taxman, who in turn, relayed them to Miss Scroggins, and so on and so forth."

"Busybodies," muttered Aunt Augusta.

The corners of Willis, Sr.'s mouth twitched, but he went on as if Aunt Augusta hadn't spoken.

"Though assured that reports of a fire at Fairworth House had been greatly exaggerated, these greathearted and thoughtful women—"

Aunt Augusta snorted derisively.

"—felt compelled to see for themselves that all was well with their dear friend, *Lady Sarah*." Willis, Sr., eyes swiveled briefly toward Sally, then focused implacably on the five women opposite him. "They convened an impromptu meeting during which they debated the advisability of visiting *Lady Sarah* so late at night and decided unanimously that she would welcome their support and encouragement regardless of the lateness of the hour." He stopped talking, raised an eyebrow, and cleared his throat loudly.

"Yes, William." Peggy Taxman spoke stiffly, as if the words were choking her. "We're . . . pleased . . . to know . . . that you're well . . . *Lady Sarah*."

"Very pleased, Lady Sarah," echoed the Handmaidens, looking daggers at Sally.

"You see, Lady Sarah?" said Willis, Sr., beaming like a manic game show host. "Your loyal friends—"

"Stop it, William." Sally's face was a mask of anguish. "You've been impossibly kind, but I can't . . . I can't do it anymore. I can't tell any more lies."

Willis, Sr.'s artificial smile vanished. He clasped his hands behind his back and bowed to Sally, saying gravely, "As you wish, Mrs. Pyne."

"Mrs. Pyne?" said Henrique.

"Yes, *Mrs. Pyne*," said Sally, her voice trembling. "That's who I am, Henrique. I'm not Lady Sarah. I'm *Sally Pyne*, the widow who runs the teashop in Finch. I'm the stupid fool of a woman who put on airs and graces in Mexico, just for a bit of fun, then kept playacting because she knew that a man like you would never waste his time on a plain lump of a woman like me."

Henrique attempted to speak, but she waved him to silence.

"Fairworth House is William's home, not mine," she said, blinking back her tears. "He concocted this whole scheme to protect me from *them*." She pointed a shaking finger at Peggy Taxman and her companions. "If you'd come to the tearoom, Henrique, if they'd found out how foolishly I'd behaved in Mexico, they would have hounded me until my dying day. I couldn't've stood it. I would've had to leave Finch and start over somewhere else and I don't *want* to live anywhere else." Her chest heaved as she gulped for breath. "So now you know. You know who I really am and you know what I've done. I'm not proud of myself and I won't blame you if you walk away."

"Walk away?" said Henrique. "And lose my backgammon partner? Are you stark staring mad, woman?"

"No, that would be me," said Aunt Augusta.

"H-Henrique," Sally stammered. "Y-your accent . . ."

"Is as phony as your tiara, my dear," said Henrique, who suddenly sounded as English as Mr. Barlow. "Since it seems to be a night for confessions, I'll make one to you. I'm no more Henrique Cocinero than you are Lady Sarah. Henry Cook's the name. How do you do?" He caught Sally's hand in his and shook it firmly.

"Henry Cook?" she said faintly, the color draining from her face.

"Born and raised in Putney," he said. "I've worked

the Carribean cruise ship circuit for the past thirty years as a general entertainer. You know the sort of thing: acting, singing—"

"Juggling," I put in, entranced, "magic tricks."

"That's the ticket," he said, nodding amiably. "I retired last year and found myself at loose ends. When I met you I got so homesick that I thought I'd come back to old Blighty and look you up. Now I won't deny that marrying a rich woman seemed like a good idea at the time, but blimey, I couldn't've done it if it meant being Henrique for the rest of my life. I don't fancy being loved for my accent."

"B-but I *do* love your accent," Sally faltered.

"This I will do for you whenever you desire it, *querida*," Henry purred. "Just not all the bleedin' time, all right?"

"So *that's* why you liked Deirdre's cooking," I said, clapping a hand to my forehead. "It really did remind you of your mother's."

"After dining on steak and lobster for the past thirty years, a bit of plain cooking hit the spot," said Henry, patting his ample stomach.

"Are you telling me that we're *both* big fat liars?" Sally asked incredulously.

"That's right," Henry replied cheerfully. "And I'm not planning on going anywhere unless you ask me to leave."

Sally gazed into his eyes for a breathless moment, then cupped his round face in her pudgy hands and said, "I'm not asking you to leave."

"Good," said Henry. "Because I love you, Sally Pyne,

and I intend to marry you." He kissed her full on the lips, then inclined his head toward the Handmaidens. "And you don't have to worry about those spiteful old cats. If they try to dig their claws into you, they'll have to deal with me first."

"*Spiteful?*" cried Opal Taylor.

"*Old?*" protested Millicent Scroggins.

"*Cats?*" yowled Selena Buxton.

"I've never been so insulted in all my life," huffed Elspeth Binney.

"You ain't heard nothin' yet," said Henry. "Hunting season is over, ladies. My Sally is off-limits." He stood and drew Sally to her feet. "Fancy a stroll in the garden? You and me have a lot to talk about, starting with this 'plain lump of a woman' rubbish. You're my pleasingly plump little pudding, and don't you forget it." He tucked Sally's hand into the crook of his arm and strode jauntily out of the drawing room, looking as if he'd just won the lottery.

"To love someone as she is," Willis, Sr., said quietly, "this is the very essence of love."

The sound of a suppressed sob came from my left and I turned just in time to see Peggy Taxman dash a tear from her eye.

"I've known Sally Pyne for nearly fifty years," she said gruffly. "How could she think I'd hound her out of Finch? I only wanted her to tell the truth about that letter from Mexico."

"And now she has," said Willis, Sr. "Thank you for your cooperation, ladies. Though it turned out to be unnecessary, it was greatly appreciated. Please allow me to escort you to the door."

"Uh, William?" said Millicent, peering inquisitively at Aunt Augusta.

"Not tonight, Miss Scroggins," Willis, Sr., said with a pleasant smile. "I have contributed enough grist to the rumor mill for now. The rest will have to wait. Mrs. Donovan? Will you please close the draperies?"

He drew a white linen handkerchief from the breast pocket of his dressing gown and gave it to Peggy Taxman as they led the Handmaidens out of the drawing room. Deirdre made short work of the drapes, then returned to her chair to speak in undertones with her husband.

"Lady Sarah is Sally Pyne," Kit recited softly. "Henrique Cocinero is Henry Cook. Deirdre Donovan's a Fairworthy and Declan's a thief. Aunt Augusta's a stowaway and Peggy Taxman is capable of feeling remorse." He gave a low whistle. "Lori, you must *always* let me come with you when you're staking out a house."

"Some night, huh?" I said, shaking my head bemusedly as I leaned back in my chair.

"Frederick," murmured Aunt Augusta. "It's a good name. Dimity would have liked it."

"*Who?*" I exclaimed, sitting bolt upright.

"Dimity Westwood," she answered dreamily. "She lived in a cottage not far from here. We were great chums, Dimity and I. Used to climb trees together, get into all sorts of scrapes. She gave Frederick to me on my tenth birthday."

"Dimity Westwood gave Frederick to you?" I said, gaping at her.

"On my tenth birthday," she repeated, smiling, "to

keep me company when I went away to school. He's been with me ever since."

My mind went into overload mode until another question raised its hand.

"Did Dimity Westwood give you the seedcake recipe, too?" I asked.

"She copied it from her mother's cookbook," Aunt Augusta replied. "It isn't to everyone's taste, but I've always loved it. Deirdre makes it for me now." The old woman closed her eyes, rested her head against the back of her chair, and drifted off to sleep.

Before I could even begin to digest what my dazed brain hoped would be the last of the evening's revelations, Willis, Sr., stepped into the drawing room, closed the door behind him, and resumed his seat in the Chippendale armchair. I tried to read his expression, but it was like trying to read granite.

"I shall now summarize the matters that were under discussion before Mrs. Pyne's friends came to call." He pursed his lips and gazed severely from Deirdre to Declan, as though he were about to sentence them both to the gallows. "You accepted positions in my household under false pretenses. You allowed an unstable woman to wander at will through my house, jeopardizing her own safety as well as the safety of every other person under my roof. You burgled Crabtree Cottage, causing Mr. Tavistock great mental and emotional distress, and you concealed the stolen item on these premises."

"We didn't intend to keep the family tree, sir," Declan said desperately. He glanced at Deirdre, who did nothing but hang her head. "We only wanted to buy

Aunt Augusta a little more time here at Fairworth. She has so little time left, you see."

"Yes, Mr. Donovan, I do see," Willis, Sr., said crisply. "I see that you and your wife have behaved with a reckless disregard for other people as well as the law."

I stared at Willis, Sr., in dismay. It seemed a bit ripe for a man who'd spent the past four days participating in an all-out fib fest to judge the Donovans so harshly. If they'd been the master criminals I'd taken them for, I would have cheered him on, but their actions had been based on love, not greed, and no one had been seriously hurt. Grant himself had admitted that a liberal application of his favorite beverage would cure his mental and emotional distress in no time flat. I couldn't understand why Willis, Sr., was taking such a hard line.

"Have you anything else to say in your defense?" he asked.

Declan swallowed hard and answered, "No, sir."

"In that case," said Willis, Sr., "I have no choice but to smooth things over with Mr. Tavistock, ask you to hire the extra help you need, and attempt to convince Aunt Augusta that I am not her deceased cousin Ernest, an endeavor which in itself may take several years of concentrated effort."

Kit burst out laughing and I glared reproachfully at Willis, Sr.

"Jeepers, William," I said. "You had me going there for a minute. I thought my sons' loving grandfather had suddenly turned into Mr. Nasty."

"Um," said Declan, peering uncertainly at his

employer. "Are you saying that we can stay, sir? All three of us?"

"It seems so," said Willis, Sr., smiling. "Have you any objections?"

Declan grinned from ear to ear. "I have none, sir, and I'm sure that Deirdre——"

"We'll stay on one condition," Deirdre interrupted, showing a hint of the spirit Aunt Augusta had in such abundance. "You must never again ask me to cook badly."

"I accept your terms," Willis, Sr., said instantly.

"If you don't mind my asking, sir," said Declan, "how did you get the ladies from the village to go along with Mrs. Pyne's charade?"

"I appealed to the better angels of their nature," Willis, Sr., replied.

"And?" I said suspiciously.

"I reminded them of how profoundly blessed they are to live in such an idyllic community," he said, waxing lyrical. "I reminded them that Finch is a place where neighbors help neighbors and friends support friends, where petty differences are set aside in times of trouble, where noble thoughts, kind words, and selfless deeds are as common as bluebells in the spring."

"And?" I pressed.

Willis, Sr., studied his fingernails. "And I may have mentioned in passing that I would take their behavior toward Mrs. Pyne into account when compiling the guest list for my next social gathering."

"Blackmail." Aunt Augusta's deep-throated chuckle

rang out unexpectedly from her place near the hearth. "Works like a charm every time. Well done, Ernest. You have to stand up to the busybodies or your life will never be your own."

"Words to live by," Willis, Sr., said wisely, "if one lives in Finch."

Epilogue

$\mathcal{J}$f one lives in Finch, one learns to expect the unexpected. Opal Taylor, Elspeth Binney, Millicent Scroggins, and Selena Buxton—whom Bill has taken to calling "The Four Handmaidens of the Apocalypse"—became Henry Cook's greatest admirers after he rented a room in Mr. Barlow's house and took up the position of assistant manager at the tearoom.

Aunt Dimity believes that the ladies revised their opinions of Henry for two principal reasons: They wished to stay in Willis, Sr.'s good graces and they were dead set on having a hand in planning Sally Pyne's June wedding, which is sure to be *the* social event of the summer.

Bill credits their conversion to simple math skills. He says it must have dawned on them at some point that Henry, by removing Sally from the ranks of eligible widows, had vastly increased their own chances of landing my father-in-law.

I'm convinced that the Handmaidens like Henry Cook for the same reasons everyone else in Finch likes him. He has a huge heart, a sunny disposition, and a great sense of humor, one aspect of which became evident when Bill explained that *cocinero* is the Spanish word for *cook*.

It's not hard to figure out why Sally Pyne likes Henry. He's a bilingual sweet-talker with a mile-wide romantic streak and he's completely nuts about her. They spend most of their evenings at the pub, where Henry juggles, performs magic tricks, and serenades his *querida* with songs that evoke images of lovers strolling hand in hand along moonlit, jasmine-scented beaches.

Though Sally has added flan and sopapillas to her menu, she continues to make her sublime jam dough-nuts and we continue to stuff our faces with them. She sent her granddaughter home at the end of August with a sackful of them and Rainey started the school year with a fresh appreciation of the hard work involved in running a small business as well as the mind-blowing knowledge that true love can blossom between two peo-ple who are well past the age of eighteen.

Peggy Taxman hasn't clashed with Sally once since their nonconfrontation at Fairworth House. I don't know whether Peggy's finally recognized how impor-tant Sally's friendship is to her or whether she's just leery of tangling with Henry, who has a seasoned enter-tainer's way with zingers. Mr. Barlow, who's known the two women for as long as they've known each other, is taking bets on when the truce will end. Bill's money is on Guy Fawkes Day, but I'm holding out for Christmas, when competition for roles in the Nativity play will be at its fiercest.

Grant Tavistock demanded no explanations when Willis, Sr., returned the Fairworthy family tree to him and Willis, Sr., offered none, asking simply that Grant finish the work he'd begun. It took Grant a couple of weeks to restore the family tree to its former glory, but it now hangs in a place of honor in Aunt Augusta's room, above a glass cabinet containing her father's snuffboxes and her mother's silver, sheep-shaped salt and pepper shakers. The brass compass remains on the map case in the library. Where it belongs.

Aunt Augusta insisted that Willis, Sr., retain custody of Frederick and ordered him to memorize *Notes on Sheep*.

"Best book ever written on the subject," she told him. "Read it myself when I was a girl. Chock-full of useful information."

Her subsequent disquisition on prolapsed uteri, scabies, and the squits, given with great enthusiasm during one of Deirdre's superb Sunday dinners, may explain why Willis, Sr., has not yet acquired his own flock of Cotswold Lions, though he has made a large donation to the Rare Breeds Survival Trust.

Declan hired Mr. Barlow and two Sciaparelli boys to help him with the gardening and Deirdre demonstrated her deep understanding of village politics by hiring every available woman in Finch to help her with the housework on a rotating schedule. By doing so, she avoided the deadly appearance of favoritism and reduced to a bare minimum the Handmaidens' opportunities to explain to Willis, Sr., how kind they were being to Sally Pyne.

When Deirdre found out that I lived in Dimity Westwood's old cottage, she presented me with a fragile slip of paper that had been handed down to her by Aunt Augusta. It contained Aunt Dimity's handwritten recipe for seedcake.

I studied the slip of paper on a fine evening in late

September, while I sat in the study with the blue journal opened in my lap.

"Your writing hasn't changed much," I observed.

I'm sure it was much neater then. Our schoolmistress had the face of an angel, but she would rap our knuckles with the edge of a ruler if we failed to meet her exacting standards.

"Looks can be deceiving," I acknowledged. "Your masquerade proved that."

I couldn't have predicted that Henry Cook would be wearing a mask of his own. I'm glad he's taken it off. I'm glad that all of the masks have been discarded. I had Sally's best interests at heart when I hatched my little scheme, but honesty really is the best policy.

"Fairworth House was wearing a mask, too," I said, struck by the comparison. "I thought the place was beyond redemption but William looked past the overgrown ivy and the broken windows and saw one of the prettiest houses in the county. My instincts were right about the Donovans, though. They were up to something." I smiled ruefully. "It just wasn't the something I thought they were up to."

I'm proud of the way you've adjusted to their presence at Fairworth House.

"I thank God for their presence at Fairworth," I declared. "They could have left Aunt Augusta to rot in a nursing home, but they took her into their hearts and they jumped through a thousand flaming hoops to make sure she could live out her days in a place she's loved since childhood. I can't think of anyone—including myself—better qualified to take care of William."

I still find it hard to believe that Gussie's back at Fairworth.

"I still find it hard to believe that you call Aunt Augusta 'Gussie,'" I said, rolling my eyes. "She told me that the two of you used to get into all sorts of scrapes."

We were notorious apple thieves. Gussie was the ringleader, of course. She was a pistol.

"She still is," I said. "She keeps rearranging the furniture, but William says she's a better decorator than the one he hired, so he's letting her get on with it. It won't surprise me if she lives long enough to see a new branch sprout on the family tree."

Has Deirdre indicated that a blessed event might be in the offing?

"No," I said, "but my instincts are telling me that she and Declan will be creating a nursery in their apartment in the not-too-distant future. And I'm learning to trust my instincts."

I do hope you're right. What good is a family tree if it stops growing?

"William considers the family tree to be Fairworth's greatest treasure," I said.

I hate to contradict him, but I must. Ancestors and artifacts are lovely things to have, but a house's greatest treasures are the people who live in it. Without William, Deirdre, Declan, and my old friend Gussie, Fairworth would be nothing more than an empty shell.

"Speaking of which," I said, sitting up excitedly, "I almost forgot to tell you that someone's bought Pussywillows."

The cottage next door to the tearoom? How delightful. It's been on the market for ages. Do you know who the purchaser is?

"She's a well-dressed, sweet-faced widow in her

early sixties named Amelia Thistle," I replied promptly, having done my homework.

Oh, dear. The Handmaidens won't be pleased when they hear about her.

"They already have and they're not, but I am," I said, grinning. "What good is an English village if it stops growing?"

I said good night to Aunt Dimity and Reginald and went upstairs to bed, wondering what role Amelia Thistle would play in village life. For all I knew, she could be a convicted felon with a rap sheet as long as my arm or a tedious taxidermist from Topeka.

Looks, as I had discovered, could be deceiving.

Aunt Dimity's Seedcake

Makes one cake

Preheat oven to 350 degrees Fahrenheit. Grease and line a 6-inch-round, 3-inch-deep cake pan. (A soufflé dish will work.)

8 tablespoons softened butter (1 stick)
²/₃ cup sugar
2 teaspoons caraway seeds
2 large eggs, beaten
1¼ cups unbleached flour
3 tablespoons cornstarch
¼ teaspoon baking powder
1 teaspoon ground cinnamon
¼ teaspoon ground cloves

In a large mixing bowl, cream the butter and the sugar, then work in the caraway seeds. Beat in the eggs a little at a time. In a separate bowl, stir together remaining ingredients, then fold them into the mixture with a large spoon. Spread mixture in the cake pan. Bake for 1 hour and 15 minutes or until toothpick inserted into cake comes out clean. Allow the cake to cool for a few minutes in the cake pan, then carefully turn it out onto a wire rack to cool completely.

AVAILABLE FROM PENGUIN

MORE STORIES OF AUNT DIMITY

Aunt Dimity Down Under
ISBN 978-0-14-311865-7

*Aunt Dimity Slays the
  Dragon*
ISBN 978-0-14-311658-5

*Aunt Dimity: Vampire
  Hunter*
ISBN 978-0-14-311479-6

Aunt Dimity Goes West
ISBN 978-0-14-311291-4

*Aunt Dimity and the
  Deep Blue Sea*
ISBN 978-0-14-303830-6

*Aunt Dimity and the
  Next of Kin*
ISBN 978-0-14-303654-8

Aunt Dimity: Snowbound
ISBN 978-0-14-303458-2

*Aunt Dimity Takes a
  Holiday*
ISBN 978-0-14-200393-0

Aunt Dimity: Detective
ISBN 978-0-14-200154-7

*Aunt Dimity Beats the
  Devil*
ISBN 978-0-14-100219-4

Aunt Dimity's Christmas
ISBN 978-0-14-029630-3

Aunt Dimity Digs In
ISBN 978-0-14-027569-8

Aunt Dimity's Good Deed
ISBN 978-0-14-025881-3

*Introducing Aunt Dimity,
  Paranormal Detective*
ISBN 978-0-14-311606-6

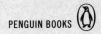

PENGUIN BOOKS